HIDDEN GATES

HIDDEN GATES

D.T. DYLLIN

DRAGONFAIRY PRESS
ATLANTA

HIDDEN GATES

This is a work of fiction. All characters, organizations, and events portrayed in this book are products of the imagination or are used fictitiously.

Copyright © 2013 by D.T. Dyllin
All rights reserved

Cover art by Lindsay Tiry, with contributions by Rebecca Sampson & Julia Starr. P.J. Stone Gates Trilogy logo by Jordan P. Fremgen.

Published by Dragonfairy Press, Atlanta
www.dragonfairypress.com
Dragonfairy Press and the Dragonfairy Press logo are trademarks of Dragonfairy Press LLC.

First Publication, January 2013
Trade Paperback Edition, February 2013
Trade Paperback ISBN: 978-0-9850230-5-8

Published in the United States of America

Library of Congress Control Number: 2012956372

*For my dad,
who planted the seeds of inspiration,
one Unc Nunkie and Tik-Tok at a time.*

1

"Hey P.J." Evan's raspy voice commanded my attention from beside my locker. I glanced over to meet his deep brown eyes with surprise. "I was wondering what you were doing this weekend?"

"Me?" I squeaked. Evan Thompson was actually speaking to me, *and* he knew my name.

"Yeah, you. I don't see anyone else around, do you?"

My eyes traveled the length of the empty hallway and back. *When did that happen?* "No, I just—" I was silenced when Evan brought his hand up to caress the side of my face before slipping his fingers into my hair. The contact of his skin on mine made me tingle with awareness as his powers slid into me.

"How have I never noticed you before?" His voice had dropped down into a more intimate tone, and his eyes flashed with lust just before he pushed me back against the lockers and captured my lips with his. I groaned with pleasure as his tongue slid into my mouth to intertwine with mine, and his muscled body pushed firmly against me. The hand that wasn't holding me captive by my hair moved down to—

"What?" I said with annoyance as I felt someone pinch the back of my arm, startling me back to reality.

I looked up to see my best friend Bryn's dark blue eyes glittering with amusement. "Day dreaming again? Who was it this time? Let me guess." He leaned back in his seat and scanned the room around us. When his eyes came to rest on Evan Thompson, who just happened to be sitting in the exact spot my vacant gaze had been fixated on for the past half hour, he rolled his eyes. "Really? Evan Thompson? Like you have any chance at all with him."

I shot Bryn an evil glare. "Hey! I might not have had a shot with him last year, but this year is different."

Bryn interrupted me with another eye roll. "Here we go again. Just because your tits have grown like half a cup size isn't going to change anything. Trust me when I say you're probably the only one who can tell the difference."

I brought my arms up over my—*fine*—less than ample bosom, to protect them from his hurtful words. "You noticed," I grumbled, in protest.

He chuckled. "Only because I noticed you prancing around like they're suddenly D cups."

"Okay, this is just weird. Can we *please* not talk about my cup size, or lack thereof anymore? You may be my best friend, but you're still a guy. Besides, I have plenty of other qualities that might interest someone like Evan Thompson." Bryn gave me a pitying look before going back to doodling on his folder, letting me know he thought our conversation wasn't worth his time anymore. "Fine. Whatever, Bryn *Aries* O'Bannon." I hissed. "Nobody asked you anyways."

Bryn clutched the sides of his desk and turned to deliver me a death glare of his own. "Quiet, Paige *Joplin* Stone. You wanna use my middle name for everyone to hear, then two can play at that game."

HIDDEN GATES

"Shut up!" I cringed at hearing my middle name said out loud. "My name is *P.J.*"

His lips curved up slightly at the corners. "What was that, *Paige Joplin Stone?* I couldn't quite hear you."

A few kids turned around in their seats, their interest piqued by my and Bryn's exchange; not that I could blame them, there usually wasn't much excitement in study hall, but why did my conversation have to suddenly catch everyone's attention? Realizing I could be blown out of the water and my entire high school career ruined, I shot Bryn a pleading look. "Okay. Fine. I'll shut up if you do. Just please don't say that name out loud *ever* again."

Bryn gave me his patented lopsided grin, complete with dimples, and ran his hand through his thick black hair as he met my eyes. "Well, I don't know. What are you willing to give me for my silence?"

Now I was starting to get angry. Most of the time, Bryn was great, my partner in crime since we were five, but lately he was becoming relentless in his harassment of yours truly. And truth be told, he knew way too much about me for it to be even the tiniest bit amusing, case in point with my middle name. Bryn was the only person, outside of family and staff at my school who was privy to such top-secret information. It would be hard enough to make it through high school relatively unscathed without such handicaps as everyone knowing your middle name is Joplin because your quirky mother's favorite singer is Janis Joplin. "I swear to God, Bryn, if you don't shut up right now, I'm never going to talk to you again."

Bryn laughed. "You'd never be able to find someone who puts up with you the way I do, and you'd come crawling back to me in less than a day."

"I hate you," I grated through clenched teeth.

"You love me." His eyes twinkled brighter, which only made me want to scratch them out.

"No, I hate you," I repeated with more vehemence.

"Whatever you say," he said as he returned to his stupid doodle.

I sat and stewed for the rest of the period until the bell—or buzzer, if I really wanted to get technical—signaled it was time for lunch, thank the heavens. I gathered my stuff, jammed it all into my bag, and bolted for the door. I usually waited for Bryn since we always ate lunch together, but since I was still mad at him, I didn't bother. I had made it about halfway down the hall before he caught up with me.

"Awe, come on, I was only kidding. Don't be so touchy." I turned my head to avoid eye contact with him and sped up my pace. He matched my speed with ease on his longer legs. Damn Guardian growth spurts—only a few months ago I was almost as tall as him, but now he towered over my 5'9", which isn't exactly short for a girl, I might add. "Okay, I'm sorry. Is that what you want? An official apology?" When I didn't respond, he continued, "Someone like Evan Thompson would never notice you because you would never even blip on his radar. You've seen the trashy girls he's with all the time. You're too good for him. It was kind of a compliment, what I said before—in a backhanded sort of way."

"Very backhanded," I grumbled. "Besides, it's not like he can *really* be with any of those girls—not in the long run anyways—he's a Gatekeeper." No, he couldn't be with a *regular* human—or Regs as we referred to them—at least not settle down with one, because our world has rules. Our world—*my* world—is very different from the one most people know. In my world, there are portals—gates if you will—that link our dimension to thousands of other dimensions. Living close to these gates are small groups of people, with special gifts, that

HIDDEN GATES

have existed as far back as recorded time. These people—*my people*—exist to protect our dimension from any outside threats. We pass down our genetic gifts from generation to generation, which ensures the future safety of the earth. So it's kind of important to keep our bloodlines strong.

Evan, as a Gatekeeper, would be expected to choose a Seer as a future mate. We can go out and date whoever we want, and technically, have kids one day with whoever we desire, but it's been ingrained since childhood that it's our duty to pass on our DNA for the protection of the planet. *Talk about pressure.* I, being a Seer, can only reproduce another Seer if I have a child with a male descendent from a Seer line or a Gatekeeper. An anomaly of Guardians is that they only produce male children, so if I were to have a child with one, I would put a halt to the possibility of another Seer being born, as only girls possess active Seer powers. Seers are the most important group among our people; no one else can really do their job if there aren't any Seers around. Therefore, a lot of work goes into perpetuating our lines. *Yeah, being a member of my world kind of puts a kink in my love life.*

"That part doesn't matter. You deserve someone better, someone who can appreciate you for who you really are."

"I don't think that guy exists, Bryn. My choices are kind of limited," I said with a sigh. "You're right when you said no one else would put up with me. At least when I'm forced into a marriage one day with someone that repulses me, I'll still have you to comfort me as I cry myself to sleep every night."

"Awe, come on, I was just giving you a hard time, and you know it." He ducked to bump my shoulder with his. "We both know it's the other way around. Who would put up with me and my—"

"Dark and broody moods?" I interjected. "You're quite right. Me and only me. You shouldn't antagonize me, Bryn.

What you really should be doing is kissing my feet." I smiled up at him. "Kissing my toes and massaging my feet, for putting up with you all these years. How Tammie did for an entire year is beyond me."

He scowled at me. "I broke up with her, remember? Not the other way around."

"And I don't understand why." I studied his face for some kind of clue. Tammie Masterson had been Bryn's girlfriend for well over a year. I'd never really liked her because he was way too good for her, but that aside, they had seemed pretty happy together—although she was constantly jealous of all the inside jokes Bryn and I shared. But whoever dated Bryn was going to have to deal with that because I was here to stay—one day Bryn would be my personal Guardian, and there was no interfering with that relationship. Everyone knows a Guardian's most important job is protecting his Seer—*as it should be.*

"I really don't wanna talk about this right now."

"But I do. Why won't you tell me why you guys broke up? You used to tell me everything. It's been almost a whole month, and I still have no clue what happened between you guys. Aren't I your best friend anymore?"

Bryn's eyes darkened. "You know you'll always be my best friend. There are just some things I can't talk to you about." When my lower lip stuck out at him, his face softened. "At least not right now."

I took his hand in mine and gave him my best puppy dog eyes. "Please, Bryn. Please tell me. I'll do anything you want. Pah-leeeeeezzze."

He stared at me, and his brows drew together. "Be careful what you say." He turned and started walking again. "What I want might be more than you're willing to offer me." I heard him mutter the last part under his breath. His comment completely confused me. *What could he possibly want from me that he would think I wouldn't give him?* He was my best friend in the world, and there was nothing I wouldn't do for him—nothing.

I scurried to catch up to him. "Bryn, what are you talking about? I hope you know I would do anything for you. You know that, right?"

"Just drop it. I told you I don't wanna talk about it." We walked a few moments in silence before he spoke again. "So what time did your mom say for us to come over tomorrow night, again?"

Bryn's and my birthdays were a day apart. Mine was today, and his was tomorrow. Somehow we had ended up having a joint sixth birthday party, and it just kind of stuck, becoming a tradition with our families to combine our celebrations. Since our families were so close, no one objected—in fact, quite the contrary. "I don't know, six-ish I guess. You know"—I interlaced my fingers with his—"I'm still older than you for a few more hours. Older and wiser."

You know that saying . . . *speak of the devil and he shall appear*? Well, in this case, the devil was a *she* because Tammie chose that exact moment to walk out of a classroom just as we were passing it. She stopped abruptly and looked up at Bryn like a deer caught in headlights. The two of us dwarfed her small about five foot frame, and she self-consciously ran her fingers through her long blond curls. "Hey, Bryn. I was hoping I'd see you today. I wanted to wish you Happy Birthday, and I was hoping that maybe . . ." Her voice trailed off as she took in the sight of Bryn holding my hand. "Oh, I see," she said crisply. "I can't say that I'm surprised." She whirled on her heel and headed off in the opposite direction at a dead sprint.

Realization dawned on me, and I dropped Bryn's hand. "Really? Is that what you don't wanna tell me? Does she really think something is going on between us? Is that why she was always so jealous of me?" I laughed. "That's ridiculous, absolutely ridiculous."

Bryn's face clouded over. "Yeah, absolutely ridiculous," he said through clenched teeth. "Look, I forgot my math book and I need it to finish up some homework before next period. You go ahead and have lunch without me, and I'll see you later." Bryn turned and jogged off in the opposite direction of where Tammie had gone, before I could argue with him.

"Weird," I muttered to myself. *His locker isn't down that way, and we don't even have any math homework. I'm in the same class. What just happened?* I had a sinking feeling that I really didn't want to know.

2

"Do you think Bryn's been acting weird lately?" I asked Jenna between bites of pizza.

Jenna sat gazing off over my shoulder, eyes shining with adoration while she twirled a purple piece of hair around her finger. "How am I supposed to know? You guys have your own language, one that even I've never been able to understand."

I frowned at her. "I don't have time for your stupid Speaker jokes. I'm being serious here."

Jenna turned her deep brown eyes on me, a smile breaking across her face. "So am I—being serious, that is. You guys are a mystery even to me."

"What's that supposed to mean?" I so wasn't in the mood for one of Jenna's cryptic conversations right now. Speakers had their own unique brand of humor, one that I had a hard time getting on board with most of the time, mostly because I didn't get it. As a Speaker, everything in Jenna's world revolved around language because she has the ability to understand any language of any species. For her to say that Bryn and I had a language of our own that she didn't even understand was only something she would find amusing.

Jenna's gaze slid back over my shoulder, her eyes glazing over again. "Evan Thompson really is hot. All that lean golden muscle, topped with his golden brown hair, and chocolate eyes that I could melt into—Mmmm, mmm, mmmm—tasty. I would love to feel more than just his Gatekeeper magic sliding into me, if you know what I mean."

"Hey," I said with annoyance. "You can pretty much date whoever you want. Don't dip into my shallow pool." I sighed, letting go of my hostility. "Not that it matters anyways; I have about as much of a chance with him as you do."

Jenna raised one dark eyebrow at me. "Actually I do have a chance with him. At least if I'm only interested in getting into his pants." She paused to flip her purple hair over her shoulder. "And darling, I most certainly am."

I groaned. "Jenna, come on. You're not going to sleep with him."

"Who said anything about *sleeping* with him?" She giggled. "If I have my way with him, there definitely won't be any *sleeping* involved."

"Whatever," I mumbled. And she would, Jenna was the type of girl who could just go up to a guy like Evan and offer him sex. Me . . . not so much. I was beginning to think I was the last card-carrying member of The Flying V Club in my entire school. Hell, I'd barely gotten to second base. I was definitely way behind my peers in the sexual experience department, even though it was by choice. I still had the same hormones pressuring me on a daily basis that my friends did, but I wanted something more than just the physical, call me crazy. And even though I daydreamed about a lot of guys, when it got down to it, I wasn't really interested. Some days I envied Jenna, with her constantly changing hair color and brazen attitude towards life. She did whatever she felt like whenever the whim hit—again, me . . . not so much. I seemed to always fall victim to over-analyzing everything. I couldn't do anything without dissecting it twenty different ways, and by that time, the opportunity to be spontaneous had passed me by.

"Oh, why don't you just do it with Bryn and get it over with?" Jenna asked, breaking into my thoughts of self-pity.

"What? You can't be serious!"

"I never kid about sex and . . . well, sex. Sure he's not long-term material with him being a Guardian and all—yours to be specific—but why not at least do it for the first time with someone you trust? And you do trust him, don't you?" She eyed me speculatively, as if trying to decode something in my face.

I flushed under her scrutiny. Sure Bryn was hot, but he was my best friend, and one simply didn't do those kinds of things with their best friend. Besides, there could be no future between us, so what would be the point really? "Umm . . . I can't sleep with him, *especially* because he's going to be my Guardian. I won't even bother ticking off the rest of the reasons because there's only one that's really important: he's my best friend, and even if I wanted to—which I don't—he's not interested in me like that."

"Sure he's not," Jenna said dryly. "I'm sure, since he's a guy, if you offered him sex, he'd turn it down."

"I'm not doing that, and he wouldn't be interested anyways. Don't be ridiculous," I snapped. First Tammie and now Jenna, when were people going to get it through their thick heads that nothing had or would happen between me and Bryn?

"Speaking of Bryn," Jenna murmured.

I turned just in time to see Bryn enter the cafeteria. His dark blue eyes scanned the room and lit up when they landed on me. As he began to head our way, I couldn't help but notice again how much he'd grown recently. Since coming into his powers, he'd sprung up to almost 6'4", and instead of being long and lanky like most boys his age, he had already filled out quite nicely. I smiled up at him as he pulled out a chair beside me and curled gracefully into it. He ran his hand through his thick black hair and gave me his lopsided grin complete with dimples.

I smiled back at him. "Hey. I thought you had some work to do or something."

"Yeah. I guess I got stuff mixed up, because as it turns out, we didn't have a math assignment." *Huh.* Maybe I was reading too much into things, as usual, and Bryn had simply gotten confused; it happens to the best of us sometimes. "So what were you guys talking about?"

"You," Jenna said.

"Nothing," I said at the same time. I gave her a dirty look before turning back to Bryn. "Well—"

"What about me?" Bryn's blue eyes glittered with curiosity, and I knew I had to work fast. If I didn't change the subject soon, Jenna would tell him exactly what our topic of discussion had been about.

"So Jenna actually thinks she has a shot with Evan Thompson," I blurted out in a Hail Mary effort.

Bryn tilted his head at me, giving me a look that said he knew I was changing the subject, but then he turned to Jenna and grinned. "What, you just gonna walk over and offer to do him?"

"How'd you guess?" Jenna laughed.

"Gee, I don't know," Bryn chuckled into his sandwich. "Because maybe that's what you always do."

Jenna pretended to turn pensive, twirling a purple piece of hair around her finger again. "Huh. Well, I guess you're right, I *do* always do that."

Whew. Crisis averted. No need to put any ideas about Bryn and I having sex into his head. I was fully confident that he didn't think about me in that way, but he was still a guy;

HIDDEN GATES

Jenna was right about that part. Then again, better safe than sorry; time to bring up a new topic completely off boys and sex. "So how's your bad ass in training stuff coming along?" I directed my question at Bryn.

"Fine, I guess."

"What about you?" Jenna interjected. "Any premonitions"—from the corner of my eye I could see Bryn furiously waving his hand at her in a slashing motion—"... yet?" Jenna finished up hesitantly.

I scowled. *Damn it.* Just when I'd gotten my mind off of one problem, I had to be reminded of another. "Nothing. I've got nothing. So maybe I won't have to worry about you dipping into my shallow pool after all because maybe I can date whoever, too." Most Seers my age had at least gotten some small premonitions. Me—not even a blip on my premonition radar. Maybe I was some weird Seer anomaly that was born without powers. If that were the case ... well, at least my dating worries would be over. *Hooray?*

Bryn sighed loudly. "Some Speaker you are. Do you not know what this means?" He waved his hand in front of his neck in a slashing motion again.

Jenna scrunched up her face at him. "Obviously not."

I placed my hand on top of Bryn's. "It's okay. I might as well face the truth. Something went wrong with me, and I'm never going to actually *see* anything."

Bryn interlaced his fingers with mine and gave my hand a squeeze in an effort to comfort me. "Maybe the problem is you're putting too much pressure on yourself. Just relax."

"And you know what's a great thing for relaxation? Sex," Jenna added.

I groaned. "Come on, Jenna—seriously—enough already."

"Fine. Oh, hey, you gonna go to Ryan's party tonight? It's going to be awe-some," Jenna asked, finally changing the subject. *Thank God.*

"I don't know. Maybe. Our birthday celebration isn't until tomorrow night, but I'm just not sure if I feel like dealing with another of Ryan's parties." I slumped back into my seat, withdrawing my hand from Bryn's, causing him to frown slightly. Normally I'd be all gung ho about going to one of Ryan's parties and scoping out the place for any eligible males who I could maybe actually date, but at the moment, the thought was just depressing. *Who am I kidding anyways?* I wouldn't find anyone but the usual drunk fools interested only in sex and nothing more. "You going, Bryn?"

He shrugged his shoulders. "I am if you are. Could be fun."

"Pleeeaase," Jenna pleaded while clasping her hands in front of her. "You can get ready at my place, and we can go together."

I sighed. "I don't know why you always beg me to come to these things since you ditch me for some guy practically before we're even in the door."

"Don't worry, I'll be there," Bryn chimed in.

"Fine," I agreed, knowing I was sure to regret my decision, but at least I'd get to hang out with Bryn and have a few beers.

Jenna gathered up her things and smiled at me. "Good. Just come over to my house after dinner, and we can get ready." And with that, she headed off in Evan's direction, but not before pausing to adjust her v-neck T-shirt to better show her cleavage—which I admitted with envy, was much more impressive than mine probably ever would be.

"So, should I just meet you guys there?" Bryn asked, causing me to drag my eyes away from Jenna and her soon to be spectacle with Evan.

"Yeah, I guess. By the way, you ever going to tell me what happened with you and Tammie?"

Bryn's jaw ticked with sudden tension, and he ran his hand through his hair. "Why won't you just let it go, Peej?"

HIDDEN GATES

I smiled to myself. Despite Bryn changing so much on the outside lately, most of the time he still said my name so it sounded like one syllable, something he'd been doing since we were kids.

"You know I can't do that. It's just not possible. So you might as well just get it over with and tell me now so you can save us both all the trouble."

Bryn stood abruptly, pushing his chair back with enough force to hit into the wall behind us. "Let. It. Go. There are just some things that I can't talk to you about. You better get used to it now." He then turned and stalked out of the cafeteria without finishing his lunch.

Huh. Then again, maybe I wasn't reading too much into things; Bryn was definitely acting weird.

3

"I can't believe I let you talk me into this," I hissed at Jenna as I tried to pull down the hem on my dress, which was much too short. Of course, when I managed to do that, I then had too much cleavage showing, and I had to try and pull the dress back up. Either way, I had *way* too much skin showing. Little black dress, my ass . . . how about *too* little black dress.

"Oh hush. I would kill for your legs. Instead, I have to make do with these stubby little things." She motioned briefly to her legs. "And it's too late now. We're almost there."

I gulped as Ryan's house came into view, framed in the window of Jenna's bright yellow Volkswagen bug. She pulled up and parked at the curb, turning to me with a serious face. "So . . . what do you think of the new hair color? Too much?"

She had gone from a dark purple color to a shade of red that matched most fire trucks. It would definitely turn heads; I just wasn't sure it would be in the way that she wanted. I tried to remain tactful though. "If attention is what you crave, then you definitely chose the right color."

She frowned. "You don't like it, do you?"

"It's not that I don't like it—it's just—well, I liked the purple better." And that was very true. I liked the purple a whole lot better.

"But now we both get to be redheads." Her peach glossed lips turned up in a smile. She really didn't care that much that I didn't like her new shade of hair. Besides, it would probably change by next week. It was a wonder all of her hair hadn't fallen out yet.

"Yeah, but only my shade of red can be found in nature," I said dryly. Why anyone would purposely dye their hair red was beyond me. My natural color was a bright strawberry blonde, which I had managed to darken to a nice auburn shade through the use of frequent Rainbow Henna applications. I was still stuck as a redhead, but at least I liked its current darker hue. As we exited her car and headed up Ryan's walkway, I began fidgeting with my borrowed dress again. I felt like an adult trying to squeeze into little kids' clothes, and I suddenly wanted to go home very badly. "I don't think I should be wearing this in public," I grumbled more to myself than Jenna.

She turned a very annoyed face towards me. "Okay. I'm done. You look super hot, so stop complaining. I don't wanna hear another word about it." She reached up and turned the knob on Ryan's front door. We were greeted by loud music and even louder voices. Jenna smiled up at me, took my arm, and pulled me over the threshold. We'd barely made it two steps before she spotted Evan. "It looks like I have a date with destiny," she said, dropping my arm and heading towards Evan with a huge grin on her face. When he saw her approach, he let his gaze travel over her from head to toe, a grin of his own spreading across his face. I guess he liked what he saw and was going to take her up on her offer from earlier. I turned away abruptly, not wanting to see any more.

HIDDEN GATES

"Hey." I looked up to see Bryn standing nearby, his blue eyes taking in my teeny tiny dress. "Did you let Jenna dress you?"

I laughed. "Is it that obvious?"

A slight smile tipped up the corners of his full lips. "To me it is." He reached forward and took my hand in his. "Let's get you a beer. It'll help."

"What would really help is a pair of jeans because this dress is so small it could be a shirt. I really don't know how she talks me into these things sometimes." I grimaced self consciously as we passed by a group of guys who I didn't know, all of them eyeing my bare flesh. *Thanks, Jenna.*

I stood by and attempted to adjust my dress again while Bryn filled up two plastic cups with beer from the keg for us. He handed me one and I took a sip, crinkling my nose in disdain. "Natty Lite? Ugh. At least get a decent light beer, if there is such a thing."

Bryn took a swig of his beer and chuckled at my still scrunched up face. "Underage beggars can't be choosers."

"Yeah, yeah," I grumbled, chugging down the rest of the cup. I had decided I would make up for in volume what was lacking in quality, with my beer option. Bryn quirked one dark eyebrow at me as he raised his cup to his lips again. I glared in response. "Don't you give me that eyebrow, Mr. O'Bannon," I said as I began pumping the keg for a refill.

Bryn's blue eyes met mine over the rim of his cup. "What? I didn't say a word." His lips curled up, showing his dimples.

"You didn't have to, your eyebrow said it all." It was then I thought about what Jenna had said earlier about Bryn and I having our own language. Maybe I could see her point. "It's a party. I'm just trying to have fun." Bryn still didn't say anything but simply looked at me with his way too expressive eyes. They currently were asking me if I thought getting completely smashed was the answer to my problems. I narrowed my eyes and scrunched up my nose. *Yes, yes, it is.*

As I polished off beer number two within five minutes, Bryn decided I was temporarily cut off. I knew he was worried that I would get too chatty like I sometimes did when I was drunk, and start complaining to the wrong person about my lack of premonitions or something. I had one little incident in the girls' room at one little mixed party like this one, and Bryn has been paranoid ever since. It wasn't like any of the Regs believed me anyways; they just thought I was really, really drunk. He reached over and snagged my empty cup, set it down near the keg, then took my hand again and tugged me back into the other room. I giggled, *lookout—lightweight coming through,* and scanned the room for any signs of Jenna and Evan. Just as I had suspected—they were both conspicuously absent. "It looks like Evan took Jenna up on her offer," I called to Bryn over the much too loud music.

Ignoring me, Bryn almost pushed me down on the couch. "Sit," he ordered. "I'm gonna get you some water. Don't go anywhere." He met my eyes with meaning. "And it's probably best if you don't talk to anyone until I get back either." *Bossy much?* I giggled again as he walked away, really starting to feel the effects of those two beers. But hey, at least I hadn't thought about my dress or boyfriendless situation for a couple of minutes. Sometimes it was nice having the super low tolerance to alcohol that all Seers shared. I couldn't imagine being like Bryn or Jenna, or, well, anyone else of my kind who didn't really seem to get drunk. The best they were able to do was get buzzed. That was the reason my kind watched Seers like me so closely at parties like this one.

"Hey, pretty girl. How are you doing tonight?" A guy with longish sandy blond hair and bright crystal blue eyes sat down next to me. He was one of the guys who had been eyeing me when Bryn and I had gone in to get our beers just a few minutes ago. He was kind of cute, and I could sense some power coming off of him. It was very faint, though, and felt like tiny fingers running up and down my exposed skin, causing goosebumps to erupt all over me. I tilted my head to study him for a moment, like called to like, and I just knew. *Seer.* I mean, he wasn't—obviously—but I was picking up on the dormant power in his blood. Maybe he was exactly what I'd been looking for.

"Hey, yourself." I grinned at him feeling very relaxed. "What does it look like I'm doing?"

"It looks like you're wasting that dress sitting all alone on the couch." His eyes slid down over my body, but instead of feeling self-conscious like I did before, I felt empowered.

"Well, what do you suggest?" I said with a giggle.

"Come with me." He grinned, pulling me up from the couch. Normally going off in a party with some strange guy would seem like a bad idea, but this guy seemed harmless, and maybe he was even future boyfriend material. *So why not go with him? What will it hurt?* I smiled back at him and allowed him to lead me out the back door and farther off onto the edge of Ryan's property where there was a small patch of woods. He pulled a small flask out of his pocket, took a swig, and then offered it to me. "It's Southern Comfort mixed with some lime."

I took it from his hand and eyed it suspiciously, as if it would jump up and bite me. "Yeah, I don't know, I'm already feeling kinda buzzed."

He gave me an easy grin. "It's just Southern Comfort, it's not that strong; give it a go."

Well, I didn't want the happy buzz I had going to wear off, so what would one little taste do to me? I brought the flask up to my nose for a quick sniff before taking a shot's worth into my mouth. "Blak. That stuff is horrible." I winced at the slight burn it left in its wake.

He took the flask from my hand and drank again before screwing the top back on and replacing it in his pocket. I was still reeling from the horrible taste of the Southern Comfort when he pushed me up against a tree and shoved his tongue down my throat.

Now I was already feeling buzzed from the two beers I had chugged; add in the Southern Comfort and toss in this guy throwing me up against a tree, and my whole world started to spin. "Hey." My protest came out in a slur as he started to slobber all over my neck. "Hey, wait a second. Stop." I tried to push him off of me, but he was a lot stronger than he looked. His hands were roaming all over my body, and when he reached down to hike up my dress, stark panic began to take over. "Stop," I squeaked.

"Awe, come on, baby, it'll be good. Just relax."

That's when it hit me. I didn't even know this guy's name, and I had wandered off into the woods with him when I was already halfway toasted. How stupid could I get? "Please. Stop," I pleaded, my words sounding more slurred than I would have liked. "I'm a virgin."

He laughed. "Yeah, I don't believe that for a second." He fumbled with the zipper on the side of my dress, and I heard a rip. I was kicking and fighting the best that I could, but I was no match for this guy in my current state. He had me pretty firmly pinned. I thought about screaming but realized that probably no one would hear me over the loud music inside the house. Why, oh why, had I gone off with this guy? It looked like the price I was going to pay for my stupidity was losing my virginity to a guy I didn't even know. I thought of Bryn at that moment for some reason, not because I was wishing he'd come to my rescue, even though I was, but because his face appeared in my mind's eye, completely unbidden.

HIDDEN GATES

"Please, I don't want this. I'm not lying—I'm a virgin." I whimpered as his hands skimmed up and over my underwear. Bile rose in my throat. I didn't want to lose my virginity this way—it just wasn't fair.

"Get the fuck off her!" Suddenly the guy was pulled from me and thrown to the ground. I was so happy to see Bryn I could have cried, and as soon as I was out of this mess I probably would. "I should break your face. I should break every bone in your body," Bryn snarled.

I'd never seen Bryn look so—so dangerous. His long black hair had fallen forward into his face, and his dark blue eyes raged with violence. He reached forward and picked up the wanna-be rapist by the neck with one of his large hands, holding him a good few inches off of the ground. A low growl emanated from the back of his throat, and I could have sworn, for the briefest of moments, his eyes sparked an even brighter blue, as if they glowed.

"Please. I'll leave," Wanna-be Rapist sputtered while gasping for air. Bryn released his grip and let him drop to the ground with an audible thud. "I'm leaving," Wanna-be Rapist said, with an edge of panic in his voice. Apparently, I wasn't the only one who thought Bryn looked dangerous. He scrambled up and ran off faster than I'd seen anyone run while intoxicated. Or maybe that was just me?

Bryn watched him go, and then he turned to look at me, his face softening. "You okay, Peej?"

I blinked up at my savior—*Bryn*. Bryn, who I'd known practically all my life—suddenly he looked like a stranger. He really was becoming a Guardian—*my Guardian*—and for some reason, in my current state, that upset me. I didn't want things to change; I didn't want to lose him. I could no longer hold back the flood of tears that had been threatening to escape my eyes. I slid down the tree, sobbing hysterically.

Bryn dropped down on one knee and tipped my face up with his long fingers to look at him. His face was contorted with some emotion I couldn't read. "He didn't—he didn't—I thought I got here in time."

"No. He didn't," I croaked. "But he would have; he was going to."

Bryn exhaled one long breath and, wrapped his arms around me, hesitantly at first, but when I sank into him, his hold grew fiercer. "What were you thinking? Going off with him? I told you to stay put." His voice was harsh, making me cry harder.

"I don't know. I wasn't—thinking, that is. I'm sorry, Bryn, so sorry." My apology, like my thoughts, was slow and muddled.

He let go of me and tipped my face up towards him again so he could look into my eyes. "Hey, why are you apologizing to me? I was just worried is—" He stopped talking as I brought a hand up to caress the side of his face. I'd never really realized how truly beautiful Bryn was. I mean, I noted on some level he was hot, but I didn't actually take notice. I studied the face that had been one of the most important ones in my life since I was the age of five. I let my gaze roam from his dark blue eyes that were currently churning like a storm at sea; to his high sharp cheekbones; to his full, perfectly shaped lips. The contrast between his strikingly blue eyes and his black hair was nothing short of perfection. Bryn had the most beautiful face I had ever laid eyes on, I decided.

"Do you think I'm pretty, Bryn?" I whispered. His brows furrowed as he looked down at me. "Because I think you have the most beautiful face I've ever seen." *Did I actually just say that out loud?*

"Peej—"

I brought my index finger up to his lips slowly, as if my hand weighed more than it normally did. "Shhh . . . No, really. Do you think I'm pretty?"

HIDDEN GATES

He swallowed, causing his Adam's apple to dance up and down in his throat nervously. "No—I think you're beautiful."

I frowned at him. "You're just saying that so I don't feel bad, you know, because I said you're beautiful."

"No. I mean it." He tucked a piece of hair behind my ear, his hand lingering a moment too long. "So beautiful." His lips met mine with an undercurrent of electricity. The kiss started out soft and sweet but began to gain momentum quickly. I gasped as his tongue slid in to deftly take control of my mouth. An unfamiliar feeling of liquid heat pooled in my middle, causing a moan to escape from me as I wrapped my arms around his shoulders in an attempt to pull him closer. It was like my body was on fire, and Bryn was the only one who could bring me relief.

And just as suddenly as it had begun, the kiss ended. Bryn stood quickly, leaving me on the ground to stare up at him in a daze. He swore under his breath, turning away from me to run his hands through his hair. "That shouldn't have happened." His voice broke an octave lower than normal, causing my stomach to do a little flip flop.

"Bryn." His name, carrying an unsaid plea, felt new and unfamiliar on my tongue. I wanted his lips on me again, so much so that almost being raped didn't even feel relevant anymore. Following my duty didn't seem relevant anymore either. Nothing but tasting Bryn's lips again mattered in that moment. "Bryn," I said again, bringing the fingertips of my hand to touch my lips, imagining his were still locked with mine. It didn't matter that he was a Guardian and I was a Seer; he was Bryn—*my* Bryn.

Bryn turned back towards me, acknowledging my silent plea with wide eyes. Tension was etched into every line on his face. "You're drunk, and that shouldn't have happened."

Maybe I was buzzed, but I wasn't drunk. And for the life of me, I couldn't remember why kissing Bryn was such a bad idea. I might have had the memory a moment ago, but it was now buried beneath the fog in my brain. I'd never imagined kissing someone could feel so—*right*. So there was no reason why it shouldn't have happened or why it shouldn't happen again. "Why?" I whispered. "Why shouldn't it have happened? I want—I want you to kiss me again." When Bryn didn't move, I felt my cheeks heat with embarrassment. Again, how could I be so stupid? Of course Bryn didn't want to kiss me again, we were friends—best friends. He obviously didn't think of me in a sexual manner—like I had told Jenna earlier in the day.

Bryn's dark blue eyes held so much sadness, I thought it might be possible to drown in them. "I'm a Guardian, Peej. That's why it shouldn't have happened."

"Oh," was all I managed. How could I have forgotten? *Maybe I am drunk.* Of course—there was no possibility of a future for us. I would marry a Seer descendant or a Gatekeeper one day, not a Guardian. I brought my fingertips back up to touch my lips—they yearned to be pressed up against Bryn's again—and suddenly none of that mattered anymore. "I don't care," I whispered, gathering my feet under me and pushing off them to stand. I swayed for a second, dizziness temporarily tilting my world, before Bryn caught me in his big strong arms. "I don't care," I whispered again as I looked up into Bryn's beautiful face from only mere inches away.

"You should care," he replied.

"I want you"—even as I was saying it I could hardly believe the words that were coming out of my mouth—"to be my first time." Not stopping to get a reaction from Bryn, I took a step back and tugged my tattered dress from my body. I stood in front of him in only a little black thong and matching lace bra. Goosebumps erupted over my skin in response to the cool night air.

HIDDEN GATES

"Peej—" Bryn's voice cracked, and I averted my eyes, not wanting to see any kind of rejection there. I was hoping I hadn't misread what he had just said. He didn't say he didn't want me, just that we couldn't be together because I was a Seer and he was a Guardian.

"Don't you want to? Be my first? I thought you said you think I'm beautiful." Still not wanting to meet his eyes, I watched his fists clench and unclench.

He strode forward and took my face in his hands. "I want it so much it hurts." There was a fierceness in his eyes that I'd never seen before, and I realized I liked him looking at me that way. We had somehow found our way back to the same tree that the wanna-be rapist had been trying to take advantage of me against, but none of that mattered once Bryn claimed my mouth again. I eagerly welcomed the taste of him on my tongue, the feel of his callused hands on my skin, and the press of his body against mine. I gasped into his mouth as he ground himself against me, feeling that part of him pressed so intimately against me was a shock—even if it was a good one. When I instinctively wrapped my long legs around his waist, I felt Bryn freeze. "We can't," he protested against my mouth as he pulled away from me. "We just can't."

"Bryn, no—," I started to protest, but he didn't let me finish.

"No, we can't," he growled. "God knows how much I want to, how long I've thought about it. That's why Tammie and I broke up—because it wasn't right; I couldn't get you out of my head. It wouldn't have been right to be with her when I was thinking about you the whole time. But it doesn't change the fact that you're a Seer and I'm a Guardian. You're too good for me, out of my league."

I blinked at him in surprise, letting his words fully sink in. I was the reason he broke up with Tammie? He wanted me? Like *really* wanted me? "You can have me." And I meant it,

I realized as I said the words, that I always had—and always would be—his for the taking.

"Be careful, Peej." His voice was low and husky. "If you keep offering, I might just take it."

I stepped into him, resting my hand on his arm. "I wouldn't offer it if I wasn't willing to let you have it." His sea storm eyes threatened to pull me under, to wash away any thoughts of anything but him. "Don't you see? I'm not too good for you; if anything, it's the other way around. You're always watching out for me, taking care of me—what have I ever done for you except be a major pain in your ass?"

A slight smile curled the corners of his lips up. "You don't even know how great you really are, which is part of why I love you." As soon as he said the last part, he clamped his mouth shut, his face going taut with tension again.

My mouth dropped open, ready to catch any nearby flies. "You love me?"

"Yeah, you know that; of course I love you," he said gruffly, not meeting my eyes.

"No—you *love* me?"

Bryn stood still and silent, hardly breathing.

"How long? Just—how long?"

"I don't know." His voice was so low and soft that if I hadn't been standing so close, I never would have heard it. "Maybe always. It just took me awhile to figure out what my feelings really meant."

As his words sunk in, it made me question my own feelings. Could I be in love with Bryn and not even know it? I thought about all the times I'd gone out of my mind when he'd been with Tammie, even though I thought it was because he was my best friend, and I was just jealous of his time. But maybe not, maybe it had been more. Next, my mind flipped through all the times when I'd gotten petty with girls when I felt like

HIDDEN GATES

they were trying to flirt or make a move on him. Again, I had thought it was just because I was jealous of his attention. But it was more than that, I realized—much more. I had always thought of Bryn as mine. He belonged to me. His smile, his eyes, even the mix of his deodorant, soap, and individual scent that made him—*home*; I'd come to think of him as home. Everything about Bryn was home for me. "Every time I'm with you, it's like coming home," I murmured.

"What does that even mean?"

I stepped closer into Bryn, pressing my body tightly against his. "It means I love you, too." Why did it take almost being raped for me to figure it out? Now I understood why I'd thought of Bryn when the wanna-be rapist had his hands all over me. It was because his was the face that I loved, the one I truly longed for, the one I wouldn't have been able to look at again, if he hadn't arrived in time to stop it from happening.

He opened and shut his mouth as though he didn't know what to say, before his face hardened with determination. "You'll get over it when your mom starts setting you up on dates with guys you can actually be with, guys that a real future is possible with."

I began to feel my thoughts sharpen, the effects of the alcohol finally beginning to wear off. I let out a strangled cry of frustration. "But I don't want other guys—I want you." *If only I'd figured it out sooner.*

"I won't be strong enough to watch another guy walk away with you once I've had you. It's just better for me not to know." His voice turned pleading. "Let it go, Peej. I'm going to be your personal Guardian one day. I won't be able to handle it if we have some kind of thing like you're suggesting. I know I'm a guy, but I want more than just sex with you."

"I'm not trying to suggest that we have some little thing that's just about sex. Didn't you hear me? I love you, too."

"Put your dress back on. *Now*," Bryn said between clenched teeth. Instead, I unhooked my bra and let it slip from my arms. I loved him, too. I wanted him. Why couldn't he see that wasn't something someone like me would just throw away?

Bryn groaned, his eyes locking onto my nearly naked body. "You'd put it all on the line for me, give it all to me, wouldn't you? Because you think you have a choice." His voice came out sounding strained to the point that it almost hurt me to hear it. "But you don't have a choice. *We* don't have a choice. *Put. Your. Clothes. Back. On. Now.*"

"No." I raised my chin at him defiantly. "There's always a choice. We'll find a way. You're not going to run away from this—from me."

"Put. Them. Back. On. *Now*." Bryn snarled at me. He'd never talked to me like that before, and even though I wasn't afraid of him, it still made me back up a few steps. Unfortunately for me, my balance wasn't what it should have been, because even though my thoughts were clearer, I was still buzzed. The ground came up to meet me so fast that I banged my head on the hard dirt.

"Ow," I grumbled, suddenly feeling nauseous. "I don't feel so good anymore." I rolled onto my side just in time to throw up everything I had in my stomach. *Fabulous*. I closed my eyes and wished the ground would open up and swallow me whole. "Go away, Bryn. Just leave me." *My humiliation is complete.*

"I'm not leaving you. Don't be stupid. I'm going to give you my shirt; it should cover you better than Jenna's dress did, anyways."

"Why can't I just put the dress back on?" I mumbled.

"Because it's ripped, and you just threw up on it." If I didn't know better, I'd swear Bryn was laughing at me. *No. He wouldn't dare.*

HIDDEN GATES

"Okay. But you can tell Jenna what happened." My world was spinning, and all I wanted was to go to sleep, until a thought occurred to me. Bryn would be walking around with his shirt off in front of everyone—everyone as in all the other girls at the party. Jealousy spiked through my fuzzy, probably concussed brain. "No. I'll wear the puke dress," I mumbled, my eyes still shut. I had no desire to see whatever was swimming in his beautiful sea storm eyes. But I felt Bryn lift me up in his arms, already bare-chested. *When did that happen?* "You can't walk around without a shirt on," I stated with annoyance. Why did he not understand this?

He chuckled. "I think me walking around without my shirt on is going to cause less of a stir than you doing it."

"I said I'd wear the puke dress," I grumbled. What did I have to do to make him understand? *Geez.*

"What's your problem with me being shirtless?" I could hear the amusement in his voice.

"Because you're mine." I snuggled in tighter to his muscular chest. "And I don't want the Jennas of the world to get a good look at what they've been missing and steal you away." I inhaled deeply, letting Bryn's scent surround me in comfort—*home.* As I began drifting off to sleep, I heard Bryn whisper something that I'd never forget.

"There's never any danger of that. I'm yours. Always."

4

At first I thought it was a dream. Something pulled me up and out of my body—an invisible power—not a completely unpleasant feeling, just different than anything I'd ever experienced before. Off in the distance, a weird purple light pulsated, and the draw of it made me feel like I was caught in a tractor beam. I focused my mind completely, and the light drew closer to me—or I drew closer to it; I wasn't really sure which. I arrived at the origins of the purple light, and I found myself so completely riveted that it was as if I were mesmerized.

The air around me felt cool, and yet it was charged with an electric current, almost like static electricity. All the hairs on my body stood on end. In front of me, it appeared as if a piece of sky had been ripped into the side of the forest, the jagged edges swaying in time with pulsating shades of purple and blue. The shape of it was irregular, moving as I imagine pure energy does, with a kind of pattern that no naked eye could pick up on—even a Seer's naked eye. It was absolutely beautiful, and a sort of pity washed over me for all of the Regs that would never get to see such a magnificent sight.

As I stood, or hovered, or whatever; shapes began to emerge from—*the gate. Yes*—I realized I was seeing one of the gates for the first time; truly *seeing* it. But my elation was short-lived as the shapes took form in front of my eyes. They looked human, and yet were *other*. There were so many of them—too many to count—and I couldn't tell any of them apart; they all appeared uniform in appearance to me. Huge eyes bulged out of their too tiny, pinched faces. Luminescent, dewy skin glowed with a soft light that picked up on the gate's hues, making them all appear to pulsate with their own lights. They glided out of the gate slowly, their thin bodies levitating inches off the ground. As I stared at them, a chill ran up my spine. I couldn't shake the feeling that these creatures were dangerous, and they were creeping into my world completely unnoticed. Where were the other Seers? Why weren't they here watching this with me? Where were the Gatekeepers to shut the gate on these pesky humanlike creatures? And where were the Speakers and Guardians to tell them to return to whence they came or they'd get some major smackdown laid on them?

I seemed to be the only silent witness to the breach of our world. And then, just like that, they blurred off into the distance, too fast for my eyes to track. With horror, I realized they had disappeared, and I had no idea where they'd gone. They could be anywhere—anywhere at all. I had to tell everyone. Warn them before it was too late. I had to—

"P.J. Hey, P.J. Wake up," Jenna said with annoyance. "You're having a nightmare, and I'm trying to sleep."

I opened my eyes and tried to sit up, but my head was pounding. Reaching up, I grabbed my temples, almost sure I'd find brain matter of some sort oozing out. "What happened?" I tried to focus my eyes, but everything was blurry.

"I'll tell you what happened. You got too drunk, you puked on my dress—but not before managing to rip it—and then you

HIDDEN GATES

passed out. Me and Bryn brought you back to my place where I've been trying to sleep."

Events from earlier in the evening came flooding back with crystal clarity. I groaned as I tried to process everything that happened. "Where's Bryn?" was all I could manage.

"I made him go home. He wanted to stay, but I was afraid if my parents came home early and found him here, they'd blow a gasket." Jenna said around a yawn. "Now go back to sleep."

"But he's my Guardian," I groused.

"As my mom would say, he's not your Guardian yet, so go to sleep." I heard Jenna flop over on her bed.

"Wait. I had a premonition. We have to warn people." Finally that got a real reaction out of her, but not the one I expected.

"You got drunk, hit your head, and passed out. You didn't have a premonition, you just think you did." Jenna flung a pillow that hit me in my face. "Now go to sleep."

"Fine," I muttered to myself as I stumbled out of Jenna's guest twin bed. If Jenna wouldn't listen to me, I would find someone who would. As I made my way out into the hallway, I tripped over something in the middle of the floor. "What the hell?" I yelled as I lurched forward in the dark. Strong, familiar arms caught me before I face-planted.

"What are you doing?" Bryn stage whispered. "Go back to bed."

"What are you doing in the middle of the floor?" I asked incredulously. "It's a good way to get kicked in the head, and send someone hurtling to their death, I might add."

"I wasn't in the middle of the floor, I was leaning against the wall. You just don't have any depth perception."

"Hey. It's dark. I—"

The hallway light flicked on, and a very annoyed Jenna glared out from under a tangled mess of red hair. "What the hell? I told you to go home."

Bryn glared back at Jenna. "I couldn't just leave her. I was worried. Besides, if someone hadn't let her go stumbling around in the dark, you would've never known I was here."

"I'm not her babysitter," Jenna snapped.

"How about trying to be a concerned friend?" Bryn growled.

My friends were completely exasperating. "I have no time for this. I have to warn everyone about the premonition I just had."

Bryn's head snapped back towards me. "What? What'd you see?"

"Nothing. She was drunk and hit her head, remember?" Jenna said with a sigh. "So can we all just go back to bed, please?"

Bryn studied my face for a second before responding. "Do you really think you had a premonition, or do you think Jenna could be right?"

I met Bryn's blue eyes and shivered, thinking of the kisses we had shared earlier. Recognition of my reaction to him played briefly across his face before he looked away. I swallowed, trying to fight the sudden dryness in my throat. It finally dawned on me that I still had Bryn's shirt on and almost nothing else on underneath. He hadn't bothered to find another shirt, so he stood in Jenna's hallway in nothing but his jeans and socks. I found myself wondering if Bryn was a boxer or brief kind of guy, or maybe he went commando? I wanted nothing more than to close the distance between us, and run my hands over his finely honed muscles and smooth skin; to dip my hands underneath the waistband of his jeans so I could find the answer to my question.

"What's wrong with you guys? I'm getting some really weird vibes from you two right now." Jenna looked back and forth between the two of us. "Well?"

HIDDEN GATES

I couldn't let Jenna know. What happened between Bryn and I, and the potential of what could happen between us in the future—that was staying between just the two of us. I had to say something to distract her fast. "It felt like a premonition, but I don't know. Bryn—what do you think?"

He was careful not to meet my eyes again as he spoke. "If it was something that major, then someone else had to have seen it—another Seer, I mean. You should just go back to sleep, and we can figure it all out tomorrow."

"Yeah, I guess." Standing out in Jenna's hallway made the premonition, or whatever it was, seem too surreal to be plausible. Besides, Bryn was right, how could it be possible for me to have been the only one to see such an important vision, especially when I'd never had any before? Chances were, with having hit my head and having been buzzed, I'd just had a very realistic dream. And of course, in my dream I'd be the only one who could save the day. It was an excellent way for my psyche to make up for the fact that I hadn't had any real premonitions yet—just give me the Mac Daddy of all premonitions to make myself feel extra special. On to more important issues, I supposed. "Are you going to keep sleeping in the hallway?"

"Probably," Bryn said while running a hand through his black hair. "It would make me feel better to kind of stand guard for you, since I will be your Guardian one day." He met my eyes with meaning. Yeah, yeah; I knew what he was trying to get at, and I didn't care. I let my gaze briefly pass over his smooth, muscular upper body before returning to his perfectly chiseled face.

"You could keep a closer watch if you stayed in Jenna's room with us." I bit my lower lip and smiled at him. "I mean, you could always stay in my bed, with me, so you could keep a *very* close eye on me."

"Oh, hellz, no," Jenna interjected. I had almost forgotten she was standing there. "If he wants to be all creepy and stay in the hallway, fine. At least he has a leg to stand on with the whole future Guardian thing with that situation. But if my parents caught him in bed with you, no matter how platonic we all know it would be, there'd be no escape from punishment for any of us."

I raised my eyebrows at Bryn, asking him a silent question. How platonic would it be now that we'd crossed that line? Would he be able to just hold me like he used to under the guise of friendship now that he knew that I loved him and wanted him, too? From the tormented look on his face, I was guessing the answer was no. Was he imagining what it would be like to be naked in bed with me right now? I sighed loudly thinking about it myself.

Jenna looked at me sharply. "Seriously—what is going on with you guys?"

I forced a yawn. "Going back to bed now." Luckily it was always easy to distract her.

"Finally," she muttered, flicking the hallway light off. I stumbled back into bed and crawled under the sheets, shutting my eyes against my pounding head. I thought with how crappy I felt, the minute my head touched the pillow I would have had an instant ticket to dreamland, but instead, all I could think about was Bryn; Bryn, and his half-undressed state, currently residing right outside Jenna's door. It was like the kiss we shared earlier had unlocked all these feelings that had been pent up for years. I sure would have liked to unwrap him as a birthday present. *Ugh. I'm starting to sound like Jenna.* The fact was that I just wanted to be near him—something that I always craved; it was just that now I actually knew my motivations.

I stumbled out of bed again and crept back into the hallway. This time I had a pretty good idea where Bryn had situated himself so that I wouldn't trip over him again. I heard him sigh in the dark as I dropped to all fours and reached my hand out to search for him.

"What are you doing?" he whispered, tension evident in his voice.

"Where are you?" I asked ignoring his question. I felt his hand take mine in response, tugging me forward. "You'd think Seers would have better night vision," I grumbled. When I found him there in the dark, I pushed my way under his arm to snuggle up close to him. "I still don't feel good." I ran my hand slowly over his chest and inhaled his scent deeply. *Mmmm... there is nothing like the spicy aroma of Bryn mixed with soap.* I was sure I could make a lot of money if I bottled and sold the purely masculine—and suddenly very sexy—scent that was all Bryn.

It seemed like every muscle in his body tensed. "So go back into your nice, comfortable bed."

"But you always make things better when I don't feel good." I pouted. There had always been something comforting about Bryn's presence. I couldn't even begin to count how many times we'd spent the night together with me in his arms. Of course, things were a little different now that we'd crossed a line earlier.

"Things are different now," Bryn said warily, saying the same thing I'd just been thinking.

"So what? Now I can't be close to you anymore?"

"You know what I mean, Peej."

"Just hold me," I snapped obstinately. I wasn't going to let him push me away—literally or metaphorically.

I heard him sigh in the dark again, just before his arms encircled me. I snuggled into his side, my head on his chest, and I brought one leg up and over his. I was happier than a clichéd bug in a rug. The tension I felt in his body only seemed to last a few minutes before his breathing became more even as he drifted off to sleep. Feeling so safe and content in his arms, I wasn't far behind.

5

Things were pretty awkward between Bryn and me that morning when we woke up. He still insisted on keeping his hands to himself, much to my chagrin. And as soon as he disentangled from me, he left so fast I was surprised there wasn't a Bryn shaped hole in the door. *When did things get so complicated?* Oh, that's right—last night when I'd drunk too much, stripped, and threw myself at Bryn, then proceeded to puke and pass out in front of him as well. *Talk about putting in a good night's work.*

I was currently getting ready for our families' joint birthday celebration. It was generally pretty low key—just our families, a nice dinner, some cake and ice cream to follow, and then, of course, presents. I usually had a good time sharing the birthday spotlight with Bryn, but I had to wonder how high the tension meter would be registering between us tonight. If the nervous flutter in my stomach was any indication, fairly high.

"What's wrong, peanut?" I lifted my eyes to see my mom standing in my bedroom doorway, her face reflected in the mirror of my vanity. Her green eyes blinked at me with concern from her small, finely featured face. I noticed that she had styled her shoulder length reddish hair into a neat updo. A chignon maybe? She never wore very much makeup because she had a simple, natural beauty; today was no different.

"Nothing. Why?" I said absently as I set down the lip gloss I had just applied.

"Oh, I don't know, maybe because I've been standing here saying your name for the last five minutes."

I gave my mom the best smile I could manage. "I just have some things on my mind. Nothing's wrong exactly."

She gave me a knowing smile. "A boy wouldn't have anything to do with what you're thinking about, hmm?"

My mom was pretty cool as far as moms were concerned, but I also knew I couldn't talk to her about Bryn. She wouldn't approve of me wanting to be with him unless he suddenly became a Seer descendent or a Gatekeeper. Still, nothing wrong with testing the waters a little. "Well . . . I don't know . . . It's just—have you ever wanted to be with someone that wasn't who everyone expected you to be with? You know, when you were younger, before Dad?"

My mom came farther into my room and looked at me with understanding. "Oh, I see. You have a crush on someone you know you shouldn't."

"Well, not exactly." I knew no such thing. My feelings for Bryn were too right to be wrong—as cliché as it sounded.

My mom sat down on my bed. "Let me guess, an ungifted human or a Guardian?"

"How did you know?"

She laughed. "Oh, honey, the forbidden fruit is always the sweetest when we're young. But those kinds of things pass—puppy love always does."

"But what if it doesn't? What if it's more than puppy love?" Too late for the *what if* it's more than puppy love part.

HIDDEN GATES

"Don't be silly, of course it'll pass." She studied me for a moment before her smile seemed to up in wattage. "It's about time I start setting you up with some eligible young men, men who you could have a future with." *Oh no, I can't believe it's come to this.* Eligible young men meant only Seer descendents and Gatekeepers who were actually future husband candidates for me. It was very common with parents amongst our people to make introductions of the kind my mom was referring to. There is even a term for it—*Suiridhe*; it means wooing—or rather, forced wooing. Somewhere along the line, the younger generations had begun calling the whole process Sudding—maybe because we felt like we were getting hung out to dry after the wash, not really getting much of a say about who we eventually settled down with.

Parents paid attention when couples in my community had children, and they took notes as those children grew up. My mom probably had a list of guys that she thought I should give a chance—literally. Some parents, like mine, would give their children a little bit more say in the process, but when it came down to it, the final choice was out of my hands. Families with the most coveted, gifted children, like Seers, always held the advantage. *Bonus for me.* So all my mom had to do was start making phone calls to the eligible guys' parents, and soon enough, I'd have guys lined up around the block to date me, whether they wanted to or not.

My mind flashed to Bryn telling me just last night that my feelings would all pass when my mom started setting me up, that I would move on and leave him behind. Bryn had known it was only a matter of time before my mom started my Sudding. After all, I wasn't officially dating anyone, and I had just had my eighteenth birthday. "Aren't you worried about my feelings for this other guy?"

My mom got up from my bed and headed for the door before turning to fix me with her gaze. "No. I don't worry about you, honey, because when it comes down to it, I know you'll do the right thing. I'll see you downstairs when you're ready." She pulled my door shut behind her, leaving me alone with my thoughts.

My worst fears were coming to fruition. I was going to be set up with guys who weren't Bryn, and I was expected to one day pick one of them. An arranged marriage it was not, but it suddenly felt eerily close. The thought of letting anyone else but Bryn touch me made my stomach queasy. What was I going to do? And it wasn't even an *us* against the world situation; currently it was just *me* against the world. I couldn't even get Bryn to fight for me. That's when it hit me, maybe if I could do that—get Bryn to fight for me—then at least we'd stand a chance. I smiled at myself in the mirror. *I have a plan—finally.*

I stood and briefly scanned my purple accented room, already mentally picking through my closet, before pulling my current top over my head and letting it drop to the floor. Normally, I was a bit of a neat freak, but at the moment, even I didn't have time to worry about a few misplaced articles of clothing. I reached into the top drawer of my dresser and pulled out a Snickers bar from my secret stash. I was going to need some chocolate fortification before I set to work on myself. As I munched, I glanced at the calendar hanging on my wall with September 23rd and 24th circled in purple Sharpie. Not only were yesterday and today important because they were mine and Bryn's birthdays, but the dates also symbolized a rebirth of sorts for both of us. Last night at Ryan's party had changed everything, and I was determined that it would all be for the better.

About thirty minutes later, I made my way downstairs, dressed like I was ready for a red carpet somewhere. I had

HIDDEN GATES

decided that instead of my normal casual wear, I would put on a party dress; it was a party after all. It wasn't as tiny as the one I had on last night, but it showed off what assets I had very nicely, and the green glossy material really made my green eyes pop. I also actually took the time to curl my hair and apply more makeup than just powder and lip gloss. I looked pretty damn good, if I did say so myself.

As I entered my living room, all eyes turned towards me, but my gaze sought out only one person. Bryn was sitting in his usual spot at the corner of the couch, a glass of soda in his hand, and when he saw me, the smile on his face dropped. His cerulean eyes roved over my body from bottom to top, stopping to meet my eyes before quickly looking away. And yet what I saw there before he turned was exactly what I had been going for—possession. There was some small part of him that thought I belonged to him, just like I knew he belonged to me, and seeing me dressed the way I was made him actually want to, well, possess. I smiled to myself. *Bryn is so toast.*

Everyone greeted me with a chorus of Happy Birthdays before my mom ushered us all into the dining room for dinner. Bryn and I took our traditional seats next to each other in the center of the table. "What are you doing?" Bryn whispered.

I smiled at him innocently. "I'm sure I don't know what you mean."

He quirked one dark eyebrow at me. "I don't believe that for a second."

"What you choose to believe or not believe has nothing to do with me." I widened my smile. "Now let's just have a nice dinner and enjoy ourselves."

Dinner went pretty smoothly, and I could tell Bryn was starting to relax a little. He even let me take his hand like I normally did. It was only when we were opening presents that things got more interesting.

"Kevin," my mom said conversationally to my dad, "I was just telling P. J. earlier that I think it's time for us to start setting her up on dates with some proper young men . . . you know?"

"Sure," my dad agreed.

"It's about time you started *Suiridhe*. Some of the other single Seers about your age started already. You better get going before you miss out on someone good," Bryn's mom, of all people, chimed in. It was like they were talking about going shoe shopping or something. *You better hit the sale before all the best shoes are gone.*

I stared at Bryn when I put my two cents in. "Sure. I'd love to, Mom. It's not like I have any other prospects of my own to worry about, not really." Bryn dropped my hand, and by the look on his face, I could tell that was not the answer he had been expecting from me. "The sooner the better," I added for more effect.

"Oh, good, honey, I'll get started right away." My mom called over her shoulder as she headed back into the kitchen, "Anyone need anything while I'm in here?"

"I'm going for a walk." Bryn stood suddenly.

"I'll go with you." I wasn't going to let him get away that easily.

"No," he said.

"Well, why not?" I quirked an eyebrow at him in silent challenge. He knew he couldn't make that big a deal about wanting to get away from me without raising some questions. His jaw ticked with tension, and he turned and headed for the door without another word. Of course, he knew I would follow him. "We'll be back in a couple minutes," I called to no one in particular. Bryn and I going off by ourselves was a pretty common occurrence, and no one in either of our families would give it a second thought.

I struggled in my high heels to keep up with Bryn at the brisk pace he was keeping. "Hey, wait up," I snapped.

HIDDEN GATES

"And why would I do that when I'm trying to lose you?" Bryn snapped back, ducking into the woods that sat across from my house.

"Bryn, please."

He whirled back to face me, his face contorted in agony. "What the hell are you trying to do to me, Peej? Seriously, are you trying to punish me or something?"

"No, I—"

My words were swallowed up when his mouth found mine, his tongue forcefully pushing past my lips. His heady taste and raw masculine scent invaded my senses and overpowered me. His hands tangled in my hair, and just like the night before, I found myself pushed up against a tree by Bryn. The way he was kissing me was different than before though, he was being more forceful, and there seemed to be an undercurrent of desperation. All my nerve endings felt like they crackled with his energy, and a wave of pure lust slammed into me. "I can't lose you. I just can't," he rumbled into my mouth.

I inwardly smiled. Had my plan worked that quickly? Had the mere threat of me being with someone else driven Bryn into my arms? *Time to find out.* "I wanna be with you, Bryn. I don't wanna be with anyone else. Ever."

He stilled for a moment, breaking our kiss and pulling back just enough so he could look into my eyes. "We'll find a way. Somehow, we'll find a way," and then his lips sought mine again. That was all I needed to hear. Bryn would fight for me. Somehow we would make it work.

We stayed like that for I'm not sure how long, just making out furiously in the woods across from my house. But before things could progress much farther, Bryn pulled away, even with my protesting lips trying to ensnare his again. "Not like this. Your first time can't be like this."

I tried to catch my breath as I gazed up into his beautiful blue eyes. My insides churned for him. "You can't take it back. You can't say we'll find a way and then take it back. That would be even worse than if you'd never said anything at all." *It would kill me,* but I left that part unsaid.

He cupped my face in both of his large hands and spoke inches from me. "No. There's no going back. I want this." He shook his head slightly. "No. I *need* this. I need you. I can't imagine my life without you. Just being your Guardian isn't enough—it'd never be enough."

"So what do we do?" I whispered. I hadn't thought much beyond the getting Bryn to fight for me plan, and honestly, I didn't think it would work so fast.

"For now it has to stay a secret. We can't tell anyone."

I nodded in agreement. "Of course."

"We'll both be out of high school in less than a year, and then they can't stop us—no one can stop us."

"But what about my mom and the Sudding . . ." My voice trailed off as I noticed the torment in his eyes.

"You go. You pretend. We bide our time. And we do this"—he delivered me another long, delicious kiss that left me feeling slightly dizzy—"in secret."

"Okay."

His thumbs circled my cheeks. "I love you, Peej—so much, it hurts."

I bit my lower lip as I looked up at him. His eyes spoke of promises, promises of hope and love, and I wanted nothing more than to drown in those promises. "I love you, too."

"Come on." He interlaced his fingers with mine and tugged me away from my now favorite tree in the whole world. "We better get back before they start to wonder what's taking us so long."

"But wait—" I teetered on my heels, trying not to let Bryn pull me forward. "I didn't give you your birthday present yet."

HIDDEN GATES

Reaching into my dress, just above my left bra cup, I produced a slim leather wallet.

Bryn's eyes widened slightly. "How did I miss that?"

I laughed. "Well, to be fair, I had it more under the strap, and you kind of skipped over that area of my body and got right down to business with your groping. Not to mention that you were completely over my clothes and—"

Bryn echoed my laugh with one of his own. "Okay, okay, I get the point. Can I have my present now?"

I set the wallet on his upturned, waiting palm and watched him with anxiety. The wallet was something that I would give my friend Bryn, but he was more now... so much more. Maybe he wouldn't like it. Maybe he would think it was stupid. Bryn was always such a hard person to shop for, and I'd noticed that he needed a new wallet. His old one was on its last legs, not to mention it had a Velcro closure. I mean, Velcro? Seriously? So I got him a nice little leather wallet with his initials on the front. I'd also added another personal touch on the inside...

"Is this a picture from our first birthday celebration together? What were we, like, five?"

"No, six. We didn't start celebrating our birthdays together until we were six." I was momentarily swept away to another time as I pictured Bryn as the tiny mischievous boy that I'd come to call my best friend. His black hair had fallen forward into his sparkling blue eyes, and he had given me his patented lopsided grin complete with dimples, just as he smashed a piece of cake into my face. Of course, I had reciprocated, and a full out cake war had ensued. That's when my mom had snapped the picture of us that I had put into Bryn's wallet. We were both completely covered in chocolate cake and beaming at each other.

"Peej—"

"I know it's stupid. I guess I'm just being a sentimental girl. I don't know what—"

"I love it," Bryn cut me off. "The fact that you noticed my old wallet is falling apart—I don't know, maybe I'm being girly and sentimental, too, but I think it's cool you pay that much attention to me, that you notice the little things no one else does. And the picture . . . I love it, too."

Warmth bloomed in my chest, and I smiled at him. "I'm really glad you like it—all of it."

"My turn," Bryn muttered more to himself than me as he reached into his back pocket.

When he offered me a small black velvet box, I gasped. No guy besides my dad had ever given me jewelry before. Unable to find words just yet, I took my gift from him and popped the lid off quickly. I gasped again, "Bryn, I love them! They're just the ones I wanted—the ones I told you I saw at the mall with Jenna last month." Winking at me in the dim light was a small pair of blue sapphire stud earrings. The dark blue color reminded me of Bryn's eyes when they were churning with deep emotion, and sapphire happened to be both of our birthstones. They were absolutely perfect.

"Yeah, I know. I had Jenna show me which ones."

"But how did you afford them? I mean, they weren't exactly cheap—"

Bryn stepped forward, bringing his large hand up to cup the side of my face, and the charge of electricity that passed between the two of us shut me up completely. He stared into my eyes as he spoke. "I just wanted to make you happy." I was left completely speechless, and in the thrall of Bryn's cerulean eyes. "We'd better get back for real this time"—he cleared his throat, dropped his gaze from mine, and took my hand within his—"before I do something we'll both regret."

As I trailed along mutely behind Bryn, heading back to our party, I thought if I could find my voice, I would tell him that whatever he wanted to do—*I* most certainly wouldn't have regretted it.

6

It was harder than I ever thought possible to keep things secret about what was going on between Bryn and me. Being with him all the time had become a different form of torture. Sitting so close to him, holding his hand—those things made me want to run my hands all over him, to explore the finely honed muscles that lay under his smooth, pale skin, to kiss not only his lips but his sweet, salty skin. I craved closeness to him—a closeness I wasn't even sure I understood, being that I was still a virgin. When I was around him, it was if my skin hummed in anticipation of even the slightest touch from him, and when I looked into his dark blue eyes, I knew he felt the same. We were in love, the kind of deep, soul-changing love that happens only once in a lifetime.

That being said, I was currently waiting to go on a date with someone my mom had set me up with, *someone that was not Bryn*. I had chosen to wear black skinny dress pants and a black and white striped one-shoulder top, paired with black gladiator sandals. What I really wanted to be in was jeans and a T-shirt, but I had to at least look like I was trying, for appearance's sake. Bryn knew about the date, but I couldn't shake the feeling that I was cheating on him. I wished that I'd never said anything to my mom. Instead of sitting on the couch waiting for my would-be suitor, I could be off with Bryn somewhere, his full, perfect lips pressed against my skin. I shivered at the thought. I didn't know how much longer I'd be able to keep our relationship under wraps, not with the way he made my insides churn. Every fiber in my being cried out to be with him. Surely there was some kind of physical evidence when we were near each other. Or was I the only one whose skin heated and burned like a live wire was pushing electricity into me every time Bryn was near? How had no one picked up on that yet?

When the familiar sound of the doorbell chimed, dread snaked up and took hold of my chest, leaving it tight and restricted. I fought the urge to flee out the back door and run into the strong, reassuring arms of Bryn, and the comfort I knew I would find within them. He'd seemed pretty cool about the date when I'd told him about it a few days ago. After all, he knew we had to keep up appearances, to pretend that nothing had changed between us, but a part of me wished he'd appear in a jealous boyfriend rage and demand for me to not go on this date.

"Honey, Jeremy is here," my mom called to me, her voice much too cheery for my taste. I somehow managed to peel myself off the couch and trudge towards the front foyer. "Here she is," my mom nearly sang. "P.J., this is Jeremy. Jeremy, this is my lovely daughter, P.J. Don't mind her, I think she's a little nervous."

I glared at my mom. "I'm not nervous," I said under my breath.

"Hey." I looked up to meet the eyes of the boy who owned the voice. He had a pleasant enough face, sandy brown spiky

HIDDEN GATES

hair, deep brown eyes set over a long, straight nose, high cheekbones, full, firm lips, and a square, masculine jaw—quite handsome if I was being honest with myself. I wouldn't have been surprised to find his picture adorning the walls in one of those preppy clothing stores like Abercrombie & Fitch. Jenna would already be wiping drool off of her chin if she were in my shoes. She'd probably have him half undressed by the time they reached his car. *But he's not Bryn.*

"Hey," I replied coolly.

My mom grinned at me, obviously very pleased with herself. "Now you two have a good time." She proceeded to usher us out the front door, closing it behind us with finality.

"So . . ." Jeremy trailed off before clearing his throat. "I know this is kind of awkward, but I thought we could go get something to eat and talk, try to make this as painless as possible."

I hadn't considered the possibility that maybe whoever I went out with wouldn't exactly be thrilled to go on our date either. "Yeah, okay," I agreed with a tentative smile. I followed him down to a dark green RAV4, probably his parents', I guessed, since it was the newest model, and I let him open and shut the door for me as I climbed into the passenger side. I waited in silence as he rounded the car, letting my gaze settle on a patch of trees by my house. I sucked in a surprised breath when I saw Bryn standing there. As my gaze met his, he stepped back farther into the shadows. My heart twisted in my chest from the tormented look on his face. Why had he come to see me leave on my date? Why would he do that to himself? I raised my palm to the window and touched my fingertips to it, wishing it were his heated face under my skin and not smooth, cool glass.

The engine in the RAV4 revving to life pulled my mind back to the interior of the car and the date I was supposed to be on. I willed myself to look away from the dark night, and from where I knew Bryn most surely still lurked. I glanced over at Jeremy and gave him another tentative smile, to which he returned one of his own. "Music?" he asked.

"Yeah, sure."

"My iPod is down there in the console, already hooked up. I'll let you pick our soundtrack for the evening."

I began scrolling through his music selection without another word. I decided on Seether's *Fake It* for the first song, feeling it was oddly appropriate somehow, and Genius-ed it. Once the selection was made, I turned it up loud enough to where it would make conversation relatively difficult. Jeremy obviously took the hint, and we rode in silence—except for the music—and I stared out the window, watching the world blur by without really paying attention to where we were going. When the car rolled to a stop, I glanced up to see the warm glow of *Tony's* restaurant sign shining through the windshield. Pittsburgh and the surrounding suburbs are jam packed with local mom and pop Italian places, so Jeremy bringing me to one wasn't that odd, but it definitely wasn't a coincidence that he had chosen my favorite. "My mom told you, didn't she?" I asked with a frown.

Jeremy looked at me, taking in my frown, and shot me a puzzled expression. "It's okay, isn't it? I mean, was your mom wrong?"

"No," I sighed, fingering the buckle on my seatbelt. "She was right. This place is my favorite."

"Okaaay." Jeremy drew out the word, obviously considering what to say next. "Look, I know this is all awkward, like I said before, but there's no need for it to be painful. It's not like I was exactly thrilled when my parents informed me I had a date with someone that I'd never met before. But then again, it's not as if I'm seriously seeing anyone right now anyways, hence the Sudding." He smiled at me. "And now, after meeting you, even though I can tell you're less than thrilled to be here, I'm thinking this might not be that bad a thing after all."

So much for him not being interested in me. He seemed nice enough, and I didn't relish the thought of being mean to him, but what was the point, really? "Look," I tugged on my seatbelt nervously, "I'm here because my mom has it in her head that it's time for me to start dating *proper young men*, and I'm sure I don't have to clue you into what she means when she says that, but—" *But what?* I couldn't exactly tell him that I was in love with someone else. It no doubt would get around, and my mom would demand to know what was going on, and I couldn't afford for anyone to figure out what was happening between Bryn and me.

"But what?" Jeremy asked. "Are you, well, are you—there's no easy way to ask this, so I'm just going to—are you into girls or something?"

"What?" I blinked at him in total shock. I *so* hadn't seen that question coming.

"Well, you're not married, and you're not in a serious relationship, so if you're not a lesbian, then I don't see why you can't at least have dinner with me, give me a shot. Unless you think I'm completely repulsive?" He met my eyes and grinned, knowing full well he wasn't repulsive.

An image of Bryn flashed in my mind's eye. Heat rolled over my skin in reaction to the thought of his body pressed up flush to mine, his lips trailing down my—

I had to push the image immediately out of my mind before I combusted right where I sat. I fought the very real urge to fan myself. Yeah, the thought of me being into anything but boys made me laugh. I couldn't help the smile that stayed on my lips. "Fine. Dinner. But that's all I'm promising." I'd at least pretend to give him a shot, and then tell my mom there was no chemistry or something. *Next contestant, please.*

Jeremy turned to open his door, shooting me a hundred-watt smile. "That's all I'm asking."

I unhooked my seatbelt and slid out of the door to meet him beside the car. He offered me his arm, which I eyed warily before stalking off towards *Tony's*. I'd have dinner with him, but I never said I would touch him. So far, I'd managed to avoid the connection with his Gatekeeper powers by not opening myself up to them, and by not having skin-to-skin contact. I was planning on keeping it that way. For some reason, that fact was important to me, no matter if it didn't really make any sense.

About forty-five minutes later, numerous glasses of soda consumed, and our meals completely devoured, I had discovered that Jeremy wasn't that bad.

"So then what'd you do?" I laughed, trying hard not to squirt soda out of my nose.

"So there I was, out in the woods, by myself, completely naked, no phone, no keys, nothing. My only choice was to hoof it home. Luckily, a few blocks from where I was, I found a trash bag that didn't reek too bad that covered me up until I got home." He paused to laugh himself. "You shoulda seen the look on my dad's face when I tried sneaking in the back door. Of course, he was so proud when he found out the whole thing was because I was beginning to come into my powers."

I took another sip of soda. "I never knew that could happen to Gatekeepers. I wonder if it happens to a lot of you guys?"

Jeremy averted his eyes in embarrassment. "As far as I know, I'm the only one, although I'm not going to be making my incident public, so maybe that's why I haven't heard of it happening to anyone else."

HIDDEN GATES

"Well, I'm just glad being a Seer doesn't run that risk. I have enough potential for embarrassing situations as it is. I don't need to worry about zapping all of my clothes out of existence when I go to manipulate energy around a gate."

Jeremy's brown eyes met mine, suddenly serious. "I'm guessing there'd be a lot fewer complaints if you were seen around town naked, though."

Our gazes stayed locked for a minute before I turned away and cleared my throat. "So are you better now? With your powers? That doesn't happen on a regular basis, I mean?"

"No, it hasn't happened since then." His attention was temporarily distracted as our waitress brought back his change from our check. He took out a couple of bills and left them in the book for her.

I saw my opportunity and seized it. "I guess you're ready to go then?"

"Yeah, I guess. I don't suppose—"

"No," I interrupted. "I need to be getting home. I have to get up in the morning pretty early for . . . church." Yeah, I hadn't been to an early Sunday service in—ever. But he didn't know that.

"Oh." Disappointment showed in his eyes. "Then I guess I'd better get you home."

A wave of guilt rushed over me. I mean, Jeremy was a nice and charming guy, and if it weren't for Bryn, I might have even been interested. "Thanks for dinner and everything," I said as I stood and headed for the door. He caught up with me, and we walked in silence to the car where he opened and shut the door for me again. Like before, I turned up the music for the ride home, which effectively kept him from talking to me anymore. I heaved a sigh of relief when we pulled into my driveway.

Jeremy turned the car off and opened his door. "I'll walk you up."

"Oh, you don't have to . . ." I trailed off as he was already making his way around the car. *Why can't he just take the hint already? Ugh.*

He helped me out of the car and walked beside me all the way to my front door where he paused to face me. "Well, I'm really glad I met you, P.J., even though I know you're still feeling weird about this whole thing. I'll call or text or something and maybe we can go out again. I hope you'll be more open to it since you can see that I'm actually a nice guy."

I wasn't really sure what to do. I didn't want to be mean, but I didn't want to lead him on either. Should I hang out with him again for appearance's sake, or move on to the next guy my mom probably already had lined up? It most likely would be easier to go out with Jeremy a few more times before I dropped the no chemistry line on everyone. I had to at least pretend I was giving him a real shot. "Yeah, okay."

He smiled at me, real happiness shining back at me from his eyes. "All right, talk to you soon then." He leaned in and gave me a quick peck on the cheek before I had a chance to react. Just the briefest sense of his powers slid over my skin and snapped into sync with the act of his lips brushing my cheek. My breath caught in my throat at the intoxicating rush. He paused to lock eyes with me, and gave me another smile before heading off down my walk. *Crap.* Our powers had connected, and that wasn't a good thing. With my people, power was always a very enticing lure. If Jeremy thought we had a power connection, it would only heighten anything he might already be feeling for me. I stood there and watched him leave before turning to go into my house, but then I stopped. I had to see Bryn—now. I suddenly couldn't get the tormented look he had on his face before I left out of my head.

I took off at a dead sprint for Bryn's house, hoping he would be there. As I neared his home, which was only a few blocks

HIDDEN GATES

down from mine, and crept into his backyard, I breathed a sigh of relief when I saw the light in his first floor bedroom was on. *Thank God he's home.* Making my way up to his window, I paused to listen, checking if he was alone. It would be an utter disaster if his parents found out I was sneaking into his bedroom when I was supposed to still be on my date, and not just any date, but the first of my Sudding. I smiled when I didn't hear any voices and reached up to tap on the window. A few seconds later, Bryn peered out, and then pulled up his blinds and opened his window so I could crawl through. I could hardly wait to have Bryn's arms around me, and I fully expected to be greeted with the same enthusiasm from him; and yet when I went to him, his arms stayed limp at his sides, and his eyes regarded me with dark emotion. "What's wrong?" I asked, studying his face for some clue. He didn't say anything. He just kept watching me, his eyes churning with something I couldn't read. As I studied him, I realized his whole body was wrought with tension. "Bryn?" I licked my lips nervously, noting that his eyes followed my every move. He slowly stalked towards me, backing me up against the wall. His hands came to rest on either side of my head, balled into fists. And even though he seemed so angry, so dangerous, my breath caught in my throat, and my pulse began to race with excitement. "Bryn?" I said again, my voice coming out breathy and low.

"I couldn't stand seeing you leave with him," Bryn practically growled, his voice so low I barely recognized it. "I had to fight everything in me to not come after you." His chest was heaving as he tried to keep himself calm. "You're mine. I won't share you."

"It's not real, Bryn. You know that. I'm yours—all yours."

He stared at me a few more seconds, his eyes raging with so many dark emotions. "It seemed so real, Peej—like I was losing you. It was like a nightmare I couldn't wake up from."

I reached up and cupped his face, feeling his jaw tick with tension. "I'm here now. And I'm yours. Always."

He caught my lips with his, taking my mouth forcefully, dominating me like he never had before. I welcomed the heat of his jealousy turning into fiery passion as he explored me with his tongue and mouth. Our clothes began falling away, and soon we were both left in just our underwear. Usually this was the point where Bryn and I stopped. We hadn't gone much farther than heavy petting, and neither one of us had been completely naked in front of the other. Our physical relationship was just so new that we were both in awe of the simplest things, like kissing and touching, but tonight—tonight Bryn didn't show any signs of stopping. And I sure as hell wasn't going to protest. I'd wanted to give my virginity to him since that first night in the woods. He was the one who thought it wasn't the right time or place. He assumed that as a girl, I needed more for my first time, even though all I really needed or wanted was him—that's all I'd ever need.

"I need you, Peej," Bryn rumbled as his fingers deftly dipped down under my panties. I moaned as his long fingers explored areas where no boy had ever gone before.

"Yes," I gasped into his mouth. Bryn made quick work of getting my bra and panties off, lifting me, and setting me on his bed. He joined me there, but not before sitting back to study all of my bare, exposed skin. I fidgeted under his rapt gaze. "Bryn," I pleaded, reaching for him. It was one thing to be naked with Bryn while we were kissing and touching, but I didn't like him studying me while I just lay on his bed without a stitch of clothing on.

"You're so beautiful," Bryn whispered in reverence. He then came to rest over me, his pelvis cradled in between my legs. *When did he manage to get his boxers off?* I attempted to

HIDDEN GATES

swallow back my nerves as it really sunk in that Bryn and I were going to have sex. I locked gazes with him, and his sea storm eyes pulled me under, washing away all my trepidations. "You still taking the pill?" Bryn asked huskily.

Reality check. "Yeah." My mom would be absolutely furious if she knew I was using the pill for its intended purpose and not just to regulate my period. Especially if she found out I was using it with Bryn on the heels of a date with someone she had set me up with. "What about your parents—"

"Not here," Bryn said as he dipped his head, showering me with more kisses before pulling away again. "You ready? I don't wanna hurt you."

"Yeah, I'm ready," I whispered, gazing deep into his dark blue eyes. The way he looked at me in that moment, the love that emanated from him, made me feel like the most beautiful and special girl in the entire world. Someone who looked at me that way deserved to have everything that I was—mind, body, and soul. So far, he'd only received two of those three. *Tonight he would have everything.*

As he pushed into me, filling me in a way I'd never been able to imagine, I tried to mentally prepare myself for the pain. From all accounts, the first time for a girl was almost always painful, and I thought I was ready, but no amount of mental preparation could have readied me for the level of pain I was currently experiencing. I gritted my teeth and dug my nails into Bryn's shoulders, not wanting him to know how much it really hurt. But it was short lived—the pain I mean—and slowly, ever so slowly, as Bryn rocked back and forth inside of me, the pain began to be replaced by pleasure. A deep-seated pleasure that made me truly understand, for the first time, why people like Jenna were so sex crazed.

My entire world narrowed down to Bryn and me, and I could no longer tell where I ended and he began. Surely there was nothing closer to bliss than being in the arms of the man I loved, and sharing such intimacy with him. A new type of warmth I'd never experienced before bloomed in my center. Soon it grew into a fire of need, spreading through my system, pushing outward into spasms of ecstasy. Bryn captured my face in his palms, forcing me to look at him instead of throwing my head back like I wanted. He didn't last too much longer after that, and I slumped down in his bed as if all my bones were suddenly liquefied. Never, ever, had I imagined sex would be so wonderful—the connection between not only our bodies, but our powers as well—or maybe it was just that way with Bryn.

    I smiled up at him as he collapsed above me, careful not to put his full weight on me. I ran my hands through his silky, tousled hair, and then down over his sweaty back. He shuddered at my touch, leaning forward to kiss me with a slow languidness that spoke of shared intimacies, and unspoken promises. "I love you, Peej. More than I can even begin to explain." His voice was so low and husky it seemed to brush things on my insides, making me shudder in turn.

    I gazed up into his eyes with adoration. "I love you, too," I whispered, surprised at how husky my own voice sounded. I wished I could stay in his arms forever, forgetting about the outside world and all the problems it contained. But our love wouldn't be enough to protect us from our parents' wrath if they found us like this.

    I must have frowned because Bryn's brow furrowed as he looked at me. "What's wrong? Did I hurt you?"

    "No, Bryn" I bit my lower lip, thinking about what we'd just done. "You made my first time more amazing than I ever could have imagined." He grinned at me, a look of pure male pride washing over his features. "I just wish I could stay here with you and not worry about everything else."

HIDDEN GATES

He rolled onto his back, tucking me into his side so my head rested on his chest. "I hate this, Peej. I just wanna be with you. I wanna be able to touch when I want, kiss you when I want. I wanna yell from the rooftops that you belong to me." He pulled his fingers through my hair. "I don't wanna have to watch you go out on dates with other guys." His fist balled up in my hair.

"It wasn't so bad tonight, was it? I mean, yeah, it sucked that I had to go on that date, but"—I lifted my head so I could meet his eyes—"look at where we ended up."

He frowned at me. "I'm sorry, Peej. I really wanted your first time to be more special, not in my bedroom because I was crazy with jealously over some guy that you're not even really dating. I just—"

"Shhh . . ." I brought my finger up to his lips. "I'm glad it happened. I wanna give everything that I am to you, Bryn. The rest doesn't matter. Tonight was the best night of my life so far, because I just shared something with you that I've never shared with anyone else. You own me now—heart, soul . . . and body."

"You own me, too, Peej. Everything that I have—that I am—belongs to you and only you. Always." His lips sought mine, and our kisses began to become more fevered again. I wanted so badly to stay in his arms, kissing, exploring, learning all there was to know about pleasing him, and discovering what I liked best, too. But we couldn't stop the outside world from happening; eventually it would seek us out.

"Hey. I should probably go." I started to get up, but Bryn pulled me back down to capture my lips with his again. "Bryn." I tried to chastise him, very unsuccessfully, especially since my body seemed to have a mind of its own. I groaned as he rolled me under him, obviously not liking the idea of me leaving quite yet. "Five more minutes..." I murmured, giving myself over to him.

My eyes fluttered open to sunlight streaming through Bryn's bedroom window. "Oh, shit!" I sat up with a start. Bryn reached for me without opening his eyes, trying to pull me back down into bed. "Bryn—no! Wake up! We fell asleep." His eyes cracked open, and he sat up on his elbows, drowsily scanning his room. I could almost see when realization hit him. "Oh, shit." He leapt from bed and pulled on a pair of shorts.

I, meanwhile, was frantically searching for my clothes. "Oh God—Bryn—we're going to be in so much trouble. They're going to know. They're—"

"Calm down, Peej. Don't panic just yet. My parents obviously didn't check in on me, so our cover isn't blown yet."

I grabbed my cell phone out of my purse and swore under my breath—*25 missed calls.* Just then my phone began to vibrate in my hand. It was Jenna. "Hello?" I squeaked.

"Oh my God! Where are you? Your parents were freaking out. I told them you came over to my house after your date to tell me about it and fell asleep, but they're going to be expecting you home soon."

Relief washed over me, and I exhaled the tension from my body. Our cover wasn't blown yet. "I'm on my way home now. Thanks, Jenna."

"Wait!" Jenna yelled. "I better get all the details later. It's the least I deserve."

"Yeah, okay. But I have to go now. I so don't wanna get busted."

"Yeah, yeah, yeah. Bye." She hung up in a huff. What exactly was I going to tell her? Guess I could worry about that part later. For now, the important thing was that I had to get home before anyone discovered what really happened to me.

HIDDEN GATES

"Jenna covered for you?"

"Yeah, thank God," I said as I pulled my shoes on and headed for the window.

When I'd made it through, Bryn caught my wrist and tugged me up so I had to stand on my tippy toes to reach him. "I need to see you later."

I smiled up at him. "I hope you don't think we're going to be getting naked again for the next couple of days. I can barely walk."

He delivered me one of his patented lopsided grins complete with dimples. "We can do other . . . *things*."

I'm not really sure why I had the urge to ask—no, the *need*—but I just couldn't help myself. "What was it like—with Tammie? I mean, was I as good?"

"I didn't go all the way with her. Why do you think I did? Last night was my first time, too, Peej."

My jaw dropped in surprise. "But you were with her for over a year, and you've been making such a big deal about my first time and—" *And he was so good.* How was he so good at those things if he'd never done them before?

"Girls look at their first time a lot differently than guys do. I just wanted to make sure it was special for you." He locked gazes with me. "I told you I couldn't get you out of my head. It would've been wrong to do it with her while I was imagining it was you the entire time. I knew as long as my first time was with you, it would be special for me."

My cheeks flushed. "Oh, but—"

"We did other things. Mostly she did them to me," Bryn answered before I could ask. "They were good, and I enjoyed them but . . . she wasn't you."

I knew it was absolutely ridiculous, but thinking of Tammie doing things to Bryn, and him enjoying them, despite the night Bryn and I had just shared, made jealousy flare red hot within me. "Teach me," I practically growled. "Teach me so I can do all of those things to you. I wanna learn how to make you happy, Bryn."

He reached forward, face serious, and tucked a piece of hair behind my ear. "You've already made me happy, Peej. You're so amazing—beyond amazing—I can't even describe . . ."

"You know what I mean."

"I'll be happy to teach you." Bryn mischievously grinned at me, heat shining at me from his eyes. "There are a few things I wanna learn to do with you, now that you broached the subject." He kissed me one last time, slipping his tongue in my mouth to briefly intertwine with mine, before he playfully pushed me away from the window. "Now go before I don't have the strength to let you."

"Okay." I smiled up at him, biting my lip. My steps were slow and labored as if my legs were protesting the thought of leaving him. I willed myself not to look at him for fear that I would run back into his arms. I hurriedly made my way back to my house with what I was sure was a big goofy grin on my face.

7

My mom turned to glare at me as I sheepishly entered the kitchen through the back door. "Nice of you to call to let us know you were safe. I was frantic with worry." She fidgeted with her reddish hair that was currently pulled into a low ponytail at the nape of her neck, a sure sign of her motherly anxieties, since it was clear she hadn't bothered to wash or style it. I also noted the dark smudges under her eyes, probably caused from staying up much too late worrying about me. I internally sighed. *What am I going to do with her?*

"Mom, you're always frantic with worry. It's what you do," I mumbled, averting my eyes. I was almost positive she'd be able to tell I wasn't a virgin any more just by looking at me.

"True," she stated. "But that's beside the point. Next time, at least call." She turned back to the stove to continue cooking breakfast. "And no allowance this week. I'll probably need to use the money to buy hair dye to cover all the gray you're giving me."

I just stood there for a moment, staring at her back in shock. *That's it? A week without allowance?* I half expected her to turn back around to yell at me that she could tell what I'd done, that it was obvious to anyone who had fully working eyes. But that didn't happen, and I decided not to look a gift horse in the mouth. "I'm gonna go shower," I mumbled as I scurried out of the kitchen.

Only when I was safely behind my closed door did I dare to release a sigh of relief. I pulled out my phone and texted Bryn.

In the clear, I typed before hitting send.

A few seconds later, my phone beeped in response. *Wasn't worried. Need 2 c u later.*

I'll text u when I can get away, I typed.

I'll be waiting.

I couldn't help the smile that broke out across my face. I was so lucky to have Bryn. I thought it sucked before, being separated from him when he was just my best friend—although I'm really not sure he was ever *just* my best friend—but now that we were so much more, it was almost as if I could barely breathe being away from him.

I heaved a loud sigh and made my way into the bathroom for a quick shower. I turned the water on to let it warm up as I stripped my clothes off, stopping to study myself in the mirror. On the surface, maybe I didn't look any different, but the eyes that were reflected back at me were those of a stranger. She seemed to hold some dark, delicious secret of what it meant to be touched so intimately by the man she loved, and her eyes danced merrily with the knowledge of what it felt like to be made love to by her heart's desire. She smiled at me. I smiled back. I paused another moment to study the rest of me for changes. Unfortunately, I hadn't sprouted the body of a woman overnight. I was still a tad too skinny and a tad too tall. "But Bryn thinks I'm beautiful," I murmured to myself. And that was all that mattered.

I hopped into the shower with a smile on my face, letting the hot water roll over me, relaxing my well-loved body. I

HIDDEN GATES

began humming to myself, unable to pull my thoughts away from Bryn. Snatches of last night kept flashing across my mind, making my shower take longer than planned. By the time I finally turned the water off, the entire bathroom was filled with steam. I pulled a fresh towel from the linen closet, wrapping myself in it before making my way back to my room, still humming.

"Someone's in an awfully cheerful mood today." I stopped short to see my mom standing in my room setting some folded laundry on my bed. She smiled at me, obviously thinking my good mood had something to do with my date last night, and not Bryn. "Want to tell me about it?" She looked at me eagerly, her green eyes dancing.

My face heated as an unbidden memory of Bryn and I locked together in bed flashed across my mind. "There's nothing to tell. Can't I just be in a good mood for no particular reason?"

"No, *you* can't be in a good mood for no particular reason. I know you too well, peanut." Her face was expectant, as if her words would loosen whatever secret I didn't want to tell her.

"There's nothing to tell," I repeated, fidgeting from foot to foot.

She frowned, her face showing disappointment. "Fine. If you don't want to share with your mom, I guess I can live with that. But can I assume you're going to have a second date with Jeremy?"

"Yeah," I said, leaving it at that. I wasn't lying about that part. Let her draw her own conclusions.

"Good," she said, sounding very pleased with herself. "Come downstairs when you're dressed, and I'll heat up some breakfast for you."

"Okay." I waited for her to leave before getting dressed, pausing to text Jenna before I headed downstairs.

U need 2 get here ASAP—can't deal with mom interrogating me about last night.

K. But we need 2 go somewhere so u can fill me in, she texted back, followed by, *Leaving now, c u in 10.*

I texted back, *K. Pretend we already had plans.*

She didn't text me back, but I knew she'd be on it.

I stalled a little bit longer before heading downstairs, giving Jenna time to get to my house. Just as I was coming down the stairs, the doorbell rang, and I dashed for it. "Jenna's here, Mom. Last night we made plans to hang out today," I called.

"You still need to eat breakfast," my mom called back. "Maybe Jenna will want something, too."

I flung the door open, never more relieved to see Jenna and her now *blue* hair? "That red lasted even shorter than usual," I observed.

"Yeah, well, I had to do something last night since a certain someone was M.I.A. after her date, and I had no prospects of my own," she retorted.

"Shhh," I hushed her. "My mom has bat ears. We have to eat before we go anywhere," I added. Well, at least Jenna's new hair color might distract my mom for a few minutes while I scarfed down some breakfast. I trailed into the kitchen behind her, my nerves at an all time high, when suddenly my entire world tilted.

It was like the dream/premonition I thought I'd had the other night at Jenna's after Ryan's party. I was pulled up and away from my body, drawn to the pulsating soft purple glow of the same gate. I saw in fast-forward the same imagery I had before—*There were so many of them—too many to count—and I couldn't tell any of them apart. They all appeared uniform in appearance to me. Huge eyes bulged out of their too tiny pinched faces. Luminescent, dewy skin glowed with a soft light that picked up on the gate's hues, making them all appear to*

HIDDEN GATES

pulsate with their own lights. They glided out of the gate slowly, their thin bodies levitating inches off of the ground. And then, just like that, they blurred off into the distance, too fast for my eyes to track, but this time, I followed one of the "aliens" as he left the scene. I focused in on him as he made his way to . . . Tennessee, yes. Even though I'd never been there myself, in my current state I had knowledge of this place. I watched as he glided into the bedroom of an older man—his dark hair was a similar shade to Bryn's, I noted—and well, the "alien" proceeded to ooze into him. It was if the "alien" went liquidy and flowed into the man, only to reform inside of him. He still looked like the man he had been, and yet . . . I could *see* the "alien" shining through. It was very disconcerting dual imagery that caused me to scream just as I was hurtled back into my body, everything going dark.

8

I came to slowly, my head pounding as if someone had done a tap dance on my skull. My mom stood nearby, talking in a hushed voice, "No, doctor, she passed out cold. Mmm-hmm. Mmm-hmm. Well, please get here as soon as you can. I'm pretty sure it was just a premonition, but because she's never had one before, I can't really be sure." The telltale beep of the cordless phone let me know my mom had hung up.

I sat up slowly, blinking my bedroom into focus. "I'm fine, Mom. I don't need a doctor."

"Oh, honey, you're awake. Good." My mom sat on the edge of my bed and put the back of her hand to my forehead in the way that it seems all mothers do.

I pushed it away with annoyance. "I said I was fine. I just had a premonition is all."

My mom studied my face for a moment and then smiled. "Oh, I'm so happy. What did you see?"

"It was horrible—I saw the gate and everything but then these aliens came through and then I followed this one alien, well not me exactly but my consciousness or whatever and then the alien slid into this old guy and I could see him hiding underneath him—inside him—like he took over almost like a possession." I inhaled deeply, not having bothered to take a breath during my entire long, run-on sentence of babble, but at least I'd gotten it out—sort of.

My mom's smile dropped from her face. "That's not possible, honey. There has never been a time when a lone Seer was witness to such an event. And on top of that, anytime any of the gates have ever actually been breached, the offending aliens have never made it more than a few steps into our world. That's why all of us exist, to prevent such things from happening. And usually a Seer's first vision is something pretty benign... You know that. Your first vision wouldn't be of an impending breach. You aren't ready for that yet. A Seer's mind won't show her something she's not ready to handle. I guess maybe you did just pass out from low blood sugar or something. Good thing the doctor's on his way. I don't think your little episode had anything to do with your powers. What I do think is—"

"No, Mom, it was real!" I exclaimed.

"Alright, honey. Just calm down and we can talk about this later," which meant she didn't believe me and was just patronizing me until she had something better to dissuade me with. Fine, I could bide my time, too. I crossed my arms over my chest and waited.

An hour later I had a clean bill of health, although I still couldn't convince anyone that my premonition was real. I was beginning to wonder how sure I still was about it to persist with the fight. Besides, I had more important things to worry about at the moment. I was almost to Jenna's house, and I hadn't thought of a single good lie that I thought she'd buy about where I had been last night. I couldn't exactly say I was with Jeremy because then if I slipped up about some detail from our date, she would know I was lying. A part of me wished I could just tell her about me and Bryn, but the fewer people who knew, the safer our secret would stay. *Having a secret affair just isn't all it's cracked up to be.*

I'd barely raised my hand to ring Jenna's doorbell when she was pulling me into her house, only to then drag me up to her bedroom. She flopped onto her bed and looked at me expectantly. "Spill," she demanded.

I sighed, my eyes dodging around her room, wishing I didn't have to say anything. "Well, there's really not much to spill—we fell asleep is all."

"Liar," Jenna hissed. "I'm a Speaker, remember? I can understand all kinds of language, including body language, and you"—she waved her hand in my general direction—"are hiding all kinds of secrets."

I narrowed my eyes at her. "You're a Speaker, not a mind reader. You've been known to make mistakes before."

"Not this time. Spill—now," she demanded again.

"I don't have to put up with you accusing me of stuff that I'm not even guilty of—I fell asleep, and that's all," I said.

She narrowed her eyes at me and studied my face for a few seconds before relaxing. "Okay."

What? Some Speaker she was if she actually bought that. "Okay?"

"Yeah, okay."

My phone beeped, letting me know I had a new text message. I popped it open to see it was from Bryn.

Getting impatient—need to see you. Meet me in 15 @ our tree.

My face flushed at him mentioning "our tree;" I'd come to think of it as that, but I was pleasantly surprised to know he had, too. My stomach did a little flip flop thinking about having Bryn kiss me while pressed up against my favorite tree in the whole world—where he'd finally decided to be with me.

K, I responded.

I shut my phone and looked up to see Jenna eyeing me suspiciously. "Who was that?"

"Bryn. But umm . . . I've gotta go. We'll talk more later." I hurried from her room. "Thanks for covering for me—love ya!" I called over my shoulder as I rushed through her front door, slamming it behind me. I didn't want to upset Jenna, but I wanted to see Bryn more than anything else in the world right now. The walk over was a blur. I was floating on a cloud of joyous anticipation, and I would have run, but I didn't want to arrive all sweaty to see Bryn.

I'd hardly made it a few feet into the spattering of woods across from my house when warm, strong arms encircled me from behind. "I missed you." Bryn spun me around and captured my lips with his. I allowed myself to sink into him, his scent and taste making me feel like I was being welcomed home.

"I missed you, too," I murmured, running my hands eagerly over his muscled body. It felt like I hadn't seen him in months, not hours. His hands explored me, emboldened by the night we'd shared last evening, and it wasn't long before we could have been arrested for indecent exposure.

"I'll never get enough of you, Peej. It's like a dream—us being together," Bryn rumbled. "I love you so much."

"I love you, too."

"Oh. My. God." Jenna's voice shattered our happy little love bubble. Bryn and I fumbled to put back on and straighten our clothes as Jenna stood in the clearing gaping at us. "I can't believe you didn't tell me!" she exclaimed.

"Why would I tell you?" Bryn said with agitation.

"Not you—her. I mean, I know he's your best friend and all—and now I can see why—but I'm at least your best *female* friend." She crossed her arms and glared at me with indignation.

"Did you follow me?" I couldn't believe she actually followed me—well, then again, maybe I could. I would do it if I were in her shoes. "You didn't believe me at all. You just said you did so I wouldn't think to check if you were following me."

"Exactly." Jenna smirked at me. "I knew you were hiding something really big and juicy. I just never in a million years imagined it was this." She motioned to both Bryn and me. "And you guys are in love? I mean, having sex is one thing, you know, being friends with benefits or something, but this is some really serious shit."

"You heard us?" I asked incredulously. "But if you followed me—" I stopped to stare at her for a stunned moment. "You were watching us? Oh my God, Jenna, are you some kind of perverted voyeur or something?"

"No! I'm not, I just wanted to see what I could find out, and then I got distracted by a chatty squirrel who, by the way, said he would normally be annoyed by you guys, but after the other night when he heard you professing your love for each other, he is now okay with you guys being here. I kind of thought he was exaggerating the whole love thing, but apparently not."

Damn Speakers, I inwardly cursed, *and damn chatty squirrels.* "You can't tell anyone—please," I begged.

"Well, duh. Like I said, this is some really serious shit. I can't believe you guys are in—did you guys have sex? Did you lose your virginity to him and not even tell me? Please tell me it isn't so."

I almost laughed at the expression on Jenna's face. She was more upset at the thought that I wouldn't tell her about losing my virginity than anything else. "Last night."

"I suppose I can forgive you since you've only been keeping that vital information from me for less than twenty-four hours." A huge grin broke out across her face, and she jumped up and down, clapping. "Oh—oh—I'm so excited! I need to hear every last detail!"

Bryn looked at me with horror. "Please don't. Our sex life is not up for public discussion." *Bryn and I have a sex life. We've had sex.* I inwardly sighed. *Life is good.*

"It's not public, it's just me. And I bet you're super pumped to finally have P.J. after all this time. I kept trying to get her to have sex with you, but I just couldn't tell if she was into you or not."

"What?" Bryn and I exclaimed at the same time.

"Yeah, Speaker here." She motioned at herself. "I've known Bryn had a thing for you for awhile, P.J., but you were the tough one to figure out. Sometimes I felt the vibe, and other times, well . . . I guess it was just because you hadn't figured out your own feelings yet." She nodded to herself.

So that was why Jenna was always telling me to just have sex with Bryn and get it over with. I couldn't count how many times I'd heard her say that. In fact, I distinctly remember her saying it the day of Ryan's party. "Well, you could have told me he had a thing for me."

"No, I couldn't have. You would have freaked out and run for the hills so fast none of us probably ever would have seen you again."

"She's right," Bryn agreed.

"Hey!" I indignantly looked from Bryn to Jenna and back again. "Fine, maybe that's true." I couldn't help but crack a smile. "I guess I had to figure it out myself."

"So, what are we going to do now?" Jenna asked.

Bryn scowled at her. "We? I don't think so. This is between me and Peej—"

"And me now," Jenna interjected. "Because I know the secret and all. I can help you, you know, to keep it that way."

HIDDEN GATES

Bryn glanced at me as a look of complete exasperation splashed across his face. "Why do I have such a bad feeling about this?"

I grimaced. "Because you're not stupid, that's why."

"Maybe it'll be okay that she knows," I said to Bryn, though even to myself I didn't sound convinced. "I mean, it did help to have her cover for me the other night when I stayed at your place." My thoughts were suddenly carried away to the glorious night I'd spent in Bryn's arms. It made me sad to think there wouldn't be many of those in the near future, just stolen moments like we had now. And what if we did get caught? Then maybe I wouldn't even get those.

"Hey." Bryn tipped my face up so he could capture my gaze. "Don't be sad. I know what you're thinking."

I looked into his eyes and saw the determination that lay there. The dark blue of his irises raged like a storm, reminding me that he would fight for me, and that's all that really mattered. "What if we do get caught? Then what?"

He ran his fingers down along my jaw, tracing the same path with his lips a moment later. I shivered. "Then no matter what happens, I'll find you, I'll come for you; no one can keep us apart. It's less than a year; we could make it that long . . ." His voice trailed off with words left unsaid. He was saying if we got caught, if we were separated, then when we graduated from high school, he would come for me no matter what. The worst that could happen would be being separated from him for the rest of the year. My heart ached at the thought. "We're not caught, yet. Let's enjoy the time we have together."

I buried my hands in his hair as he kissed a trail of fire down my neck. "I just wish I could have figured this all out sooner," I more mumbled than anything as I tried to at least temporarily fight the effect Bryn's lips had on me.

"What?" His voice was so low and husky it was going to be harder to concentrate than I thought.

"Us—how I feel about you. I mean, I've been in love with you, and I didn't even know it." I used the grip I had in his long black hair to pull his head up so I could meet his eyes. "I didn't even notice when my love grew to be more . . . adult. And now look at us."

"Yeah, look at us now. Although I suppose I should have guessed that one day you'd have me wrapped around your little finger. After all, you were the only girl who never had cooties as far as I was concerned." I laughed and playfully swatted at him. I'd forgotten about that. Like a lot of little boys, Bryn had gone through the "all girls have cooties" phase, but with one exception: in his case, it was more "all girls have cooties, except P.J."

"Yeah, our version of doctor has changed a little over the years." He gave me a devilish smile. "Now take off your clothes so I can give you a full examination."

"Bryn." I laughed as he playfully tugged at my clothes. It was just so right being with him—someone I'd shared almost my whole life with, someone who knew me better than any other person on the planet. It was then that my cell beeped. "Hold on," I chastised him. "It could be my mom. She's figured out how to text now, you know." The smile dropped from my face when I saw who it was—Jeremy. I opened it and read:

Was really hoping we could go out again soon.

I bit my lip in thought. I had to take into consideration a couple of different things before I just went with my gut and said no. One, for starters, was that Bryn and I had to remain a secret. If I raised too many suspicions, people would start to ask questions, and in our case, questions were bad. Another issue was that I had to take my time and act like I was seriously weighing my options with the guys my mom was setting me up on dates with for Sudding. It had to look like I was actually giving them chances. It didn't matter that the only guy I wanted to spend any time with was Bryn. I had to appear available.

I was still staring at the screen when Bryn slipped my phone out of my grasp before I even realized what he was doing. "That's a resounding no," he said, anger flaring in his eyes as he read the message from Jeremy.

"Hey, Bryn. I have to, remember?" I made a grab for my phone, but he kept it just out of my reach with his long arms.

"You don't have to anything. You went on a date with him, now it's over, time for Mr. Gatekeeper to move on along from you."

"Bryn," I whined. "Just give me my damn phone."

"Why? Do you *want* to go out with him again or something?"

Is he kidding? "Don't be ridiculous. Of course I don't *want* to, it's just I need to look like I'm giving these guys a chance. Besides, he was a nice guy; I should be able to get another date out of him without him trying something with me."

The hostile expression that settled into Bryn's face told me that had not been the right thing to say. "You are not going out with him again," he said through clenched teeth.

"Bryn, what's wrong with you? Stop acting all jealous and demanding. No matter how much I love you, there's absolutely no future for us if this is how you're going to treat me." I raised my chin and glared at him angrily. There was no way he was going to order me around. It didn't matter that I loved him. I absolutely would not tolerate that kind of behavior from him, or anyone else for that matter.

He just stared at me for another couple seconds, his jaw ticking with tension, before he visibly relaxed. His eyes slid down to the ground as if afraid to meet mine any longer. "I'm sorry, Peej, this is just so hard for me. Our relationship is so new, and watching you drive off with him before . . ." He stepped into me and wrapped his arms around my body, engulfing me. I let him hold me, finding comfort in his scent and embrace. "It was as if you reached into my chest and ripped out my heart with your bare hands, taking it with you." He ran his fingers through my hair. "I don't mean to order you around; I know you hate that kind of stuff. I'll try harder, I swear."

Just like that, all my anger towards him washed away. Maybe I'd be acting a little crazy, too, if the shoe were on the other foot. I sighed into his muscled chest. "I'm sorry, too. I could never walk away from you no matter what you did. I probably shouldn't be telling you that. It just encourages bad behavior, but maybe it'll make you feel better."

"No. I don't wanna be one of those controlling assholes. I'll try harder—really." He kissed the top of my head. "We'd better get back though. You leave first. I'll wait a couple minutes to make sure no one sees us leaving the woods together."

"Why? It's not like we're not allowed to be seen together—we're best friends. Everyone knows that." I pouted at him. He was being too cautious. That could raise questions, too.

"Just humor me, okay?" He dipped his head to deliver me one last thorough kiss that left me breathless before pushing me in the direction of my house, taking the time to swat me on the behind in the process.

"Hey!" I giggled as I walked away from him.

He delivered me one of his patented lopsided grins, complete with dimples, causing my heart to speed up. Bryn was incredibly hot. Scorching, in fact. "Sneak over to my house later, if you can."

"Yeah, okay," I said, all thoughts except ones of us together had vacated my mind. I finally managed to will my head to

HIDDEN GATES

turn back around, and I trudged through the woods wrapped up in a cloud of Bryn lust. He was better than any drug—at least I imagined. *Definitely better than chocolate* . . . That I could say with certainty.

"Paige," a voice whispered, seemingly coming from the very woods themselves. No one called me Paige. I didn't like someone calling me that because it meant they probably didn't really know me, and if that was the case, why were they lurking around in the woods waiting for me to be alone?

"Paa-aige," the voice whispered again. This time is seemed closer, and I could definitely tell it was a male voice, which made it sit even worse with me. I pivoted and dashed back in the direction I had left Bryn.

"Paige," the voice sounded like it was right on top of me, and having watched one too many horror movies growing up, I wasn't stupid enough to take the time to look behind me. I let out a scream of panic, regardless, as I tried to run faster. Suddenly my vision blurred, and I felt myself falling.

"What happened?" I mumbled, opening my eyes to see someone's shoes in my line of vision. Why were there someone's shoes in my face? No, that wasn't right—everything came back to me from right before I must have passed out—my face was in somebody's shoes. I shot up like a missile, though all I managed to do was fall over on my ass; but at least I was right side up now. I took in the sight of the man that belonged to the shoes. My gaze went up and up . . . and up to locate his face. This guy must have been at least 6'7" because somehow I could just tell he would tower over Bryn, and that was no small accomplishment. He had large broad shoulders, not often seen on someone his height, and he looked like he worked out—a lot. He had dark auburn hair, so dark I would have mistaken it for brown if not for the rays of sunshine hitting it through the trees, and it was pulled back in a low ponytail at the nape of his neck. All of that in itself would have unsettled me, but his eyes were what really caught my attention. They were so green they almost seemed to glow, or maybe they actually did. I gulped to combat the sudden dryness of my throat, my heart picking up to double time with my nerves. And yet a small spark of anger also pushed to the forefront of my consciousness. Who the hell was this guy, and why did he try to scare me? *Rude much?* I lifted my chin and met his eyes, narrowing mine to show my displeasure. "Who the hell are you?" I demanded.

He took a step forward, his spooky green eyes fixated on me, and I instinctively scrambled back a little. Maybe demanding anything of such a scary guy was not a very bright idea. After all, someone his size could do anything he wanted, and I really wouldn't be able to stop him. What I really wanted to do was scream for Bryn, but I already knew if he had been somewhere close, he'd already be here. It looked like I was on my own. As I stared at the guy intently, readying myself for anything he might do, a smile cracked across his face that quickly turned into a laugh. He actually threw his head back in the process. I stared in amazement. "I like you," he rumbled. His voice was low and husky, and it sounded as if he hadn't spoken in awhile.

Unable to stop myself, the words just spilled from my lips. "And I should care because?" I slapped my hand over my mouth in shock. What the hell was wrong with me? I had a tendency to be a smart ass, and was always quick on the draw, but now I was being just plain stupid.

He looked down at me with his spooky green eyes that seemed to glitter with amusement. "Yes, I definitely like you." He paused to tilt his head much like my dog would do. "You may call me Khol." When I didn't respond, he spoke again. "I have come a very long way to see you. I mean you no harm."

"Then why did you scare the crap out of me and then just stand there while I was lying on the ground passed out?"

"I did not mean to scare you. I am out of practice with this form of communication, and it proved to be too much for you. In time, you will grow accustomed."

"What are you talking about?" I looked at him incredulously. "What form of communication?"

"You are currently in a state similar to a dream. Right now, your consort is trying to resuscitate you. I did not mean to scare him, either. He is very worried."

Did he just say *consort*? Seriously? "Why are you here?" I could have asked a thousand other questions, but I figured it was best to skip to the most important one first.

His lips turned up at the corners in a smile. "I had a desire to meet you. Your power has been a constant draw to me the past few weeks, and I could no longer resist."

"My power?" Umm . . . what power? Last time I checked, I was running on empty.

"Yes. Your power. You are just beginning to come into your gifts. You will be a very powerful Seer, the likes of which haven't been seen for a millennia. That kind of power draws many kinds—some who will wish to steal or control it, some who will wish to destroy it, and some who will wish to protect it and you."

My mind was reeling. "Which are you?" I squeaked, almost afraid to hear the answer.

"I fall into the category of wishing to protect it . . . and you." His gaze swept over me with heat. "Yes, I do not wish to see harm come to you." His eyes flared brighter, causing me to shrink back from him even more.

"What are you?" I whispered.

"I am a friend. I hold magic that is very, very old, and which I do not wish to reveal still exists. I have placed a binding on you to prevent you from discussing me with anyone. One day I may lift it." He shrugged his shoulders. "Or perhaps not." His face grew very serious. "I know of what you have seen in your visions, because I have chosen to link myself to you. I, too, saw them. Trouble looms in the future, the kind of which this world has yet to see. Although we have not been able to ascertain how to eliminate the problem yet, for now take comfort in knowing that you are not alone." I was speechless. And I so didn't like the fact that he was claiming to be linked to me. The only guy I wanted linked to me in any way was Bryn.

He strode forward and offered me his hand. I took it numbly, figuring he'd already said he wasn't going to hurt me, and I wasn't really standing in the woods with him anyways. When he had a hold of my hand, he jerked me to him, bending down to run his face up the side of my neck, inhaling. "Mmm mmm . . . delicious. You smell of power and innocence, a very rare combination." He brought his face up so we were inches apart, his spooky green eyes illuminating his face. "I have been sleeping a very long time, and your allure is almost too great for me to resist. I could so easily take what I want from you—make you mine. And yet—" He stepped away from me, and I sunk back to the ground, my knees weak with fear. "Your heart belongs to another. I will respect that—for now." He disappeared right before my eyes as my vision went dark again.

9

My life was consistently getting more and more complicated. And to think I used to complain that my life was boring. No more boring here, that's for sure. For starters, who the hell was that Khol guy? Or maybe a more apt question would be *what* was he? Him just showing up and delivering me a portent of doom had my anxiety levels creeping up towards a full blown panic attack. According to him, both my premonitions/visions were real, and they pointed to bad things coming very soon on the horizon. If only I could get someone to believe me. Add in Bryn and my secret relationship, and me trying to pretend to date other guys . . . Well, like I said, no more boring here.

"She'll be fine," my mom talked in a hushed whisper, "the doctor checked her over again and said it's just low blood sugar . . . or rather, he couldn't come up with a better explanation. But he's sure there's nothing seriously wrong with her. She just needs to take better care of herself. I'll make sure to tell her you were worried, but you can go on home now."

"Can't I just stay a little longer? In case she wakes up. I just—"

"Awe, honey. You're going to make a wonderful Guardian one day, but today isn't that day. Now head on home, and I'll tell her to give you a call later."

But I didn't want Bryn to leave. I wanted to be held in his comforting, warm arms. My eyes fluttered open with effort. "Bryn," I whispered, feeling very tired. It probably wasn't the best idea to beg for him to stay. It might give something away, but at the moment I didn't care. I just wanted him to stay with me. "Mom, please let him stay." She frowned at me. "Mom," I whined. "He's stayed with me like a million times before, why can't he now?"

"Because, peanut, the two of you are too old for some of the things you used to do. It just wouldn't be right." I almost wanted to laugh. She'd probably have a coronary if she knew some of the things we'd been doing together. The bright side was that she obviously still thought Bryn and I were completely platonic best friends. "Besides, I don't think whoever you end up in a serious relationship with is going to appreciate Bryn being so close to you all the time."

"He's going to be my Guardian," I groused.

"Guardians don't stay in the same room with their charges, sweetie. It just isn't done. You don't see mine constantly hanging around. Your father wouldn't be very pleased if he did." She reached over and ruffled Bryn's hair. "Now head on home, and you two can hang out tomorrow."

"But, Mom—" I protested as I watched Bryn slowly leave my room, his eyes lingering on me with worry. *Graduation day can't come fast enough.* "Fine. Whatever." I glared at my mom once Bryn had left. "You're being absolutely ridiculous. What do you think is going to happen anyways?" Probably something along the lines of *exactly* what would happen. *Oh, the irony.*

HIDDEN GATES

"I just wouldn't be a very good mother if I let my eighteen-year-old daughter have her eighteen-year-old male friend stay over in her room." She had taken on the *"there's no point in arguing with me"* tone that all mothers seemed to have in their bag of tricks. Even I knew when the battle was lost, so I decided to change the subject away from Bryn completely.

"Jeremy texted me earlier. He wants to go out again."

"Really?" Hope danced in my mom's eyes. Yep, my subject change was a success; I had my mom hook, line, and sinker. "So what did you say?" She sat back down on the edge of the bed and looked at me expectantly.

"Well, nothing yet. I kind of passed out and forgot about it until now." Not to mention Bryn's mini-meltdown in between those two things.

"You said he was nice, right? And he's cute, so you should definitely say yes. Where's your phone? You should text him right away." She swiveled her head around, scanning all the surfaces in my room for my cell.

I really didn't like how excited she was. I was determined to be with Bryn, but it was going to kill me to disappoint my parents so much. If only there were a way we could all be happy. I sighed. "It's probably still in my purse."

"Oh, of course." My mom scurried over to pull my cell out of my bag in a blur of excited movements. She handed it to me and sat back down on my bed only to resume her expectant stare. When I didn't move to immediately open my phone, she sighed impatiently, "Well, go ahead, peanut."

I thought about how Bryn had reacted in the woods, and I scowled at my phone. Even though I didn't like being told what to do, I most definitely could be motivated by guilt. If I said yes to a second date with Jeremy, no matter how hard Bryn tried to hide it, I knew it would hurt him. And that was something I wasn't interested in doing. "I think I'm going to say no," I mumbled.

"What? Why?"

"He was nice and all, like I said, but there didn't really seem to be a spark with him, you know?" I raised my gaze to meet my mom's, silently pleading that she would let the issue drop. But of course, I should have known better.

"Oh, is that all? You said he didn't even kiss you yet. How can you know?"

"Because I don't want to kiss him, that's why. I also don't need to kiss Jenna to know that there's no spark between us. Should I just go around kissing everyone I see to find out who I have a spark with? Hell, why not go a step farther, why not—"

She scrunched her face up at me. "There's no need to be crass, missy. I just think you should try kissing him before you dismiss him so easily."

"I don't want to," I said.

"You're going," my mom said back, motherly determination etched into her face.

I narrowed my eyes at her. "No, I'm not. And you know you can't make me."

"No, but I can make you wish you did. You're grounded until you set up a date with Jeremy."

"You can't do that!" I screamed at her rapidly retreating back.

But the closed door staring back at me said she could. I stood and shrieked my fury. I couldn't believe my mom was trying to punish me into going out with Jeremy again. She'd never done anything so unfair before. Why was she behaving so crazily?

Anger fueled my next decision. I wasn't just going to sit in my room and take that kind of abuse from my mother. *Oh hellz no.* I was going to sneak out to find the comfort in

HIDDEN GATES

Bryn's arms that she was trying to deny. I opened my phone and texted him.

Meet me—now.

I didn't wait for his response before I popped the screen out of my window and scrambled out and down the drainpipe. I skulked across my front yard, trying to keep to the shadows created by the oncoming dusk. I heaved a huge sigh of relief as I made it into the cover of the woods across the street from my house. I only had to wait a few minutes before I saw Bryn jog into my line of sight. I rushed over to him, wrapping my arms around his waist. "She grounded me until I say yes to going out with Jeremy again." I sobbed into his muscular chest.

"But I thought you were gonna go anyways."

"No. Not after"—I struggled to catch my breath—"not after how you reacted. I couldn't stand the thought of hurting you."

His arms tightened around me. "I know why you have to go. You won't hurt me. None of this is your fault." He pulled away from me, cupping my face in his huge hands, dipping his head to kiss my tears away. His lips were soft yet firm against my skin, and I longed to lose myself under his sweet caresses.

"It's just not fair." My lower lip trembled as I stared up into Bryn's beautiful blue eyes. "I don't understand what's wrong with being with you. So what if our kids are all Guardians; I can't bring myself to care as long as I'm with you." People often ask what the meaning of life is. What's the point in all of this? As far as I can tell, life is pretty much pointless without love. If you have it, then you're truly rich, and if you don't, then nothing else really holds any value. What would my life mean if I married a Gatekeeper or Seer descendent for the sake of duty? It would mean nothing to me, even if it did to others. Bryn gave my life meaning; he made everything else worthwhile. He always had, and hopefully, he always would.

"Because you're special, Peej—so special. You deserve to be with royalty, not a Guardian like me." I opened my mouth to protest, and he silenced me with one of his long fingers. "But I'm not stupid, although I am plenty selfish. I want you all to myself. I'm not going to walk away from you so you can be with someone else, someone born into the right family. Somehow I got lucky, and you love me back. I'll fight for you as long as you want me."

"I'll always want you," I whispered.

"Then I'll always be yours," he said gruffly, his lips meeting mine in a brutal kiss, the taste of him helping to sooth my nerves. My hands slid into his silky black hair, and I moaned as I found my back pushed up against a tree. It seemed to be fast becoming me and Bryn's thing. Or maybe it was because we didn't have any other place to go.

"Take your hands off of my daughter." My father's deep voice boomed across the clearing, making me gasp with fear. *We were caught—oh God, we were caught.* Bryn and I separated quickly, but it was too late.

"Sir, I—" Bryn started, obviously flustered.

"Sir nothing." My father's voice seethed with anger, making me cringe. He stood across from us with his reading glasses still perched on his nose. He must have come after me in such a hurry that he hadn't even bothered to remove them. I watched as his fists clenched and unclenched, and his face turned the shade of a boiled lobster. "How dare you take advantage of my family's trust like this? And how dare you take advantage of the sacred trust being a future Guardian affords you?"

"Daddy, please!" I interjected. "It's not Bryn's fault. Don't—" When he turned his withering stare onto me, I temporarily lost my ability to speak.

"You, young lady, have disappointed me. We've raised you better than this. Never in a million years when I saw you

HIDDEN GATES

sneaking over here did I expect to find you in this kind of situation. I don't even want to look at you right now."

"I love your daughter, sir," Bryn stated, his voice filled with raw emotion. "All I want is to love and protect her. I never meant to disrespect anyone."

Ignoring Bryn's words completely, my father spoke to me. "Get your ass over here right now, P.J. You're not to be alone with him for one more second—ever."

Fear snaked up and wound itself like a boa constrictor around my heart. My worst fears were coming to fruition. My family was going to tear me away from Bryn, and I wouldn't be able to see him for nearly a year. I flung myself at Bryn and wrapped my arms around his waist. "No!" I screamed. "Don't do this to me, Daddy! I love him! I love him! I love him!" My volume increased to the point where I was practically shrieking. I'm really not sure what I was going for, maybe I thought if I yelled long and loud enough, I could get through to my father.

"You just turned eighteen years old. You don't know what real love is yet." My father's face and eyes had grown as hard as stone, and his sudden calm scared me more than his anger.

"Don't tell me I don't know what real love is yet!" I continued shrieking at my father. "I would die for him! I would lie down and die for him!" My chest heaved as I struggled to catch my breath. "If you take him away from me, I might die, too!"

"Teenager dramatics," my father grumbled as he stalked towards me. "You better let her go, son." My father, even though he wasn't as tall as Bryn, definitely had the intimidation factor down. He leveled his stone cold stare at Bryn, practically daring him to disobey. Bryn tightened his grip on me as I tightened my grip on him. My father eyed us both with annoyance scrolling across his face. I'd never hated my father more. He was threatening to rip my whole reason for living away from me, and he was annoyed.

"I hate you," I seethed. "I fucking hate you."

"Don't you dare talk to me like that. I'm your father," he snapped.

"That's why I hate you so much. You're my father, and you should want me to be happy more than anyone else does. You shouldn't be treating me like a child." I hissed every word with vehemence.

"Fine. You want to be treated like an adult, then you come back to the house, and we can talk about this like adults. Stop cowering in the woods, refusing to let go of *him*." He spat the last word out, not even bothering to say Bryn's name.

I peered up at Bryn, and he nodded his encouragement, although I could see the tension lining his mouth. I slowly let go of him and stepped towards my father. "Fine," I said as I stalked towards the house. The truth was that if my parents wanted to keep me separated from Bryn until I was out of their house, there was nothing I could do about it. I would be lying to myself if I thought I had any real control over anything in this situation. My father followed close behind me, not saying a word. When we crossed the street and got to the house, only then did he react. As soon as the front door was closed behind me, he grabbed me by my arm and pulled me upstairs, shoving me into my room and locking the door from the outside.

I pounded my fists against the door. "You said we were going to talk!" I screamed. "You lied to me!"

"You lied to me first," my father said through the door, "and don't bother trying to sneak out again. Your mother has Eric watching for you now." *Great*—there definitely wouldn't be any escaping now that my mother had put her Guardian on the job—her Guardian, but also Bryn's father. It would be like trying to escape from Alcatraz.

HIDDEN GATES

"Daddy, please." I softened my voice, trying a different tactic. "I love him. Don't destroy me like this." The only response I got was my father's footsteps walking away from my door and down the stairs.

I turned and sank down on my bed in despair. My only hope was that maybe my mom would side with me and convince my father to let me be with Bryn. So yeah—I had absolutely no hope at all. I curled into a fetal position and sobbed until sleep overtook me.

I awoke to the sound of my door creaking open. My room was completely dark now that it was night. My bedside lamp switched on to reveal that visitor was my mom. She looked down at me with a pained expression and sat down on the edge of my bed. "How could you?" she whispered. "You know you can't be with him, peanut."

I sat up and looked at my mom beseechingly. "Why? Why can't I be with him? I love him—so much—more than anything. How can I be with someone—someone like Jeremy—after I've discovered I can have that kind of passion with someone else?"

My mom reached out to touch me, but I shirked away. "Sometimes I forget how young you are. You're growing up so fast, and yet . . . you know nothing of the world." Her face held a sadness I'd never seen before.

"I know enough. I know that I love him. Mom, please." Fresh tears began to slide down my face.

"Bryn's going to be sent away—to train elsewhere. He'll be assigned someone to guard when he's ready."

I read between the lines. "Someone that's not me," I croaked, not wanting to say the words out loud.

She looked away when she responded. "Yes."

"No!" I wailed, dropping to my knees and grabbing my mom's hands to beg. "He's my best friend, too. He's not only my lover, but my best friend, too."

Only when shock and horror spread across her face did I realize what I'd said. "Your lover?" she breathed.

"No—that's—um—that's not what I meant. I just meant that—" God—what did I mean? Why had I said that? Why couldn't I have said boyfriend? *Because he's more, so much more,* my mind whispered.

My mom visibly paled. "Have the two of you—did you—did you have sex with him?" Her voice was trembling, and I almost felt sorry for her if not for the rest of the situation. I swallowed hard, not sure how I should answer. Maybe if I told the truth, she would take our relationship more seriously; or maybe a lie was the way to go? I was too frazzled to think clearly. My unhelpful mind conjured up an unbidden image of Bryn and I wrapped in each other's arms, and I flushed.

Her hand flew to her mouth. "Dear Lord, your face just told me all that I need to know." She stood abruptly, heading for the door. "I thought we'd raised you better than that. I thought you'd know better than to let a common Guardian defile you."

"Defile me? But I thought you said the forbidden fruit was the sweetest—I thought you'd maybe understand—"

"To daydream about, to look, but not touch, not to slum with. You gave your most valuable gift to a common Guardian. I would never have even considered you doing such a thing—even after what you'd said to me before. Especially because of what you said before—you *knew* it was wrong." She meant when I'd asked her about wanting someone I knew I shouldn't.

"No, I know no such thing. I gave it to him because I love him." I started sobbing again. I couldn't believe the things she was saying. Who was this woman standing before me?

HIDDEN GATES

Certainly not the caring, loving mother I'd grown up with. My mom would never say such things. Bryn and my family had always been like one since we were little; at least that's what I'd thought. Maybe to my parents they were just beloved servants. Maybe I'd never really understood the true class lines that were drawn within my society. How could I when I was at the top of the tier? I'd always thought of Guardians and Speakers as different, no better or no worse... just different. Maybe that's why Bryn put me up on a pedestal. I thought my people would be upset and angry about me not having a Seer child if I chose Bryn—maybe I'd become sort of a social pariah—but now I was beginning to see that I might truly be shunned. So much more was at stake than I'd ever really understood... but I still didn't care. I'd give up anything and everything to be with Bryn.

"We'll be lucky to make you a good match after this. With him being sent away, people will assume the worst, whether or not it is the truth. No decent Gatekeeper or Seer descendant will want you after you've been with a Guardian." Her face scrunched up as if she were going to cry. "I wanted so much for you..." Her voice was swallowed by a sob as she left and relocked my door.

I sat in stunned silence. The things that my mother had just said sounded like they were pulled right out of the 1800s, maybe a Jane Austen novel. *We'll be lucky to make you a good match after this.* Was she kidding? There had to be some kind of mistake. I must have fallen and hit my head, and this was all some kind of huge nightmare, a coma-induced nightmare.

My phone beeped, and I dashed for it, hoping it was Bryn—and it was.

Remember, I'll come 4 u—1 yr, was all it said.

I hastily hit send to call him, and he answered on the first ring. "Peej," he whispered, his voice holding the same kind of desperation that was currently seeping out of all my pores. "They're sending me away—now. I won't have my phone, and I don't know if I'll be able to contact you anytime soon. I'll come for you, I promise. Don't lose hope—I love you." He paused as if listening to something. "I gotta go," he said hurriedly. "I don't want them to know we talked—to know about our plan."

"No wait—Bryn—I love you, too." The phone went dead. I stared at it in shock. It was really happening; I wouldn't see Bryn until after we graduated—almost an entire year.

I threw my head back and screamed at the top of my lungs in utter agony. I was on the edge—I know that now; hysteria like I'd never thought possible was taking over my entire being. I began to wildly smash everything in my room that I could get my hands on. Anything that wasn't nailed down, I destroyed. Things I'd had since childhood, things that I cherished, were ripped apart in an outpouring of agony because none of it meant anything anymore without Bryn. I continued smashing and screaming until my voice was gone, my eyes were blurry, and my legs could no longer support me. I sank down to the floor right where I was and curled into a ball. The only sounds that registered in my ears were my own heartbeat and my ragged breathing.

Eventually, the sweet oblivion of sleep overtook me.

10

"Well, what do you suggest we do with her then?" My mother's strained whisper reached my ears from the hallway just outside my door. Did they really think I couldn't hear them? Not that I really cared what they were saying anyways, but that wasn't the point.

"It's just more teenager dramatics. She'll get over it eventually," my father stated blandly.

"She doesn't talk to anyone, she's barely eaten, and she just sleeps all the time." Of course I sleep all the time! I wanted to shout. When my dreams all seemed to contain Bryn, and my reality was lacking . . . Well, it didn't seem like much of a choice.

"She'll snap out of it. You'll see." *Yep, my father is seriously deluding himself.*

"And if she doesn't?"

"Then we'll come up with something." I comforted myself with the thought that whatever they could come up with couldn't possibly be any worse than what they'd already done. *Do your worst, nothing can touch me anymore.*

My parents' footsteps retreated down the hall, and I heaved a sigh of relief into the dark. I wished they would just leave me alone already.

"Hello, little Seer." I heard a vaguely familiar voice waft through my mind, which I attached to an image of Khol, the guy from the woods with creepy green luminescent eyes.

"What do you want?" I grumbled, not really sure if I was imagining his voice or not.

"I'm not a figment of your imagination."

"Then how did you know what I was thinking if you're not all in my mind? Besides, that's just what a figment would say." I scrunched up my face in a display of my skepticism.

"As I said before, I linked myself to you. It comes with certain advantages, such as me being able to communicate this way with you the way I did in the woods, along with being able to sense your emotions."

Advantages maybe for him, but distinct disadvantages for me. "You know, one would think that I would have gotten some kind of say in this whole linking process. I mean, I don't like you just being able to pop into my head, and I most certainly don't like you being able to sense my emotions."

I swear he chuckled. "All the most powerful Seers of old were linked to . . . *creatures* . . . such as myself. It is a great honor to find oneself linked to one of us, and you just want to throw me away. There are very few of us left, and most of us still sleep."

"Yeah, well . . ." I groused. "You won't even tell me what you are." I flopped onto my stomach as if he were really in the room and I could turn away from him.

"All in due time."

He paused long enough that I thought he wasn't there anymore. "Hello?" I mentally called.

"Watch the rerun of the evening news tonight."

HIDDEN GATES

"What?"

"Watch the rerun of the evening news tonight, and then we'll have something to discuss." And with that, I felt a mental pop that let me know he was really gone. *Weird.* Or was it more weird how casually I was accepting this new creepy guy into my life? Or maybe I'd grown up with so much weird that one more thing didn't really seem like a big deal.

I had no idea what time it was, and I really didn't care about the stupid evening news or Khol's demand that I watch it. I slid my eyes closed and wanted nothing more than to doze off again so I could dream of Bryn. But just when I was on the precipice of dreamland, my new T.V. clicked on. With a start, I sat up in bed to see who had turned it on, and as I swung my head around, I realized I was the only one in my room. With clear certainty I knew somehow Khol was responsible, especially when I saw the evening news was currently on display. "Why the hell does he want me to watch this?" I grumbled to myself, trying to focus on what was on the screen, my eyes still slightly blurry.

A blonde anchorwoman was speaking. "And tonight we have a special treat . . . We have Senator Bill Wexington in our studio. As many of you know, he's been touring our illustrious state of Pennsylvania the last couple of days, trying to garner as many votes for the upcoming election as possible. When he asked to stop by and chat with us, we couldn't have been happier."

The screen split. The female anchorwoman remained on the left side, and on the right appeared an older man with silver hair, and the title *Senator Bill Wexington* scrolled across the bottom of the screen. I slapped my hand over my mouth to stifle a scream. *I know him. I know that man.* Only when I had seen him, he had been at least twenty years younger, but there was no mistaking who he was.

As he began to talk, I saw a quick flash of the alien "under" his skin. It was like seeing two men, one a human and one an alien, taking up the same space. Their features were mingled together somehow, and yet they were separate. "Oh my God," I whispered in horror. "How is this possible?"

"Apparently your vision was one from the past. It has been many years since the creature has merged with the man," Khol's voice answered in my mind. "They are one now."

"But how? Why?" I stared at the screen, unable to look away.

"Your vision showed the how. Obviously, it was important for you to see what you were shown. As you already know, Seers see all that pertains to the gates."

"But if that happened so long ago, why didn't any other Seer have a vision pertaining to it when it actually happened?"

"I can only offer you an educated guess as to why no one else saw it when it happened. You are the strongest Seer to be born in a long time, as I've previously stated. For some reason, maybe no one else had the power to see it. You are just now coming into your powers, so you were shown."

"Oh." Yeah, that made sense, I guessed. But there were so many other nagging questions. For one, "Why can't anyone else *see* what he really is then? I'm sure I'm not the only Seer who's laid eyes on him in all this time."

"Yes, there is that as well." Khol paused for a few heartbeats as I stared, mind reeling while I watched the T.V. What did this "alien" want? Why did he lay low for all these years only to emerge now? Or had he? "There are many questions for which I do not have the answers as of yet, my little Seer."

My little Seer? "So what do we do then?" I asked, choosing to ignore his little term of endearment, at least for the moment. I was certainly not his by any definition I was aware of.

HIDDEN GATES

"We watch. We wait. We gather power. When things become clearer, we make a move."

"Great. So basically, we do nothing." I fumbled for the T.V. remote and turned it off.

Khol sighed in my mind. "Watching, waiting, and gathering power is not nothing."

"Whatever. I don't care anyways." I slid back down in my bed and shut my eyes. None of it meant anything without Bryn.

I heard a low growl echo through my mind. "Your childish woes are nothing compared to what we face. More than just you will be affected—this is my world, too." I didn't respond and crossed my arms over my chest, hoping that by being linked to me, he would pick up on what my body language was saying.

Another growl echoed through my mind. *Huh. So it worked.* "Stop being so childish," Khol snapped, anger evident in his voice.

"Leave me alone," I snapped back. I felt the mental pop signaling that he was gone from my mind, and I heaved a sigh of relief. I didn't want to deal with anything right now, let alone crazy aliens who were up for Congress or some shit.

I stared off into the dark, waiting for sleep to claim me once again so I could be whisked off into Bryn's imaginary arms. Unfortunately for me, Khol had other ideas.

A low growl sounding outside of my head caused me to sit up and almost choke on my tongue as Khol, live and in the flesh, stalked towards my bed in the dark. His luminescent eyes glowed an eerie green, casting shadows across his angry face. The room buzzed and crackled with the foreign energy of his powers, and the air seemed thicker somehow. Khol's physical presence made every molecule in my body stand up to attention and quiver with excitement. Whatever he was, my powers definitely seemed to like him.

"What are you doing here?" I gasped in shock. He said before that he wasn't going to hurt me, but it was hard to remember with the predatory look he was currently wearing on his face.

"Trying to make you understand," he spoke through clenched teeth. He stopped at the edge of my bed and glared down at me.

"What? That you're good at intimidating me? You've already made that point clear before." Then I had a thought that made me relax slightly. "Wait, are you really here? Or just here like in the woods before?" *Because he got here awfully quick. Maybe the connection was just better this time around.*

"I am here, in the flesh this time. I would not be able to make the point that I am going to otherwise." His eyes glinted with something I couldn't decipher. It's really hard to read someone with green glowy eyes, I was discovering.

"Oh." I gulped, nothing left to say. What kind of point did he have to make to me in the flesh? Was he going to smack me around? Threaten me? My mind was reeling with possibilities, compiling a list of all the horrible things he could do to me. But what he did do took me by complete surprise because it never would have made it on that list.

He leaned down faster than I'd ever seen anyone move, even fully matured Guardians, and crushed his lips to mine. When I gasped with surprise, he took the opportunity to plunge his tongue into my mouth. The white-hot heat his kiss caused to surge through my body was even more unexpected. I found myself kissing him back with enthusiasm and shuddering with pleasure as his hands skimmed down my body.

I wanted—I wanted—*Bryn.* An image of him skittered across my mind and instantly cooled my heated skin. How could I be kissing someone else—or *something* else? *I love Bryn, and only him.* "Stop!" I said, shoving Khol away from

HIDDEN GATES

me, although with how easily I did it, I knew he had let me. "What the hell was that?" I demanded, too angry to care how scary he was anymore.

His eyes met mine with heat, glowing even brighter, if that was even possible, and a satisfied smirk spread across his face. "I was teaching you a lesson."

"A lesson? Really. And what would that be? That you're an asshole that forces unwanted attention on girls that are smaller and weaker than them?" I ground my teeth together so hard my jaw started to hurt.

"No—that Bryn is not the only one who can stoke your fires, that you need to get out of this bed and start focusing on the bigger problems at hand. Your life hasn't ended because he is gone."

Stoke my fires? Who the hell talks that way? "Yeah, I have hormones, so what? And you're a really good kisser—congratulations. I'm sure practically any hot guy could come in here and get some kind of reaction out of me. That doesn't change the fact that I love Bryn and will never want to be with anyone but him. Love means something to me, and Bryn does it for me physically—*and beyond*."

Khol's smirk didn't even falter a little bit. "Bryn is not the one for you. You will figure that out eventually, in your own time. As you grow into your powers, you will find that you will crave . . . more."

More? The way he said that made it sound like he was implying he meant more than just sexually, but I had no idea what he was trying to suggest. "Whatever. Now that you tried to teach me a lesson—and failed—will you please leave so that I can go to sleep? Dream Bryn is waiting."

"I will leave and let you go to sleep—after you promise to get out of bed and resume your life starting tomorrow. Only then will I leave." Khol crossed his thick, muscular arms over his chest and narrowed his eyes at me. I didn't know him very well, but I could tell he meant business.

"Fine. Whatever. I agree. So leave. *Now.*" *Whatever.* What was he going to do, come in the morning, drag me out of bed, and force me to go to school? *Yeah, right.*

He produced a newspaper seemingly out of thin air and tossed it to me. "There is an article about Senator Bill Wexington in there. I thought you might want to read it."

I glanced down at the paper for a second, and when I looked back up, Khol was gone. *What the hell?* Oh well, at least he was gone. I turned back to the paper and searched for the article he had mentioned, my curiosity too great to ignore it.

When I was done reading the article, I was even more confused. "So aliens are fans of gun control," I muttered to myself. "So what?" *Ugh.* All the article had told me was that Senator Bill Wexington didn't stand behind the Second Amendment of the Constitution. It wasn't like he was making any highly suspicious suggestions for his campaign to get elected to Congress. I wasn't a really political person, but I knew Senator Bill Wexington wasn't the first, nor would he be the last, politician to suggest gun control in some form.

My phone beeped, signaling a new text message. My heart sped up in anticipation. Even though I knew that Bryn didn't have his phone, I kept hoping he'd find a way to contact me. So far I'd heard absolutely nothing from him, and even a text message at this point would make me jump for joy.

I peered down at my phone and heaved a sigh of disappointment. The text was from Jenna. I hadn't really talked to her since Bryn had been shipped away and I had sunk into the depths of despair, but I did grace her with responses to her text messages at least. I think she understood, mostly, that I wasn't up to talking about everything that had happened. I opened my phone and read.

HIDDEN GATES

So who was the guy who wasn't Bryn u were just making out w/ ???
My jaw dropped open. How the hell did she know?
IDK what ur talking about, I responded.
LIAR! stared back at me as her response.
I didn't know what to say. How did she know? Nausea rolled through my stomach at the thought of Bryn ever finding out. He hadn't even been gone a week yet, and I had kissed someone else, or rather someone else had kissed me. I really didn't think Bryn would see the distinction, especially because I had kissed him back, if only for a moment. My phone beeped again, and I turned my focus back to the glowing screen.
SPILL IT!
IDK y u think that . . . yeah, no. I hit send and hoped she would buy it.
My phone beeped again almost immediately.
Squirrels r chatty & nosey. Stop lying. :/
Damn Speakers! I always forget about her sneaky little spies. The image of a little voyeur squirrel hanging around outside my window and then running to Jenna to report any indiscretions on my part was absolutely horrifying.
And crazy, I typed back and turned my phone off. I could picture Jenna sitting in her room steaming mad. I would probably have a full mailbox of angry texts when I turned my phone back on, but it was better than dealing with her now.
I slumped back into bed, blinking my eyes in the darkness. I found myself feeling oddly vulnerable, as if a whole army of squirrels could be hanging out in the tree across from my window, watching me. I stumbled across my floor and pulled down the shade, checking to make sure there weren't any gaps for nosey rodents to peek through. Once satisfied, I flopped back into bed and closed my eyes, yearning for nothing more than to dream about Bryn.

11

"Rise and shine, my little Seer." Khol's raspy voice echoed through my mind.

"No. Go away," I grumbled, pulling my pillow over my head. But pillows only buffer against noise on the outside of your head, so there was no escape for me.

"You agreed to get back to your life starting today if I left you alone last night. I did, and now you are."

"I changed my mind."

"I can come in person to wake you up if you would like." I could hear the smile in his voice. I lay there for another couple of moments. I'm really not sure how long it was before I started to doze again, the threat of Khol coming in person temporarily forgotten—until my pillow was snatched from my grasp.

"Hey!" I exclaimed, seeing Khol standing beside my bed with my pillow in his hands. His tall frame seemed to take up more room in the light of day, and his dark auburn hair looked like fire in the morning sun. His mere physical presence in the same room as me still caused my body to shiver with excitement. *Damn . . . not good.*

His lips turned up into a slight smile as he gazed at me. "Would you like me to help you shower as well?" The way his creepy eyes slid over my body made me very self-conscious all of a sudden, and I pulled my covers up under my arms as a shield. I didn't want him getting any ideas and trying to kiss me like he had last night.

"Eww... how old are you anyways? You have to be at least in your mid-twenties; I just turned eighteen. If you would have caught me a few days earlier, I'd be jailbait for you."

Khol's smile faltered, but only slightly. "Seventeen is old enough where I am from. Besides, I am not human. Your laws mean little to me."

"Yeah, about that. Are you ever going to tell me what you are?" *Besides creepy, that is.*

"All in due time."

"Fine. Whatever. So I suppose that if I don't get up and go to school today, you're just going to harass me all day instead?"

"Harass? No. But I am sure we could find some very... entertaining... things for us to do to help you back on your way to recovery." His eyes slid over me again, letting me know exactly what he was thinking. "The way your power hums to me constantly, calling to me, is like a siren's song, one that I yearn to answer with everything that I am."

My heart pounded in my chest as I stared at Kohl. There was no point in denying his words excited me, or more aptly, they revved my hormones, but that was beside the point. Because I was a teenager, that really wasn't a huge accomplishment. "I love Bryn," I snapped. "There will be no answering of my siren's song by anyone but him."

Kohl moved so fast I could barely track him, and I when my eyes found him again, he was kneeling beside me, hand outstretched. "You have no reason to fear me, my little Seer." He touched the side of my face briefly, leaving heat where his fingers had skimmed my jaw line. "I will not force you to do anything you do not truly desire to do. I am well aware that your heart belongs to another. I am simply letting you know your options for when you realize he is not the one for you."

"What about the kiss last night?" I whispered, hating how my body responded to his.

"I regret having taken what should only be given freely, and for that, I apologize. I simply needed to make a point, to show you that your life will go on without him." He touched my face again before drawing back and standing once more. "I want you to be able to trust me." His face became solemn and oh so sincere; it made me want to give my trust to him—this strange man that wasn't even human.

Staring at him, my gut clenched, and I knew that I could trust him, even if he did still scare me a little. "I don't know why . . . but I do . . . trust you, that is." I gave him a tentative smile.

His answering smile was instant and bright, making him look so much more handsome and a lot less creepy. "Now go ready yourself for school, my little Seer. I will be watching." And just like that, he disappeared again.

I heaved a huge sigh, relief that I knew would be shortlived washing over me. It looked like Khol wasn't going to let me sink any farther into my depths of despair over Bryn. I glanced over at my open window, which Khol must have opened, and saw a little grey squirrel perched on a branch in the big oak tree that sat across from it. It eyed me curiously with its beady little eyes. And to think I used to like squirrels. "Get out of here!" I yelled as I stalked towards my window. "Go tell Jenna to mind her own business and to get the hell out of mine!" I pulled the shades shut again, muting the light from the bright morning. I shook my head in disbelief. What had my world come to that I was hiding from squirrels now?

Thirty minutes later I was standing outside my kitchen, listening to my mom scurrying around making breakfast, and the occasional rustle of the paper let me know my dad was also in there. I held so much resentment towards them, and I didn't know if it would ever go away. I knew on some level they were exactly the same people I'd always known, the same people who had raised me so lovingly, but they were also the people who were responsible for ripping Bryn from my life. There are so many different kinds of love in this world, and I guess when push comes to shove, the romantic soul mate kind of love trumps everything else.

I steeled my nerves and swept into the kitchen with a solemn face. All movement stopped after both of my parents turned to stare at me. I could sense my mom's relief at seeing me out of bed and somewhat normal, but I wasn't going to make it that easy for them. I marched over to the pantry, grabbed a couple breakfast cookies and a bottle of water, stuffed them into my shoulder bag, and careful not to acknowledge their presence, marched out the back door without so much as a word. Things would never be the same between us, I knew that, and in some weird way, I suppose I was mourning the loss of my parents as well as Bryn. Because when all was said and done, I had made my choice, the only choice I could make, and when Bryn came for me in a year, I would leave with him no matter what.

As I rounded the corner, I saw Jenna, with rainbow-colored hair now, waiting expectantly for me. No doubt her squirrel spy had filled her in. She wore a scowl on her face that deepened when she met my eyes. "Are you going to tell me what's going on or not?"

"What? Your little spies didn't garner enough information for you?" I kept walking and didn't wait for her. She scurried to catch up to me with her much shorter legs. "Which by the

HIDDEN GATES

way," I said without looking at her, "it's beyond creepy to have sent a squirrel to spy on me. No wonder everybody thinks Speakers are so weird." It was a low blow, and I knew it. Not many of our kind gave Jenna the time of day, unless they were a guy interested in getting into her pants, and even then, that was short lived. Speakers had a reputation on the whole as being weird, and most of our kind steered clear. I, on the other hand, had instantly liked Jenna, mostly because of her quirkiness. I had always admired her for being true to herself and not giving a damn what other people thought—unless those other people happened to be me, as was the case now.

"That was just mean," she hissed. "I'm just going to pretend you didn't say that, for the sake of our friendship."

"Just butt out of my business," I hissed back. "And you better keep your little spies away from me before I invest in a BB gun or something."

"You wouldn't." She sounded completely appalled. "You aren't that heartless to shoot a poor, defenseless little animal."

I stopped abruptly and glared down at her horrified face. "Try me." I would never shoot a cute little squirrel no matter how annoying it was, but I was hoping Jenna couldn't see past my bluff.

She crossed her arms over her chest and glared back at me. I took that as a sign she wasn't buying my bluff. *Damn Speakers.* "If you want me to butt out of your business, then I guess I can stop defending you to everyone at school, and the next time I hear another ugly rumor, I won't try to set it straight."

The blood completely drained from my face. "What are you talking about? What kind of rumors?"

Jenna's face softened to something resembling pity. "About you and Bryn, and how he got you pregnant . . . stuff like that."

"Oh God. How does anybody even know anything about me and Bryn?" Maybe school wouldn't be on my agenda for the day. I didn't know if I could face everyone if that was the kind of thing being said.

"Well," Jenna said, "I'm not the only Speaker around here that has little spies. Let's just say that a certain Miss Tina Sims is enjoying some newfound popularity over the info she's been feeding to the masses, even if most of it is bullshit."

Great. Now when I had a squirrel chilling outside my window, I had to wonder who it was spying for. At least Jenna was just spying for herself; other Speakers obviously had other agendas beyond curiosity. "Why? Why are people believing her?" I squeaked.

"Oh, P.J., you know why. People love to hear about scandal, especially when it's about someone like you, who everyone thought was a goody-goody virgin. And you can't even deny that something happened, since Bryn has been shipped off, and you went M.I.A. at the same time."

"Oh." Jenna was right. The Bryn and P.J. rumors were probably the biggest scandal that had hit in a long time. I'd probably never live it down. It was official; my social life was ruined.

We walked the rest of the way to school in silence. Only when the front doors to my new own personal hell loomed in front of us did Jenna speak. "So are you going to tell me who that guy was last night?" I knew she wouldn't be able to keep a lid on it for very long.

"Fine." I let out an exasperated breath. "His name is—" And Khol's name seemed to stick in my throat. I opened and closed my mouth like a fish trying to say his name, but nothing came out. I tried to start over again. "His name is—" And again I couldn't utter even a syllable of his name. That's when I remembered something Khol had said to me the first time I'd seen him. He said he'd bound me from speaking of him to anyone. Was that what was going on? So I tried another

HIDDEN GATES

approach. "He first came to me in the woods. He's—" *Aaaah!* I couldn't even describe to her what he looked like. "Look, Jenna, I wish I could, if only to get you off my back, but I literally can't. I'm bound so that I'm not able to. In fact, I'm surprised I can even say that much. I can't even say his name or describe him to you—the words seem to just stick in my throat."

She eyed me with curiosity. "I can tell that you're not lying, but I've never heard of such a thing. Who bound you?"

"He did."

"Are you doing it with him now? Did Bryn completely spring you, and now that he's gone, you've already found yourself another *looover?*" She drew out the word lover to make it sound completely dirty, which was about par for the course with Jenna.

"No, of course not," I snapped. "I love Bryn. End of story."

"Then why were you kissing this other guy?" Jenna raised her eyebrows at me.

"I can't tell you, but let me just say I didn't *want* to be kissing him. The only guy I wanna kiss is Bryn."

"Hmm," Jenna grunted.

It was then, as we walked up the front stairs to the school, that people began to take notice of me, and whispers seemed to follow in my wake. I kept my eyes straight ahead and pretended I didn't notice. I so wished Bryn was with me to hold my hand and make everything better. We pushed through the huge front doors and headed towards the senior hallway. My locker was in my sights when someone grabbed me by my wrist and pulled me to a halt. I found myself looking up into the dark eyes of Eddie Covington, a large Guardian-to-be who also attended our school. He was tall, like almost all Guardians, with a rather plain face and dark brown hair. I guess he could be considered cute, but next to Bryn, he would be lucky if anyone noticed him at all.

"Hey there, P.J.," he said with a smirk. "I heard you have a thing for us lowly Guardians. Now that Bryn's gone, I was hoping you might be looking to fill his spot."

"Get your hands off me." I shook free of his hand and rubbed my wrist while frowning at him. I didn't know what else to say, so I simply turned to leave.

Eddie crowded the space in front of me. "Oh come on, P.J., there's no use in pretending anymore. I have to admit you had us all fooled with your little virginal act." His dark eyes roamed over me from head to toe, and he smiled. "Most Seers wouldn't touch one of us with a ten foot pole, and here you've been, right under our noses, screwing Bryn the whole time. Us Guardians never get to *really* experience a Seer's powers. No wonder he was so protective of you. Guess he didn't want anyone getting their hands on his little prize. Although everyone should have known, with you being friends with a slut like her." He pointedly looked in Jenna's direction. "And who was the guy in your room this morning? Tina's already let all of us know about him. Another Guardian maybe—older—teaching you some things, things that maybe I'd be interested in learning." His hand snaked out and grabbed my wrist again with force. "Come on, P.J., how about showing me what you're really all about?" His grip tightened almost painfully.

"Get your hands off me, you asshole." I took a step back from him, but he followed. I knew we were in school, and I knew he couldn't do anything to me here, at least not out in the open, but my mind flashed back to the night at Ryan's party and the still un-named guy trying to force himself on me. Panic began to bubble up in me just like it had that night, especially because I knew there wouldn't be any Bryn to come to my rescue this time.

"You heard her—get your hands off her, asshole." Eddie was abruptly shoved away from me, and I stumbled back into the row of lockers behind me. Jenna rushed to my side. Eddie retreated fairly quickly, and my savior approached me. I took in his sandy brown hair, deep brown eyes set over a long straight nose, high cheekbones, full, firm lips, and a square, masculine jaw. "Jeremy?" I murmured as his brow furrowed with concern. *What the hell is he doing here?*

"You okay?"

My face heated with sudden embarrassment. Who else had seen and heard what had just gone down between Eddie and me? And the bigger question was: *would it happen again?* "What are you doing here? At my school?"

He flashed me a smile. "It's my school now, too. My family and I moved here a week before our date. I started that following week. Didn't I mention that?"

I frowned. "No, you didn't." That I would have most definitely remembered.

"Well, here I am. And just in time, I see." *Yeah, just in time to witness my complete and utter humiliation.*

"Ahem." Jenna cleared her throat, reminding me she was still there. "You never answered if you're okay. Eddie is such an asshole. Just ignore him. I always do."

I turned and met Jenna's dark eyes, which despite her outward calm, were narrowed with tension. "Yeah, just fine." *Mostly, anyways.*

"So what was that all about? A Guardian shouldn't be treating you like that." Jeremy clenched his fists with anger.

"Oh—you haven't heard. There're some rumors going around about P.J. and—" Jenna started, but I certainly wasn't going to let her finish.

"Shut up, Jenna," I hissed, turning to look at Jeremy, who now wore a slightly bemused expression. "It's nothing, don't worry about it."

"I've already heard the rumors, P.J. As the new guy around town, everyone was more than happy to fill me in on all the latest gossip." He took my bag from my shoulder and started walking, and since he had my stuff hostage, I had no choice but to follow. I assumed Jenna wasn't far behind us. "So what's the real deal? Because I'm not the type to buy into that kind of stuff."

I met his eyes briefly before studying my shoes as we walked. "I don't know. What've you heard? Although, I'm almost afraid to ask."

"Just that you're an easy lay, you prefer to do Guardians, you were sleeping with your no longer future Guardian amongst a host of other guys, that he was shipped away after he got you pregnant, and your parents forced you to have an abortion." He paused briefly to inhale. "Also it's not just our kind that's talking. You seem to be the talk of both worlds. The Regs apparently have labeled you a slut as well, not that there are that many Regs at this school."

I turned and glared at Jenna who was walking a few steps behind us. "You never said anything about me sleeping with a host of other guys, or the abortion, or the Regs."

Jenna at least had the decency to look a tiny bit sheepish for once. "I didn't wanna upset you anymore," she mumbled.

"Because finding out this way was so much better," I snapped.

Jeremy touched my arm, and I met his deep brown eyes that burned with curiosity. "So what started these rumors?"

I mulled over what I should say to him. He seemed like a nice enough guy on our date, and he had come to my rescue with Eddie, but how would he react once he knew the truth? Our school was very clique-ish. None of the Regs realized most of the cliques were primarily divided between my kind and their kind, because we didn't look any different or dress any differently. We just had a tendency to gravitate towards people we could be more ourselves around without worry of exposure. I usually just hung with Bryn and Jenna, preferring to stay out of the clique game, that way I could be friends with whoever I wanted.

Unfortunately, my little group had just been majorly downsized without Bryn as a member, and it was sounding more and more like I was the hot topic of conversation within all the major cliques in my school. I could use as many allies as I could get. "Bryn was shipped away, and you know people talk. All of a sudden I'm the biggest slut this school has ever seen, apparently." I scuffed my shoe along the ground angrily. "I've only been with one guy, for fuck's sake, and I've only had sex once. I was a virgin until recently." I inhaled and exhaled deeply, trying to calm myself. "It's so not fair."

"But it was Bryn, wasn't it? Who took your virginity?" Jeremy asked softly.

I whipped my head up and met his gaze sharply. I'm not sure what I saw there, but suddenly I wanted to tell him the truth. "Yeah, it was." I began studying my shoes again.

Jeremy's hand reached out and tipped my chin back so he could look me in the eyes. He held his power in check for the moment, which I really appreciated. "It's okay. I won't judge. I already knew you had feelings for someone else when we had our date. I was just hoping I could compete. And you were a virgin then, I could tell."

"What? How?" I asked incredulously.

He smiled. "I'm a very strong Gatekeeper. Not only can I sense and manipulate energy around the gates, but I can sense and manipulate *other* energies."

Oh, that was just fabulous. "Why didn't you tell me?"

"Yeah, because that wouldn't have freaked you out or anything. By the way—P.J., I—"

I interrupted him with a laugh, already knowing where he was going with his line of thought. "Yeah, you may have a point there." I couldn't help the smile that cracked across my face. "I've never heard of a Gatekeeper being able to do that before."

He shrugged his shoulders. "Most can't. I can. No biggie."

Obviously no longer feeling very sheepish, Jenna took that opportunity to push in between Jeremy and me. She looked up at him and batted her eyelashes. "Hi, I'm Jenna." Her voice had gone lower and huskier, and there was no doubt what she wanted from him.

Jeremy's lips twitched up into a wry smile. "You have all the subtlety of a bull in a china shop, don't you?"

Jenna blushed, and I laughed, causing Jenna to shoot me a glare. "That's our Jenna, blunt as can be."

"Well, I can be pretty blunt myself. Sorry, Jenna, don't waste your time on me, I've already got my eye on someone else." He looked at me and smiled, and it was my turn to blush.

"Jeremy, I—well, I—"

He slid my bag back onto my shoulder and winked at me. "Don't sweat it. I know you have feelings for Bryn, otherwise you wouldn't have slept with him. I can tell that's the kind of girl you are. But he's gone, and I'm here. I have every intention of wooing you to the best of my abilities." He crowded my space by stepping up to me, and for a second I thought he was going to try to kiss me.

Instead he leaned over and whispered in my ear, "I've been on a lot of dates with a lot of Seers lately because of my Sudding, and none have piqued my interest like you have. Not only are you smart, funny, and stunning, but also, your power calls out to mine. You're who I want P.J., and I don't mind waiting around until you can be mine."

My heart thrummed in my chest with him being so close to me, and it wasn't just because he was a hot guy and my hormones seemed to be set on overdrive lately. No, it was something else . . . something more. It made me think about what Khol had said to me about me eventually craving . . . well, more. Was it his power that was calling to mine like he just claimed that mine called to his? Would the yearning to discover more grow with my developing powers? "Jeremy—" I tried again, but with a smile, he turned and trotted off down the hall.

"Wow," Jenna said as she fanned herself. "Some girls have all the luck."

I grimaced. "Yeah, but it's not necessarily *good* luck."

"Only you would complain about having multiple hot guys vying for your attention." Jenna stuck her lower lip out at me.

"Too bad the one I really want has been shipped off to who-knows-where, and I'm the one left here to deal with the fallout of everything. Or do you consider it lucky, too, that everyone in school thinks I'm such a big slut now?"

"Oh, stop being so over dramatic. We're seniors, and school's ending in less than a year, not to mention when you graduate, you and Bryn can do whatever the hell you want. Things could be worse. At least you have Jeremy to keep you occupied." She smiled wistfully, and I rolled my eyes.

"Seriously, what don't you understand? I'm not interested in him like that."

Jenna sighed. "Speaker here, something that you keep forgetting. I'm totally awesome at reading body language, and yours was saying something completely different just now. You might love Bryn, but Jeremy could definitely get you going. Why not use him until Bryn gets back?"

My jaw dropped—she couldn't be serious. "Are you suggesting that I sleep with Jeremy until Bryn gets back?"

She nodded her affirmation. "Yep, that's exactly what I'm suggesting. It could be the solution to all your problems. You could marry Jeremy and take Bryn on as your lover slash

Guardian." She clapped her hands together excitedly. "It would be perfect."

Jenna was worse than a guy sometimes. Her plan was a horrible idea, even if it were something that I was interested in, which it so wasn't. I could just imagine trying to explain it to them. *Oh, hey, Jeremy, even though you're my husband, I'm going to keep on having sex with Bryn. Hope you don't mind sharing. And Bryn, you know I love you, but I need to have sex with my husband in order to try and get pregnant with his baby. You know, duty calls and all. You okay with that?* "You're absolutely insane, you know that, right?"

"Insanely smart." Jenna giggled as she absentmindedly worked some of her rainbow hair into a curl with her fingertips.

"Yeah, you keep telling yourself that." I grappled with swapping some stuff out of my locker and into my bag before I turned in the direction of homeroom with dread.

Something must have shown on my face, because Jenna looked at me with sympathy. "The first day is always the worst. People will move on to the next big thing really soon."

I inhaled and exhaled deeply, trying to center myself. Who does that ever really work for in real life? It certainly wasn't working for me. "All right, here I go." It wasn't just the rumors and whispers that I'd have to deal with that were bothering me; it was also my first day back at school without Bryn at my side. There was an emptiness like a huge gaping hole in my chest left by his absence. I moved forward on shaky legs, ignoring the small groups of people whispering about me as I passed them. The first warning bell rang, and I hastened just a little, looking back only once, wishing that Jenna could come with me. She wasn't much, but at least she would be some kind of buffer. She waved at me with fake cheer and turned to go off in the opposite direction towards her own homeroom. *Okay, I can do this.* I mentally steeled myself. Oh, for the days when my biggest worry was someone getting wind of my middle name and telling everyone.

As I entered homeroom, every pair of eyes looked up to stare. Some tried to do it more covertly, and others openly gawked. A weird kind of quiet settled over the room as I made my way to my seat. I slumped down in my chair and dropped my bag at my feet, staring straight ahead as the final bell rang. Everyone's eyes burned into me, and my face heated as the whispering began when I couldn't help but glance to my right at Bryn's empty desk. Why was everyone so completely obsessed with what was going on with me? I understood my kind being thrown for a loop with the whole Seer hooking up with a Guardian thing, but we didn't make up all of the school, and it seemed like more than just my people had taken an interest in the gossip surrounding me. It hadn't escaped my notice that not one person had greeted me when I entered the room. I had become the local pariah. *Yay, me!*

A chime echoed three times from the loud speaker, signaling the morning announcements were soon to follow. "Quiet, everyone," Mrs. Averton said loudly. I simply slumped in my seat even lower and waited for homeroom to end. This was going to be a very long day.

It was official: I was never going back to school again. Not one single person had asked me how I was doing all day, and when anyone, male or female, deigned to actually utter a few words to me, it was always some kind of lewd remark or insult. The guys all wanted to sleep with me, and the girls all wanted to scratch my eyes out because the guys all wanted to sleep with me. I was beginning to think that Bryn was the lucky one, getting shipped off to somewhere where nobody knew who he was. But then again, he'd probably be getting all kinds of pats on the back if he were the one who was left behind instead of me. It was all so unfair.

"Hey there, my little Seer." I looked up from my spot under a tree in my backyard to meet Khol's vivid green eyes. I had come to sit here after school because I wanted to be left alone, but my parents obviously wanted to be able to keep an eye on me. I guess they were worried I'd throw myself at the next available Guardian now that Bryn was gone.

"I'm not your little Seer," I snapped, focusing back down on the ground and ignoring the almost suffocating pressure Khol's appearance caused in the air. I also wasn't going to acknowledge the buzz of excitement that burned through my entire system.

Khol sat down beside me, but not close enough to touch. "Oh? But you are. We're linked, you and I."

I lifted my head to glare at him. "Look, I'm in no mood to deal with you right now. Why did you come this time? What do you want? Wait—" I glanced over towards my kitchen window to see if either of my parents had spotted Khol yet. "You better get out of here before my parents see you. After what happened with Bryn, they'll blow a gasket if they see me out here with some guy they don't know. Apparently, I can't be trusted around anyone with a penis anymore."

Khol laughed. "Well, I don't think that is true. I think they just do not trust you in general now."

"That's all beside the point. I don't want them to see you here—with me." I glanced back over at my kitchen window again. Not to mention I didn't want any little rodent spies to see me either, although it wasn't like my reputation could get any worse than it currently was.

"They are busy at the moment. I can hear them talking." He tilted his head and smiled. "And I will be able to hear them if they approach."

HIDDEN GATES

Huh. Good to know. So he has superhuman hearing of some kind. I tilted my head to study him, almost mirroring his body language. "What are you?" I murmured. The more I was around him, the less creepy things, such as his eyes, became, and I noticed other little things more. For instance how handsome he was, even with his ginormous proportions. And he had dimples. I'd always liked dimples; Bryn had dimples—*Bryn.* I mustn't get distracted by Khol's handsome face and forget my Bryn. It was as if Khol was enchanting me somehow. "Are you using some kind of . . . I don't know—power—to distract me? Some kind of whatever-you-are mojo to make me forget about Bryn when I'm with you?"

Khol met my eyes for a moment before responding. "I possess no such powers. Whatever you feel when I am near is completely you." He leaned closer to me, letting his leg brush against mine, the heat coming from him washed over me, causing my breath to catch in my throat. Maybe what Jenna had said was true, maybe being with Bryn had sprung me, and my hormones were just going crazy now. If I knew that was the case, I could control it.

"Your friend Jenna knows nothing about these things," Khol rumbled.

"Stop doing that." I scowled at him. "It's creepy."

But he said nothing; instead, he leaned into me and pushed the hair on the right side of my head behind my ear, letting his fingers blaze a trail of heat down my neck before pulling away. Warmth pooled in my core, and my breathing was coming fast and sporadic. I balled my fists at my sides in order to resist touching him. Just because my body was reacting to him didn't mean I would betray Bryn. I stared into Khol's electric green eyes as he leaned back into me, his face skimming along my neck, his breath hot, but his lips never actually touching my skin. He moved up my jaw and towards my mouth, never making contact, stopping just millimeters from me, his face so close I was afraid to breathe. "I told you, I will not take again what isn't freely given." His lips almost touched mine as he spoke, which sent a shudder down to my core. My chest heaved as I willed myself to move away, although I seemed unable to. He ran his hands through my hair, grasping tightly at the base of my neck, and oh, I wanted him to kiss me—so badly. I felt like a traitor for wanting Khol's lips on mine, but I couldn't help the desire. I didn't have to act on it though—I wouldn't let myself.

"No," I whispered. "Stop."

Every muscle in Khol's body tensed before he slowly, ever so slowly, pulled away from me. A part of me mourned the loss of his touch, and yet I knew I couldn't allow myself to feel that way. He closed his eyes and spoke, his voice low and gruff. "I want you, my little Seer. I will not pretend that part isn't true. Your power, your body, your very essence is what awakened me from my sleep. I am yours, your willing servant, linked to you first by choice and now by need."

I swallowed, trying to combat my suddenly dry throat. "Why do I seem to be the main attraction for all you guys around here lately? Why now? Why all of a sudden, when no one seemed to notice me before?" Besides Bryn that is; Bryn always noticed me.

Khol's eyes remained closed as he spoke, his head tipped back against the base of the tree. "Because you were a pretty girl who is now becoming a beautiful woman—a beautiful and powerful woman who deserves to be worshipped, one that can no longer be ignored, one that I'm trying my best to keep my word to." He moved lightening fast, like he had the night before in my bedroom, stopping with his hands cupping my face, his eyes boring into mine. "I know that a part of you wants me to kiss you, a part of you wants what I'm offering, even if you are not ready." I shuddered, unable to deny his words, knowing even if I tried, he would know. "But I will not take it from you, although a part of me yearns to do just that. I will wait." His hands trembled against the side of my face. "We have more important things to worry about than our petty desires. I will come to you later when I have myself more . . . under control." He stood abruptly and disappeared. *How the hell does he keep doing that?*

"P.J." My mother came bustling out the back door of our house towards me, barely containing her excitement. "You have a visitor."

I looked at her balefully from my spot on the ground. "I thought I was still being punished. Must be an important visitor."

"The fact that he wants to see you at all after what happened with Bryn—well, it means you still have hope, and I'm not going to let anything stand in the way of that."

"Oh, so it's a *he?* I guess it's safe to assume that he isn't a Guardian or anyone of that ilk, you know the unacceptable kind of guys for me to associate with, ones that won't be on your Sudding list." I crossed my arms over my chest and raised my chin defiantly. If my mother wanted me to see this guy, then I had no desire to do so.

"Now, don't you ruin this. I only want what's best for you, peanut," my mother whispered excitedly as I heard my father's voice growing closer. "He'll be out in a second."

"Fabulous," I grumbled. Well, I wasn't going to get up for whoever it was. I looked up to see my father escorting none other than Jeremy into my backyard. He grinned at me as my mother hurried over to join my father, and the two of them went back inside without another word. Well, I guess I could be trusted alone with a Gatekeeper, just not any Guardians. "What are you doing here?" I asked, trying not to sound too accusatory.

"Just came to see how you were doing after your first day back at school. I know it must have been pretty rough, all things considered." He sat down next to me where Khol had been, and just like him, he was careful not to touch me when he sat.

I picked at some blades of grass, averting my eyes. "Yeah, don't really wanna talk about it. But thanks anyways." I lifted my head and met his deep brown gaze, unable to keep myself from being annoyed with him. "You know, I do appreciate you helping me today, and being so nice—I do—"

"But? I sense a 'but' coming." Jeremy eyed me with his deep brown, soulful eyes.

I sighed. "Yeah, there is, if you come over like this, my mom is going to start printing up our wedding invitations and naming our first child. She seems to think you're my only prospect at the moment, and well, I'm sure you know how it is."

"Yeah, I do. My mom is the same way. It's just, well, I wouldn't mind all of that—with you."

My mouth dropped open. "What? You can't be serious? You barely know me. You can't—"

"There's just something about you," he interrupted. "I can't quite put my finger on it. I wanna be with you, P.J. I thought girls all believed in the whole love at first sight kind of thing. I mean, I don't love you." Jeremy flushed. "Not yet anyways—but I could. I know that I could."

"Whoa, whoa, whoa. You know I love someone else. You *know* that. It's been like a week since he was ripped out of my life. And I don't plan on giving him up so easily." Seriously, what had I just asked Khol about guys noticing me so much more all of a sudden? I'd gone from a drought to a flash flood. But the one I really wanted was nowhere to be found.

Jeremy frowned, picking at some blades of grass himself. "You *love* him? No, I didn't know that part. I just knew you had feelings for him."

HIDDEN GATES

"Even if I had feelings short of love for him, it's still only been a week." I sighed. "Look, Jeremy, you're wasting your time with me."

"So what do you plan on doing? He's a Guardian, P.J., and even though I would never judge you for your indiscretion, are you willing to give up your friends and family for him? Are you willing to become an outcast to be with him? To be completely shunned from our world?"

I didn't even have to think about it. I would do anything to be with Bryn. "Yes," I whispered. "I would do anything to be with him."

"Oh," Jeremy said. "Even still—I can't just give up on you. No girl has ever gotten into my head like you have. I can't stop thinking about you. And your power—the way it feels when it connects with mine is beyond believable."

I let out a frustrated groan. "I don't wanna hurt you, Jeremy. Despite not wanting to be with you romantically, I still like you. I still want to be friends."

"Friends," Jeremy grunted with displeasure.

He then abruptly leaned into me, crushing his lips to mine. I barely had time to mentally process what was going on before his tongue was sliding into my mouth, and just like with Khol, I found myself kissing him back. And as much as I hated to admit it, my body responded to his as well. His hands snaked up into my hair, his thumbs pressed against the sides of my jaw, and I couldn't help but let out a little moan. *He's such a good kisser*, I numbly thought as his tongue massaged and played with mine.

And then it happened—I wasn't quite sure what it was at first, but I somehow knew it had something to do with his powers and my powers intermingling. I was yanked out of my body like when I had visions before, and yet at the same time, I was still very aware of Jeremy's body touching mine. I gasped into Jeremy's mouth as a vision slammed into me—white-hot light, images coming at me almost too fast to interpret. It was more of an impression than a vision, but it was bad, very bad—those things, those "aliens" in so many people. They were everywhere, hiding and yet in plain sight. They had a plan, a plan they'd already set in motion. I could almost *see* it, and yet it was just out of my grasp.

Then I was jolted back into my body when I felt myself begin to peak. Jeremy's powers swirled in and around me, pummeling all of my senses at once as he kissed me. His hands slid down my body to pull me closer to him. Everything about the kiss was overwhelming and all encompassing, and yet he wasn't actually doing anything with his hands or body that should have caused that kind of reaction in me. My whole body was spasming with ecstasy from little more than a kiss. I moaned into his mouth, my hands digging into his shoulders. He then pulled away, staring down at me as my eyes fluttered open, little aftershocks still racking my body. I bit my lip, not knowing what to say to him.

He didn't seem to have the same tongue-tied problem. "That was amazing," he murmured.

"What—what was that?" I sputtered, guilt crashing over me like a tidal wave, threatening to drown me. First Khol and now Jeremy . . . what would Bryn think?

"I'm not one hundred percent sure. I can manipulate all kinds of energies, but I've never been able to do *that* before. It was like I could feel our powers intertwining when we touched, and then . . ." His voice trailed off as he flushed, a small smile playing across his lips. "You did, didn't you? You know?"

I blushed and averted my eyes. I supposed I might as well be honest with him because I got the sense that he already knew what he had done to me and he was just pretending that he couldn't tell. After all, how could he not know when he

HIDDEN GATES

had known before that I was still a virgin just by reading my energies? "Yeah," I breathed, still not looking at him. "You?" I couldn't help but to be curious. I wanted to know if he had been affected the same way I had been.

"Yeah . . . no. I have a little bit more control than that over myself."

I narrowed my eyes at him angrily. "So what are you trying to say? That I have no control over myself? Do you think I'm easy or something because of what happened with Bryn?" I knew my anger was misplaced. Jeremy seemed like a genuinely nice guy, and I didn't actually think he'd meant anything by his comment, and yet I needed to be angry with someone. I needed to yell at someone because I hated myself for betraying Bryn. "You did that on purpose, didn't you?" I hissed.

"No, and you know I didn't. Don't be mad at me because you feel like you betrayed Bryn or something. Maybe it's better you figure these things out now before it's too late." Was I that obvious that he knew right away why I was really angry?

"Too late for what?"

He stepped towards me, and I backed up, causing him to throw up his hands in a sign of defeat. "Before you two do something really stupid, and then you figure out down the line that he isn't right for you."

"And I suppose you think you're right for me?"

His brown eyes flashed with emotion as his lips pressed into a thin line briefly before responding. "Yeah, I do."

"And why is that? Because you just made me . . . well . . . you know?" I couldn't bring myself to actually say it.

Jeremy grunted, his lips turning up slightly at the edges. "Partly; you can't deny we have good chemistry, P.J."

"I have *better* chemistry with Bryn. I love him. I don't love you." It was just like a guy to think everything was all about sex. There is more to chemistry than just sex. Okay, fine, sex plays a huge part in it, but other things go into the mix, like emotions—emotions like love.

"So, you're not even willing to give me a chance after that? Won't you at least go out on a second date with me? Didn't that kiss at least warrant that much?" Jeremy's face was pleading and not the least bit arrogant or cocky. I would have at least expected a touch of egotism after that little performance. Hell, I would be a little smug if the shoe were on the other foot, and yet his deep brown eyes only held a kind of desperation. "Please, P.J., give me a chance, a real chance. That's all I'm asking for."

I looked away from him, not wanting to see his sad eyes anymore. I wasn't cruel after all. "I can't. I'm sorry. I love Bryn."

"If you love him so much, then you shouldn't be worried about going out with me again. You could go out with me, give us a real shot, and if you really love him as much as you say you do, well then, I won't be able to steal you away. You owe it to yourself to find out, don't you think?" I didn't say anything, not really liking where the conversation was going. "The only reason to not go out with me is because you know you don't really love him, at least not the way you say you do. Don't you think you owe it to him to find out if you truly love him?"

"Stop," I said, my shoulders slumping. What if he was right? What if I was afraid to give anyone else a shot because I didn't think I could be faithful? Would Bryn want to be with me if he doubted how much I really loved him? I knew Jeremy was trying to twist things to his advantage, trying to manipulate me into going out with him again, but even I couldn't deny he made some very valid points. "All right," I stated flatly. "I'll go out with you again." I raised my eyes to meet his merrily dancing brown gaze as a huge grin spread across his face. "But none of that again—don't do that to me again." I bit my lower lip and eyed him warily. *This could all be a huge mistake.*

HIDDEN GATES

Jeremy's grin turned sly. "I can't make that promise. I'm going to use every God given gift to try and make you mine."

"Jeremy—" I groaned, my face turning into a scowl.

"Nope. You already agreed to go. I'll mention it to your mom on the way out—you know, so you can't back out of it later." He turned and loped back towards my house.

"That's playing dirty," I called to him with annoyance.

He glanced over his shoulder at me. "Yep, but at least I'm in the game."

I turned and braced myself on the tree, running my fingertips idly over the bark, freezing when the texture of the wood dipped down into small jagged indentations pressing up against my skin. When Bryn and I had been little kids, we had both carved our names into the trunk of the tree that I was currently touching. We hadn't put our initials together inside a heart or anything like that. We hadn't known about such things as love yet, but both our names did grace the trunk of this tree. And I had unerringly found the grooves in the trunk that spelled out Bryn's name. I stared at it as big fat tears began to slowly slide down my cheeks. I'd just betrayed him—twice—and both times while his name hovered above me. My heart hadn't been in the kiss with Jeremy, nor the almost kiss with Khol, but my body had been, and it had called for more, not to mention its reaction to the actual kiss I'd shared with Khol in my bedroom last night. Bryn had been gone just over a week, and I'd already been unfaithful to him three times all in all. What kind of girlfriend did that make me? Not a very good one, that much I knew.

I loved Bryn, with all of my heart. I loved him more deeply and completely than I ever could anyone else. And he made my blood boil every time he was near me . . . So why did my body respond so willingly to both Khol and Jeremy? And how could I put a stop to things when they obviously were both dead set on having me for themselves? *Maybe in a year when Bryn comes for me, he won't want me anymore.* Maybe he'll realize I'm the one that's not good enough for him.

12

The rest of my evening after Jeremy left passed by in a fog. All I could think about was how I had betrayed Bryn with both Khol and Jeremy. And now, as I lay in my silent bedroom in the pitch black, shades drawn to protect against the prying eyes of nosey squirrels, I fought a sick feeling in my stomach that just wouldn't go away. I didn't deserve Bryn and his love. How could he ever forgive me? I had to tell him what had happened, of course, but what if I didn't get the chance until a year was up? What if he came for me like planned, and I had to tell him what had transpired between me and two other guys? I could almost picture the betrayed expression on his face. Would he hate me? Would he walk away from me forever?

"I feel your tormented emotions, my little Seer. Why are you torturing yourself?" Khol's low voice cut through the thick silence of my room.

I raised my head to see him kneeling beside my bed, his electric green eyes glowing in the dark as he studied my face. He was one of the reasons I was feeling this way, and yet I had to talk to someone. "I betrayed Bryn." A sob erupted from my throat when I heard myself say the words aloud. "He won't want me now, after what I've done. And I can't really blame him; I'm not good enough for someone like him."

Khol snorted. "You know nothing of men if you think what you've done will turn him from you. He will want you until his dying breath."

I blinked in confusion at Khol. "Shouldn't you tell me that he's not going to want me anymore, and that he'll hate me, so you can swoop in and make your move?" Isn't that what a typical guy would do anyways?

Khol snorted again. "I won't resort to cheap tricks of manipulation to win your affections. You would only resent me in the end. When you finally come to me, it will be because you are truly mine, and there will be no doubts to hold you back." He flashed me a smile in the dark. "And when you are mine, you'll come to me alone for satisfaction, all other touches will leave you cold in comparison after I've branded you."

I shuddered, goose bumps erupting all over my skin. There was something ancient and knowing in his words. His mention of branding me wasn't just an innuendo. It meant something more, but I wasn't exactly sure what. It was like that with Khol sometimes. He would say something that seemingly meant one thing, but I could pick up on an undercurrent of something else hidden between the lines. I'm not sure if he meant for me to feel those things, or if it was just a side effect of our link, but regardless, they were there. "I'll always crave Bryn," I said.

"When all others turn to dust, there will only be you and me."

Fear raced up my spine. I wasn't afraid of Khol, just his words for some reason. "What's that supposed to mean?"

He stared at me for another moment, his face devoid of all emotion before he replied, "We must discuss the vision you had earlier . . . when you were kissing the Gatekeeper."

HIDDEN GATES

I eyed him warily, knowing he was purposely not answering me, changing the subject to something I couldn't ignore. "Yeah, fine. What about it? I couldn't quite make everything out. It was more of an impression than a vision."

"To you maybe, although that could be because you were otherwise occupied." He shot me a wry smile. "But I was able to look closer at your vision and discern what seemed to be just beyond your grasp." I waved my hand at him to continue. "We've figured out what they want—these creatures."

"And?" I squirmed impatiently.

"They want this world for themselves. They wish to rule it, and to enslave humans. They've done it before, to other worlds. They implant themselves amongst the residents of that world, slowly take over, and once they have complete control, they use up all the resources. Eventually there is nothing left, and they move on."

"Holy shit!" I exclaimed. "It's like this movie I saw where these aliens attacked, trying to kill everybody so they could use our world up. Actually, it's kind of like a lot of movies I've seen." I frowned, wondering if someone, somewhere, was trying to tell us something.

"But unlike in your fantasy movies, the mass public doesn't know these aliens are among us. They look like regular humans to them. If you came forward, you'd probably be locked away and labeled insane," Khol stated matter-of-factly.

And he was right. I couldn't just point to people like Senator Bill Wexington and yell, "Alien!" People would lock me away and throw away the key. "So what do we do then?"

"We're coming up with a plan. In the meantime, you must just stay aware."

"Great. More of doing nothing. And who is this *we* you keep referring to? I'm hoping you're not using the royal we or something, because it's going to take more than just you and me to take care of this problem." I noticed on several occasions Kohl had said, "*We* are working on it" and "*We* are coming up with a plan." Just who was this *we?*

"More of my kind. Most of us still slumber, as I said, but you and your powers have awakened more than just me."

My eyes widened. "Umm... so should I expect more pushy visitors like you to just drop by and harass me?" *Oh, please, no.*

"No." Khol's jaw hardened into stone. "They are not to make direct contact with you. If any of them approach you, and trust me, you will know, call for me immediately, do you hear me?" He reached up and grabbed my shoulders. "Others of my kind are not as in control as I am. They won't be able to hold themselves back from you." Anger flared in his iridescent eyes, so great that I shrank back from him. "They will try to take from you what doesn't belong to them. They are too young and do not understand. I would kill them for it, but some of them would see it as a risk worth pursuing."

"And what makes you different from others of your kind?" I croaked while staring at Khol's tense face.

"I have lived many lifetimes longer than most of them, and I understand things they do not. There is no need to fear them. They listen to me. I am their leader. But there is always a chance that one of them won't be strong enough to resist your call, and he will try to come for you." I shivered at the thought. Kohl reached one hand up and pushed my hair out of my face. "I will protect you. Please, I did not mean to frighten you." When I didn't say anything, Kohl leaned in closer to me. "Do you trust me?"

I did. For some reason I did trust him—truly. "Yes. I told you before that I did, and I still do, despite everything."

"Good." He let go of me, his face growing pensive. "And don't worry, we won't sit by and observe for much longer. The time for action is growing near. Your very existence speaks of things to come. These creatures may think this world is ripe for the picking, and in many ways it is, but there are those of this world who will fight hard enough and champion the weak. The creatures will not win."

Purpose swelled within me. I remembered thinking before that life had no meaning without love, and that was true, but what good was love if we weren't free to express it? Things needed to change, old ways needed to die in order to make room for the new, and these aliens needed to leave my world the hell alone so we could live in peace. Getting rid of the aliens was the first step, and then it would be time to change the thinking of my people so Bryn and I could be together and not be shunned by our own kind. That's when a thought hit me. "They're behind all the chaos, aren't they? All the chaos and tension that's been worsening in our world?"

"Yes. Not only do they want to use this world and suck it dry, but they enjoy the chaos. It makes them stronger and us weaker, in a manner of speaking."

"Oh. You mean like united we stand, divided we fall?" I asked excitedly. Who knew history class would actually serve a purpose in my real life?

Khol smiled. "Yes. Precisely."

Khol looked like he was going to say more, but I interrupted. "And I wasn't going to say anything, but what's up with how you talk? It's so *do not* this and *will not* that and all old fashioned in some ways."

Khol chuckled. "It's because I *am* old fashioned. As I've said, I was asleep for a very long time. I've been trying to update my manner of speaking. Haven't I been improving, my little Seer?"

I scowled at him for calling me *his* little Seer again, but I supposed there was no point in arguing with him at that moment about it. "Yeah, I guess. I mean, before you probably would have said something like, 'Have I not been improving?' . . . or something like that."

"Yes, indeed."

"And you just backslid." I laughed at his perplexed expression. "Nevermind, forget it." I smiled up at Khol for a second before I sobered. "I wanna do something. I need to help stop these assholes."

"Even when it's time to move, you will not actively participate." Khol knelt back down and ran his knuckles along the side of my face, causing me to turn into his touch, much to my dismay. He was so hot, and I wasn't just talking about how he looked, I was talking about his body temperature. I knew I must feel like ice to him, and I wanted to luxuriate in the warmth his caresses could bring my body. "You're too precious to endanger in that way. And not just to me, I mean your visions. We would all still be in the dark about this if it weren't for you. Without you, we wouldn't stand a chance."

"But I can't just sit by and do nothing. I need to help, too." I locked eyes with Khol and watched as his gaze dipped to fixate on my lips. I knew he was thinking about kissing me, and it made me tremble with longing. I inwardly cursed myself for being so weak. I'd chastised myself all afternoon and evening for what I'd done with both Khol and Jeremy, and now faced with it again, it looked like I hadn't learned my lesson.

Just for a brief moment I swore I saw fire dance behind the black irises of Kohl's eyes. Instead of being afraid, I felt myself being drawn closer to him, like I was a moth and his flames compelled me to touch him. I reached out and pressed my thumbs on the outside corners of his eyes. "What are you?" I murmured as he slid his eyelids closed, a small tremor running through him.

"Someone who can't seem to get control of himself when I'm around you." His voice was almost hoarse. "Your power sings to mine, like calls to like, and I desire nothing more than to forget my honor and claim you for my own when I am with you."

"But you won't." I swallowed nervously as his eyes snapped back open to resume staring at my lips. "Because I trust you."

Khol pulled away from me and stood on visibly shaky legs, a small smile tipping the corners of his lips up. "Ah, and that's the truth of the matter. I will not betray your trust. It means too much to me. So remember, my little Seer, if you lose your trust in me, you lose all that stops me from taking what I truly desire."

I licked my lips nervously, Khol's eyes following the movement. "And we're not just talking about sex, are we?" I don't know where I found the courage to ask, but I had to know.

A dark laugh filled my dark room, making me want to pull the covers over my head and hide like a little girl. "No, my little Seer, we are not talking about just sex. I want more—ever so much more from you than just that."

"What? What is it you want from me?" I said with shaky breath. How could I trust someone who scared the crap out of me on so many levels?

"When you are ready to know what I am, then you'll be ready to know what I want from you. Until then, you can know nothing more than that one day you will belong to me."

I raised my chin to meet his eyes defiantly, despite the tremor of fear coursing through my veins. "I'm already Bryn's. He belongs to me, and I belong to him."

Khol grunted. "It's time for me to go . . . for now." And just like usual, he simply disappeared.

I stared wide-eyed into the darkness of my room, the depth of it seeming that much deeper with the absence of Khol and his luminescent green eyes. I had so much to think about and none of the emotional experience to deal with any of it. A part of me longed for the innocent times before I had figured out my feelings for Bryn and we had slept together. To me, that night at Ryan's party was a clear demarcation of before and after, simple and complicated. I may not have officially been with Bryn, but I'd at least had him in my life, and without Khol and Jeremy hanging around trying to muck everything up, not to mention guys like the still un-named punk from Ryan's party and Eddie from school. I used to think I wanted attention from guys, and well, what is it they say? *Be careful what you wish for.* And going along with that line of thought, I had once wished so hard to come into my abilities as a Seer. That night at Ryan's didn't just mark a change for my romantic life but my life in general, because it was that night at Jenna's when I'd had my very first vision.

I was tired of not doing anything. I hadn't done anything when Bryn was sent away. I hadn't done anything about the visions I'd been given. I hadn't done anything but lay around and feel sorry for myself, and I was tired of it. But what could I do, really? I was just one eighteen-year-old teenage girl with no remarkable powers beyond having visions. My gift seemed to mirror the state of my life. I was a perpetual spectator, and I didn't know how to join the game.

I'd lain awake all night, ruminating about what I could do about all of the many issues I was facing, trying to formulate some kind of plan to take some action, and I'd come up with nothing. Nada. Zilch. Zero. And now I found my mind wandering to thoughts of Bryn. He was never far from my mind lately, even when I was liplocked with someone else. I lost myself so much in my imaginings that I could almost touch him, smell his scent wrapped around me as if I were really in his arms. It reminded me that even though I was attracted to both Khol and Jeremy, Bryn was *home*. And I would always choose him over anyone else—always. Missing him so much was torture. I hadn't been separated from him for more than a few days since we were kids. It was truly like losing a part of myself. Nothing seemed exactly real without him to share it with. He was the one person who I always ran to tell all about anything of importance. Not being able to share the recent events of my visions made them all seem like a dream, I realized. Everything felt completely surreal without Bryn. I pushed my face deeper into my pillow and sobbed.

"Oh, peanut," my mother's pained voice said as the bed shifted under her weight. I just wished she'd go away. I didn't want comfort from one of the people who had ripped Bryn from my life. It was partly her fault I was so miserable.

Her small hands softly stroked my hair. "I know you're upset now, but it's for the best, you'll see." I had to fight the urge to lift the pillow from my head and scream at her. Instead, I burrowed deeper into the comforting fluff. "It could be worse. At least you didn't end up pregnant, and then you'd have to marry the first Seer descendant or Gatekeeper that would have you. At least this way you won't have to live a lie the rest of your life. You can move on from your mistake." I'm not really sure what it was that tipped me off. Maybe it was the catch in my mother's voice, or the knowing way she seemed to speak, but that's when it hit me.

I slowly lifted my face from my pillow, my eyes widening to twice their normal size. "Oh my God," I whispered with shock. "Oh. My. God. Is that what happened to you? Am—am I even Daddy's real daughter?"

"Of course you're your father's, don't be ridiculous. I just knew . . . a friend . . . a friend that had that happen, is all," my mother snapped with as much indignance she could muster, but she wasn't fooling me. I could see the panic that hid beneath the surface of her faux anger. I'd hit it right on the nail. *Holy shit* . . . I wasn't even biologically the daughter of the man I'd grown up thinking was my father.

I reached over and grabbed my mom's hand. "Tell me," I demanded. "I have a right to know. Wait—does Daddy know? Does he know I'm not really his?" My mother's shoulders slumped in defeat, and she looked at me with tears welling in her eyes. It was then, for the first time, it occurred to me how young my mom was in comparison with all my other friends' moms. "How old were you?"

"I love your father. I don't want you to ever doubt that," she stated with a shaky voice. "It's just I was young—so young—and he was—well, he was—he was like nothing I'd ever seen before."

"He couldn't have been a Guardian, that much I know, because I would've been a boy," I interjected, speaking my thoughts out loud.

"No, you're right. Your father"—her voice shook—"your biological father, I mean—he wasn't human. Or not like any human I'd ever met before. He had these eyes—these iridescent blue eyes—and powers I've never seen before or since. He, well, I couldn't seem to resist him." My mom swallowed and looked away, unable to meet my gaze. "I gave myself to him completely. I thought I was in love. I would have done anything to be with him. But when I found out I was pregnant, he disappeared. I never heard from him again." My mother's tears spilled from her eyes. "He just left me all alone. I didn't know what I was going to do, and then . . ." She paused to compose herself, wiping the tears that were flowing down her cheeks. "Your daddy . . . well, he was in love with me, and when he found out I was in trouble, he wanted to take care of me, of *us*."

"What was his name, my father?" His eyes . . . although they weren't iridescent green like Khol's, I knew the second my mother had described him that whatever Khol was, my biological father had been as well. The shock of what that meant coursed through my system. "I'm not even fully human?" It came out sounding like a question, but it was meant more as a statement.

"You're human—you're my daughter—"

"And something else. I'm human, and something else." My voice started getting all shrill like it did sometimes when I was freaking out. And let me tell you—*I was freaking out.*

"Yes, but—"

I didn't let her finish. She didn't even know what I was. She didn't have the answers that I really needed, but I knew who did. "What was my father's name?" I asked again, my voice going up another octave.

"Dragos. His name was Dragos." My mother wore a defeated look on her face. "But he doesn't matter. The only father you need to know about is the one who raised you."

"I need to know *what* I am. Can't you understand that? It changes so many things. What if—what if I can't even have Seer children? Isn't that the only reason why I supposedly can't be with Bryn? Because of my duty? But what if that doesn't even matter?"

"No, no, that's not how it works. That's—"

"You're in denial. That's what all of this is. You don't wanna face the fact that none of the rules may apply to me. Get out. Leave me alone," I growled. A part of me hated seeing my mother cry, but a larger part felt even more betrayed than I had before. *How could she have kept this from me?*

She silently stood and made her way to my door, her face pale and her lips pressed together in a thin line. "I love you, my little peanut. None of this changes that. And your daddy—none of that matters to him. You're his daughter, and he loves you, too." I didn't respond, and I didn't look at her; I just waited until my door clicked to signal she'd left.

"Khol," I growled. "I know you can hear me, or sense me, or whatever. Get your ass here now."

He appeared in my room like he always did. One minute he wasn't there and the next he was. His green eyes glowed in the dark as he peered down at me. "So you know," he stated without any preamble.

"Yeah, I do. At least the bit that I'm obviously part whatever you are. Care to share with me whatever that is now?" I glared at him, every muscle in my body tense as I waited for his answer.

"You are half *Arach*. Your father and I are both full blooded. We are what you might call Dragon." *Dragon? This isn't real. Dragons don't really exist.* "And most people wouldn't believe you exist, either, or the creatures you've been having visions of exist." Khol smiled tightly as he studied my face for a reaction.

"Is that why my powers called to yours? Because of what I am?" I asked numbly. It was like a part of me was in complete shock, and at the same time, there were so many questions that seemed imperative to ask.

"Yes, and why you awakened not just me."

"So you can, like, turn into a dragon?"

Khol nodded once tightly. "Yes, a Dragon is my other form."

Other form? My head was spinning. "Can I? Or will I be able to . . . ?" My voice trailed off, not able to truly fathom the possibility.

"No. You were born with only one form. It's very rare for a mixed blood to have a second form."

I laughed tightly, on the verge of hysteria. "Good to know. I—" The room began to spin, but I pushed on with my questions. "What do you want with me? Really?"

Khol dropped to his knees in front of me, cupping my face with his hands, locking gazes with me. "With my kind—*our* kind—when the female is ready to find a . . . mate, she sends out a call with her magic, letting the male Dragons know she is willing. The strongest and most powerful have rights to her first, the right to try to claim her. I want to be your mate, P.J."

"Mate? What does that even mean?" I squeaked.

"I'm attempting to explain in a way that you might understand. The bond I'm referring to—we call it *Anam Cara*—loosely translated it means soul friend or soul mate. Humans have been using our term for centuries, but it means so much more for a Dragon—more than mere words. It refers to the soul-deep bond we form with our desired partner. Our kind, once we find our desired partners, bond for the rest of our days."

"And how long is that? How old are you exactly? How old am I going to live to be?" If I were a computer, I'd have been reading *Error, error, does not compute*.

"A very, very long time."

"Oh." *Bryn—what about Bryn?* At first I thought my new found heritage might enable me to be with Bryn, but what if it meant he would die centuries before I did? "*When all others turn to dust, there will only be you and me.*" I mumbled the words Khol had said to me the last time I'd seen him. "That's what you meant, isn't it?" I looked at him sharply. "You don't care that I'm in love with Bryn now, because you think once he dies, it'll be just us, that I won't have a choice." *Oh no.* The thought of me burying Bryn tore at my insides.

"Yes, you'll come to me eventually, and I'll claim what rightfully belongs to me." Kohl's eyes blazed brighter. "I would prefer to have you now, to make you my *Anam Cara*, but I can be patient when I need to be."

So many things that Khol had said to me were beginning to make sense. "And why do you think that I'm going to be yours? Even if I go along with the logic that my magic calls to yours, and that I'm eventually going to crave more—I'm assuming that has to do with our shared blood—then why you? Why not some other Dragon?"

A low animal-like growl escaped from Khol, and his voice seemed to echo inside my head as well as outside of it. "I am Lord Kholkikos, ruler of the *Rua Arach*, and you will be *mo Anam Cara*."

"Lord, huh? Well, aren't you special? Isn't there a king or something? Why are you the ruler of, well, of whatever you just said?"

Kohl studied me for a moment, and I raised my chin defiantly at him as I met his gaze. His lips turned up slightly at the corners. "I do like the fact that you are so . . . feisty. I find that an extremely attractive, and yet completely annoying, character trait." I scrunched my face up at him, and he chuckled. *Glad I could amuse.* "*Rua Arach* means Red Dragon, and no, there are no kings, only Lords of each faction—the red, the black, the silver, and the gold."

My curiosity piqued again, I temporarily dismissed Khol's display of testosterone-generated possessiveness. "Red Dragon—is that what I am, too?"

Khol's hand snaked out to take some of my hair in his hand, and he wrapped it around his knuckles, pulling me closer. "You may deepen its shade, but you can always tell what faction a Dragon is by the color of their hair. The older a Dragon is, the deeper the shade of their hair becomes. One day you won't need to darken your hair any longer. It will be this way naturally."

"Really?" I couldn't help the smile that spread across my face, and I immediately chastised myself. With everything else that was going on, I was worried about my hair? *Ugh. Vanity be thy name.* "So, still, that brings me back to my earlier question: Why do you think I'm going to be yours? Who's to say

HIDDEN GATES

I wouldn't choose another Dragon Lord, like maybe a black, or silver, or—is that why you're so hot all the time?" My face flushed. "Temperature-wise I mean? And I swear I saw flames in your eyes before. Is that—"

"No," Khol growled again. "You belong with me. You will be my *Anam Cara—mo Anam Cara.*" He ignored my other questions and tugged me by my hair closer still. "I am the strongest of the Red Dragons, and you belong with your own kind." His lips met mine with a brutality I'd never experienced before. His teeth scraped against mine, and his tongue dove into my mouth to claim and possess, not merely explore. I cried out as he pressed himself into me, the heat of his body engulfing me and making me crave more.

It felt so right, and yet—*Bryn*—I could never betray Bryn so completely. I shoved at Khol, and he reluctantly relinquished possession of me. "You said not without my permission," I growled at him, barely recognizing my own voice. "And you don't have it. Only Bryn does."

Khol's eyes crackled with flame briefly as he studied me. "Have you lost your trust in me then?"

I remembered what he said before: if I lost trust in him, then he'd claim what he felt was his—me. But if I trusted him because he wanted my trust, he wouldn't cross that line. "No. I trust you to back off now that I've warned you."

Khol smiled ever so slightly and nodded with approval. "You learn the game quickly, my little Seer." With that, he decided to just up and *poof* away again.

"Hey," I called. "I had more questions for you." The marked silence was my only answer, and I heaved a huge sigh. Lately, every time I thought my life couldn't get more complicated, the universe proved me wrong.

13

High school is a joke. What's the point of it anyways? What have I ever learned there except how cruel other people can be? I thought about how much I hated my school, or more aptly, the people in it, as I morosely studied the bright red scroll across my locker that declared me to be a *slut*. The culprit was probably somebody like Eddie, who wished the writing on the wall was just that. Maybe a couple of broken fingers would keep my tormentor from a repeat offense. Whoever said violence isn't the answer obviously didn't attend public school. A half Dragon descendant with a pesky alien invasion problem to worry about shouldn't have to deal with such bullshit.

"Hey." Jeremy's voice pulled me from my inner musings of vigilante justice.

I quickly swiveled around and tried to block the words on my locker from his view. "Hey," I muttered back, my face heating from the look on his, telling me I had, in fact, failed in hiding anything from him.

He pushed around me and scowled down at my locker. "Who the hell did this?" he asked through clenched teeth.

I shrugged, looking at the ground. "Could be any one of many. Who can keep track of everyone who thinks I'm a slut at this school?"

Jeremy's scowl deepened. "Yeah, they just wish you were, from what I hear."

"My thoughts exactly." I started walking, hoping he would follow. I was tired of staring at my stupid locker.

"Well, at least it's the end of the day, and with any luck, the janitor will have it cleaned off by morning," Jeremy added hopefully.

"Yeah, okay," I mumbled, already too low to be cheered up. My day had sucked once again. It was beginning to follow a pretty routine schedule of me being ostracized intermingled with being harassed. I might as well don a huge letter A on my chest to complete my transformation from relatively popular class senior to the most talked about and hated girl in my entire school. What really got me was that there were plenty of girls who actually did sleep around, and none of them were being persecuted the way I was. It just didn't make sense to me. I figured if I actually were what everyone was accusing me of, then no one would say anything, but because it was a lie, everyone was torturing me for something I didn't do. *Ugh.* I might still be in high school myself, but even I could admit that most of us were absolute idiots.

"So when do I get my second date?" Jeremy asked as he slid my bag off of my shoulder to carry it for me.

I eyed him thoughtfully as something occurred to me. Bryn was probably the hottest guy I'd ever laid eyes on, and he was mine. Now he had been shipped off, and Jeremy, the new hot guy, was falling all over himself to date me. Having seen myself in the mirror one or two times in the past eighteen years, I could see why no one would believe either of them would be into me unless I was putting out. I groaned at the realization.

HIDDEN GATES

"What?" Jeremy said. "Too soon? Don't forget though, you did agree. You can't take it back now."

I rolled my eyes, glad to see that my reputation was of so little concern to him. All he was worried about was locking me down for his, same as Khol. Too bad neither one of them seemed to want to acknowledge the memo that I was already taken by Bryn. "No, it's not that. It's just that a thought just occurred to me, and well, I think you wanting to date me isn't exactly helping my cause at school lately."

Jeremy frowned. "You're not trying to find a way to wiggle out of our date, are you?"

"If I said no, would you believe me?" I batted my eyelashes at him and donned my best innocent face.

"Yeah, no, not even for a second." Jeremy laughed.

"Well, even if I am trying to wiggle out of said date, the other part is still true. You're not helping my reputation by wanting to date me."

Jeremy's face became all skepticism. "Mmm-hmm. And I guess you're now going to try and enlighten me as to how."

"Of course. The explanation is simple, all you have to do is to look at me, and then look at both you and Bryn." I waved my hand in the classic etcetera motion to let him know he should be able to continue with my line of thought on his own.

"I've never seen Bryn, and I couldn't pick him out of a lineup, but I still get what you're implying." He narrowed his eyes at me. "It's absolutely ridiculous."

"No, it's not. I know what I look like. Of course, everyone thinks I have to be putting out in order to get the two of you interested. There's no other logical explanation in their minds."

Jeremy stopped and pivoted on his heel to face me, his face intense. "You obviously need glasses." He began walking forward, crowding my space until I was pressed up against the wall. His arms came up to cage me in, and I looked around to see the few people that were left in the hallway stop to stare. *Great, this is all I need.* But all thoughts fled my mind when Jeremy's lips met mine. When his tongue intertwined with mine, I had to concentrate not to curve myself around him as a small moan escaped from me. His power rose up sharply to coax mine out to play, but I fought against that, too. He pulled away slowly, his face still much too close for comfort, and I gazed into his deep brown eyes, which had flecks of gold in them, I noticed. "You're stunning," he murmured, dipping his head to kiss me lightly on the lips. "Everyone's just jealous."

Completely flustered, I ducked under his arm and dashed for the main doors to make my escape. As I hurriedly made my way down the front steps of my school, I heard a male voice call out to me. "After you're done with your latest victim, you should gimme a call, P.J." I whipped my head around to see that the voice emanated from Evan Thompson. Well, what do you know; he'd finally noticed me. I responded by waving my middle finger at him. He laughed. "Yep, you guessed right. That's exactly what I had in mind." Deciding I didn't have the energy to deal with Evan and his sophomoric attempts to be clever, I picked up my pace and turned in the direction of my house.

It happened quickly. It was a little different each time, except for the part where I felt like I was being lifted out of my body, but I knew a vision was about to hit me, and I tried everything I could to stave it off so that I wouldn't hit the pavement. I clutched blindly at something to hold me up, but my body crumpled to the ground, my awareness quickly shifting elsewhere.

It was like standing in the middle of a 3D movie; it was if I could reach out and touch everything, and yet I knew it wasn't real. I stood in the middle of a high school, but it wasn't mine. Kids passed by me, making their way to their classrooms. It appeared to be early morning the way everyone was making

HIDDEN GATES

their way inside through the front doors. I focused on a boy standing near me. He pretty much had the market cornered on the whole Emo look, and he topped it off with a long black trench coat. Something about him really drew my attention, and as I moved my gaze up to study his face, I instantly knew why. I gasped as I realized he had one of those alien creatures riding along inside of him. It was just like with Senator Bill Wexington: I could see the alien shining through from the inside, and yet the features of the boy weren't any different on the outside. The dual imagery freaked me out as usual, and I was unable to look away. That's when Emo Boy reached into his trench coat and pulled out a twelve-gauge shotgun. He just reached in as if it were the most natural thing in the world and began shooting. I heard screams of shock, pain, and utter surprise as shot after shot rang out in the small hallway, but I didn't look at the carnage that I was sure was all around us, no—I was riveted by the small ghost of a smile that turned the corners of Emo Boy's lips upward, even as I saw the creature within him beaming. I tried to spring forward and tackle them as he stopped to reload, but I found myself unable to move, and I remembered I wasn't really there, that this was all a vision. With that realization, I was yanked away from the scene, but not before I let my eyes drop to see a girl's body lying bloody and lifeless on the floor. She was in a uniform, I realized, a cheerleader's warmup uniform, red and gold with what looked like an Indian decal emblazed on the front of her jacket. I was trying to commit the images to memory because I knew it was important somehow, when everything went black.

Voices began to filter into my subconscious as I began to wake up. "Don't move her. She could be injured from the fall." A guy's voice, older, probably a faculty member, commanded.

"Why'd she pass out? She was just walking and then boom." A girl's voice chimed in.

"She'll be fine. I'll take care of her," Jeremy's familiar voice stated calmly. "I've seen this happen before, low blood sugar. I'll take her home and make sure she sees her doctor." Strong arms picked me up and began to walk with me; my head lolling against someone I assumed was Jeremy. Surprisingly, no one put up any protest, not even the faculty member.

"Hey, wait up," another male voice called, but Jeremy didn't break his stride. "I said to wait up."

"Yeah, I don't think so," Jeremy said, although I felt us suddenly come to a halt.

"She had a vision, didn't she? I usually don't sense that kind of thing, but I could almost feel the energy around her. It's the only thing it could have been, but I thought she hadn't come into her powers yet."

"Get out of my way," Jeremy's voice vibrated with anger. We started moving again, and I thought whoever it was had gone away, but I was wrong.

"Do you think it was important? The vision she had? She must be pretty strong for me to sense it."

Jeremy sighed, obviously realizing the same thing I had: this guy wasn't going away until he got some answers. "Yeah, she's stronger than even I thought, and I can sense a ton more stuff than most Gatekeepers."

"Yeah? Huh."

"Yeah."

"Well, all right, I guess I should get going then."

"It's about time," I grumbled, letting Jeremy know I was awake. I lifted my lids to meet his deep brown concerned eyes, the gold flecks in them seeming to dance in the light.

"You feeling better?"

"I feel fine. Just drained, like I need a nap or something." Jeremy nodded, looking pensive as he continued to carry me. "You can put me down now, you know. I'm perfectly capable of walking on my own."

HIDDEN GATES

Jeremy smiled down at me, his eyes sparkling. "I was kind of enjoying having you in my arms."

I scrunched up my face at him. "Well, the fun is over. Put me down." He reluctantly set me down, and I swayed ever so slightly and reached for his arm for support. Quicker than I had time to orient myself, Jeremy swooped me right back up into his arms. "Hey!" I protested.

"I'm not going to have you fall over and actually hurt yourself. You were really lucky you didn't crack your head open on the pavement before. You need to learn how to control your visions better."

I glared up at him. "They're kind of new, and for whatever reason, whenever you kiss me, your power seems to feed them or something." Narrowing my eyes at him, I snapped, "So stop kissing me, and I shouldn't have any more problems."

"Or I could only kiss you when you're lying down." Jeremy chuckled at his own comment, but I didn't miss the blatant innuendo.

"Not going to happen."

"Okay, how about leaning against a wall?" His eyes twinkled mischievously, and I hated that a part of me thought he was being cute.

"You know, I really don't have time for this. I have a vision to figure out and . . ." My voice trailed off as I questioned what I was about to say. And what? What could I do except talk everything over with Khol as I'd been doing with my other visions? Unless . . . "And—and stop." I finished my sentence in a whisper. I wanted to stop being a bystander in life, didn't I? Well, this would be the perfect way to begin. Somehow, I just knew my vision was of the future. And if it hadn't happened yet, there was still time to stop it.

Jeremy gave me a puzzled look. "That's not really your job yet. Leave it to the other Seers, the ones that have had years of training and experience."

"Yeah, that's kind of the problem. I think I'm the only one getting these visions."

"How is that possible?" Jeremy's eyebrows practically touched his hairline.

I studied Jeremy while I mulled over what I should say to him. I'd been in this situation with him before, and I had decided to go with the truth. The question was, should I again? After a quick deliberation, I decided that I had nothing to lose. If he didn't believe me, then at least maybe he'd think I was crazy and leave me alone. Either way wasn't a bad outcome because if he did believe me, maybe he'd help, even if it were a long shot.

So I told him all about my visions, leaving out the parts about Khol because I couldn't have told Jeremy about him even if I'd wanted to, and I most certainly didn't. Khol was my deep, dark secret, along with my recently discovered half Dragon status.

"Holy shit," Jeremy breathed when I'd finally finished. "You're telling the truth. I can tell these kinds of things, plus I could tell you had a real vision back there . . . holy shit." He seemed more than a little shell-shocked. I decided to stay quiet to let him process everything. I could almost see a million different things running through his mind until a determined look settled on his face. "What do you need me to do?" And just like that, I had another ally.

"You—you wanna help me?" I stammered with surprise. I was hoping he would, but I hadn't really expected it.

He looked at me like I was crazy for questioning him. "Yeah, of course I'm going to help you. I'm not just going to let you run off trying to deal with this stuff by yourself."

"Yeah—uh—well—" I blushed with embarrassment. "I don't actually have a plan. More like a plan to have a plan."

At this point we arrived at my front door, and he set me back on my feet, handing me my bag. "Can I come in? To talk about this?"

HIDDEN GATES

I bit my lip in thought. "No, we better go around back so my parents can't hear. Whatever we plan, we can't let them know."

Jeremy nodded once tightly. "Good idea." He bent down to scoop me up again, and I hastily sidestepped him.

"I'm feeling much better now, and if my parents see you carrying me, they're going to freak out, even if my mom does like you being here with me." *Liked him being there* with me was the understatement of the year. *If she could marry me off to Jeremy this instant, she would.*

Jeremy silently regarded me for a moment before agreeing. "Okay. I guess I can see your point." He still didn't look happy though.

I slowly made my way around the back of the house, trying to look as nonchalant as possible and not as if I was about to plot anything. Jeremy kept in step beside me, walking just a touch too close for my comfort, probably afraid I was going to topple over again. It was nice to feel cared about, but sometimes the men in my life took things a bit too far. I mentally paused. *The men in my life?* When had I started thinking of Khol, Jeremy, and Bryn as the men in my life? Bryn should be the only man in my life, at least if I was only counting from a romantic perspective. A sick feeling settled in my stomach, and I pushed it aside because I had more important things to worry about at the moment, like saving some innocent lives.

Jeremy and I settled against the same tree that we had been under the other day when he had kissed me. At the thought, my face heated, and I hoped he didn't notice. "That was some kiss, huh?" I looked up at him and blanched. I shouldn't be here with him again. Every moment I spent with Jeremy or Khol was a small betrayal of Bryn, not to mention the times we'd kissed.

"Yeah, I don't really wanna talk about that. We're here to figure out what to do about my vision." I closed off my emotions and met Jeremy's inquisitive gaze with cold indifference.

"And when exactly were you planning on filling me in?" Jenna's angry voice came from behind me. "I wouldn't know anything if not for the local friendly woodland creatures."

I swiveled my head around to glare at Jenna and her rainbow colored hair. "Nosy rodents are more like it. Are you having me followed all the time by them now? Because that's so not okay, Jenna."

"It's the only way I can find anything out from you lately. I would never have known about Bryn, I would never have known about that other guy who you can't talk about, I would never have known about your visions, and"—she waved her hands at Jeremy—"when were you going to tell me about him? Are you still my best friend or what?"

I crossed my arms over my chest and sighed. "Of course I am. But that doesn't mean I have to tell you absolutely everything."

"That's exactly what it means!" Jenna cried out in frustration.

"Umm . . ." Jeremy chimed in. "What other guy that you can't talk about? Do I have more competition than I know about?"

"No," I said with annoyance.

"Yes," Jenna said at the exact same time.

Jeremy frowned, looking back and forth between the two of us. "Well, which is it?"

I stood and threw my hands up in the air. "Bryn doesn't have any competition. He's the one I love, and all you guys can stop sticking your tongues down my throat, because it isn't going to do any good. When all is said and done, Bryn is who I'm going to be with."

Jeremy frowned. "So you're kissing this other guy, too?"

"No!" I exclaimed. "He's kissing me, just like you are. I'm not kissing anybody!"

HIDDEN GATES

"Does he go to our school? And you were trying to blame me for not helping your reputation." Jeremy stood and stalked closer to me. "All I want is a little honesty here."

"Yeah, what he said," Jenna threw her two cents in.

I gritted my teeth and tried to swallow back my anger. We had to get through this so we could come up with a plan to stop my latest vision from coming true. "No, he doesn't go to our school, he's—well, he's—" Like before with Jenna, I physically couldn't utter a word out loud about Khol. "I'm bound magically not to be able to talk about him. The only reason Jenna knows anything about him at all is because of her little spies."

Jeremy glanced at Jenna for confirmation. "That's true." She nodded. "And that's another reason why I have to sic my spies on you: because who knows what else is going on with you lately that you can't tell me about? Your life has gotten very weird lately."

"Says the girl who has rodents spying for her," I grumbled under my breath.

"All right. I get it, okay," Jeremy said with a closed expression. "Your life is very complicated right now, and apparently I have more competition than I originally thought. I guess I can deal with that."

"I really don't care if you can or cannot deal with it, Jeremy. I said I'd go on a second date with you, that's it. You know how I feel about Bryn. And this other—guy—he knows, too. It's not my fault you both seem to have thick skulls and aggressive tongues." I took a couple deep breaths before continuing. "None of that is relevant right now. What is important is figuring out what to do about my vision and saving some innocent lives."

"I agree," Khol's voice said, startling me. All three of our heads whipped around to watch as Khol strode towards us in all of his otherworldly beauty. Although I'm not sure if I can really describe it as otherworldly since he was, in fact, from our world, even if he didn't look it. *Dragonly beauty?* But I didn't know what other Dragons looked like; it could just be Khol who was so magnificent.

"Focus, my little Seer, you have time to contemplate my good looks at another time," Khol said with amusement.

"I'm not doing anything of the sort. You're not a mind reader, so stop pretending to be," I snapped as my cheeks heated. I was beginning to wonder if he really was able to read my mind and just wasn't telling me.

"No, you just broadcast your emotions very loudly, my little Seer." That was twice in a row he'd called me *his little Seer,* and I couldn't help but think it was partly for Jeremy's benefit, who currently looked like he was ready to do battle with Khol.

"Oh. Oh my God. You didn't tell me—" Jenna scooted closer to me and dug her nails into my arm. "You didn't tell me he was so hot," she whispered.

"I couldn't describe him to you, remember?" Jenna's whole body trembled, and I wouldn't have been surprised if she suddenly stripped off all of her clothes and threw herself at Khol right then and there. It would have been almost funny, if I suddenly didn't want to smack her so badly. I didn't really want Khol for myself, but Jenna certainly wasn't going to get him either. I stepped out of her grasp and approached Khol. "What are you doing here now? I thought you didn't want anyone to know about you?"

"It is unpreventable now. I can't let you risk yourself like you're planning. I'll simply bind them like I did you." Khol was glaring at Jeremy, his body mirroring Jeremy's fight stance.

"He can bind me anytime he wants," Jenna purred quietly at my side.

"Shut up, Jenna," I snapped. "Stay away from him."

HIDDEN GATES

"Oh. Oh, I see. You think he belongs to you, too. Not fair."

"No, I don't think that, it's just..." It's just what? Why was the thought of Jenna going after Khol pissing me off?

"I do belong to her, little Speaker, as she belongs to me," Khol rumbled, his eyes still on Jeremy.

"Like hell she does," Jeremy said. "I don't even know what you are. Your energy is like nothing I've ever seen. P.J., Jenna, get behind me."

Khol laughed. "I would never hurt her, but if I did seek to, you would never stop me... *boy*."

Jeremy glanced over at me. "I said to get behind me." His jaw was set determinedly.

"Paige," Khol rumbled, his voice going low and smooth, "Come to me. If you want to stop your vision from becoming reality, I'm the one you should seek for help, not a *boy* like him. I won't stand by and watch you be injured." The way he said *boy* made it sound like an insult, although calling a guy Jeremy's age a boy, no matter what, is kind of an insult, at least to him, I'm sure. "P.J.," Khol said again, and this time his voice seemed to be in my head.

"Yes?" I whispered. His power rolled out of him and wrapped itself around me, causing me to shudder. Before, when Jeremy had kissed me, his power had tried to coax mine to come out and play, and I was able to push it aside with concentration. But Khol's power demanded where Jeremy's had coaxed, and I was unable to deny its call. I knew Khol's power called to the Dragon half of me. He was calling a different side of me than Jeremy had been in touch with. Again I thought about what Khol had said to me about coming to crave... more... because right now, in this moment, I wanted nothing more than to go to Khol and lose myself in his sweet embrace. I was connected to him, and I could almost hear his thoughts as he longed for me to do just that. "It's natural for you to want me to claim you. If you were a full blooded *Rua Arach*, you'd already bear my *Anam Cara* mark." His voice was like a gentle caress inside my mind, and I knew that Jenna and Jeremy didn't hear what he was saying to me.

My vision had narrowed down to take in nothing but Khol and his beautiful face, and I felt myself moving towards him. What would it be like to let him have what he wanted? What would it be like to give myself over to the temptation he was offering me? To sink into his welcoming embrace, to taste the fire he offered with his touch, to be swept away in the burn he had awakened in me?

"Tell me who you yearn to be with. Tell me who you want to lay claim to you," Khol continued to speak to me alone in my mind, and I could hear an undercurrent of something else, a chant of some sort.

Even as I moved towards Khol, suddenly my vision filled with an image of Bryn so realistic, I thought for a second he was standing right in front of me. "Bryn." His name on my lips was uttered with reverence, a small prayer to the only man I would ever truly love. His sea storm eyes churned for me, threatening to pull me down in their undercurrent. His patented lopsided smile, complete with dimples, weakened my knees, and I knew in that moment that even though Khol and Jeremy both stirred longing in my body, no one would ever possess me the way that Bryn had. He owned my heart, body, and soul. I was his until my dying breath.

"No. That's not possible," I heard Khol growl. The undercurrent of the chant died abruptly along with the image of Bryn. I cried out in dismay at losing it, even if I knew it wasn't real. I dropped to my knees and hugged myself. "You will be mine," Khol growled.

I looked up sharply, sensing something about to snap in Khol, something that I couldn't let happen. I met his determined eyes with mine. "I trust you Khol. I trust you to help me with all of this, and I trust you to wait like you said. I trust you."

His iridescent green eyes flared brighter as he looked at me. "I will not break your trust, but I cannot be in your presence any longer for the moment. Call for me when you need me for your plan. I will always be there for you when you need me." He met my eyes with a longing so intense I shivered, and just like all the times before, he simply disappeared.

I began to sob as I realized that ridding myself of Khol wouldn't be an easy task. He wanted me, thought of me as his already, and he wasn't even human. What if he eventually lost his patience and hurt Bryn? What if he tried to kill him? I had no idea if a Guardian would be any match for a Dragon, and I really didn't want to find out. I would protect Bryn at any cost, but that was something to worry about at another time. I needed to focus on figuring out a plan to stop my latest vision.

I wiped at my tears with the back of my arm and turned to face Jeremy and Jenna. The two of them started to rush towards me, but I lifted up my hands to stave them off. "No, I'm fine. And even if I weren't, we don't have time to worry about it now. We need to figure out what to do about my vision. We have to save all those people."

Jeremy's face was lined with tension, and his eyes seethed with anger, directed towards Khol, I assumed. "Fine. But we are going to have a conversation about what just happened. I need to know how to protect you from—whatever he is."

I wasn't going to argue with Jeremy that it wasn't his place to protect me, or that I didn't think he really could anyways, so I decided to placate him for the time being. "Okay. But not now."

"And me," Jenna chimed in, studying my face with that look she got when I felt like she was seeing too much. "I need to know *everything.*" She caught my eyes and narrowed hers at me. Yep, she picked up on a lot more than I'd probably wanted her to, damn Speakers.

"Yeah, okay." I growled. "But not now; now is the time to plan out what we're going to do to stop my vision."

Both Jeremy and Jenna nodded agreement in unison. It almost made me want to laugh—almost.

14

We had been able to narrow down where the school from my vision was by the cheerleader uniform that had been on one of the victims. Then, by browsing school websites, I had recognized the entranceway from my vision as well. As luck would have it, the school was only a thirty-minute drive from where we were, which would have given us plenty of time—if it hadn't taken us all night to figure out where we were going.

We were currently all packed into Jenna's bright yellow VW Bug, speeding towards our destination. And by all, I meant me, Jenna, Jeremy, and yes, even Khol. Why Khol had felt the need to go with us in the car was beyond me, but I had a sneaking suspicion it had something to do with Jeremy, and that he wanted to simply spend more time with me. Ever since that lifelike vision of Bryn, Khol had been almost clingy. *Dragons, clingy . . . Who would have thought?*

"So when we get there, you point out this guy to us, and Khol and I will take him out. You and Jenna aren't to go anywhere near this mess, in case something goes wrong," Jeremy stated firmly.

"Yeah, sure, whatever," I grumbled, none too happy with the situation. I wanted to help, too, damn it! But after the umpteenth time of me arguing my case, and both Jeremy and Khol threatening to tie me up and to not let me go at all, I finally gave in. I should have been happy that they could at least agree about something—but I wasn't. My plan to get off the sidelines wasn't exactly panning out for me.

"Sure, no problem," Jenna added, obviously not feeling as put out by everything as I was. I shot her a glare. Maybe if we had both argued my point with Jeremy and Khol, we would have won. "Stop glaring at me, P.J. I'm not going to take your side just for the hell of it. They're kind of right about this one, as much as I hate to admit it."

I replied by turning away to glower out the window. Maybe she was right, but I didn't have to let her know that.

"There is no point for you to be there after you indentify this boy from your vision. I would only be worried about you if you were there with us. That could cause me to make a mistake," Khol spoke softly, bringing his warm palm up to touch my cheek from the backseat. I hated the fact that my body wanted to lean into the warmth he offered, hated that my body wanted more—so much more—from him.

"Hey. Get your hands off of her," Jeremy growled. "She isn't yours."

"Oh, but she is mine, and I will touch her whenever and however I wish." Khol shifted as he pushed his massive frame into the space between the front two seats and pulled me to him, crushing his lips to mine. I barely had time to process what was going on before Khol's tongue invaded my mouth in an aggressive kiss. Sparks of warmth seemed to erupt across my skin as all coherent thoughts fled my mind. Then the car swerved, and Khol pulled away from our embrace.

HIDDEN GATES

"Stop! Just stop!" Jenna yelled. "No kissing and no fighting in my car! We're on a mission here, people, and it doesn't include a sword fight over who gets to mouth rape P.J. first!"

I slumped back into my seat, my face heating. "That wasn't my fault, and no one gets to mouth rape me because I already belong to Bryn." I peered around the edge of the seat to see Khol and Jeremy glaring at each other. What was I going to do with the two of them? They just couldn't seem to get it through their thick heads that I belonged to Bryn already. If anyone got to mouth rape me, it was going to be Bryn. Of course, we would have to be using a very loose definition of rape if that were the case. In fact, it would only apply if rape suddenly meant *willing participant* when it came to Bryn.

"We're here," Jenna said as she threw the car into park. My head snapped up to see a high school that looked pretty much like any other high school, except this one apparently had murderous aliens enrolled.

I gulped, the reality of the situation finally hitting me. We were going to do this; we were actually going to do this. I kept staring at the school as I stepped out of the car and began walking up the front walk as if caught in a tractor beam. I heard Jeremy and Khol talking to me, and yet I couldn't look away, especially when I saw the girl from my vision—the cheerleader—alive and well, and talking animatedly to a group of girls. "This is it. This is really the place," I whispered. I felt a large warm hand wrap around mine, and I looked up to meet Khol's electric green eyes. "Won't your eyes, and well, how you look, stand out too much?" A thought that—as bizarre as it sounded—I hadn't even considered until that moment.

"No," Khol said with a tiny smile. "I can look human when I want to." And just like that, his eyes went matte to look like regular, everyday, green eyes. Nothing else changed really, but with his eyes looking normal, the rest of him looked normal, too. Well, if you could overlook how drop dead gorgeous he was . . . So okay, maybe normal wasn't the best word to use to describe Khol, but he did at least look human.

"Why didn't you ever do that before? I mean, at least when you first met me, so I didn't freak out as much?"

"I wanted you to see me as I truly am. I want no secrets between us."

"Oh," I said and looked away. *He is good.* And yep, if Bryn weren't in the picture, I'd probably already have given him what he wanted: me. I cleared my throat and scanned everyone around us as we moved closer to the front doors. I glanced back to see Jenna waiting in the car with a frown on her face as she watched us. I hated to admit it, but I kind of, sort of wished I were back there with her.

"Ready?" I heard Jeremy ask as I reached for the front door of the school. I turned to take in his solemn face and then looked up at Khol, who had an almost identical expression plastered across his own. I nodded once in affirmation before stepping into the main entrance of the school.

All noise seemed to stop for me. It was as if the ocean were rushing inside my ears, and a weird sense of déjà vu settled over me. I scanned all the faces around me, intent on finding the one I was looking for, but I didn't see him yet. What I really wanted to do was yell at everyone to run, to warn everyone that a crazy alien masquerading as one of their peers was about to use them for target practice. And yet I knew it would be useless. Hell, maybe the alien would shoot me first, if that's what I did, because he would know I knew the truth, and he would try to take me out. "I don't see him," I whispered, hoping Khol and Jeremy heard me. Khol simply squeezed my hand, and Jeremy stayed silent. I knew they were both scanning the crowd for danger, not liking that I had to identify the alien from my vision for them. If this guy didn't show up

HIDDEN GATES

soon, the both of them would probably carry me back to the car because they didn't like putting me in danger any longer.

And of course, that's when I saw him. His dark Emo hair was hanging in his face, and as he walked in the front door, he flipped his hair out of his eyes and looked right at me. I felt myself go ashen as I tried to alert Khol and Jeremy, my voice seemingly stuck in my throat. The Emo kid's eyes narrowed as he studied me, wariness showing as he took in the sight of Khol and Jeremy flanking me, even if they hadn't spotted him yet. My arm rose on its own volition and pointed straight at Emo Alien Boy. "That's him," I squeaked, tugging on Khol's arm. "That's him," I squeaked again.

Khol moved first, shoving me behind him, just as Jeremy reached for his power to do—well, I'm not exactly sure what because Emo Boy wasn't going to hang around to let me find out. He pivoted on his heels and made a mad dash for the front door. "Go!" Khol commanded, "I'll protect her." Jeremy barely glanced at Khol before he took off running after Emo Boy. I started to move forward in an attempt to engage in the chase, but Khol had other ideas. He swung around, scooped me up in his arms and suddenly we were back in my bedroom. He deposited me on my bed before giving me a stern face and narrowing his eyes at me, which, by the way, were glowing again. "Stay," he growled before disappearing.

I stared in shock at the empty spot where Khol had just been, anger slowly bubbling up to the surface of my consciousness. I couldn't believe he'd just done that to me. And why the hell hadn't he just *popped* the lot of us over to the school instead of making us drive if he could transport other people?

"You get your ass back here right now, Khol!" I hissed into my empty room, knowing he would somehow hear me, or at least know what I was feeling. I got no response. A few moments went by, and then a few more, and still nothing. That was it; I wasn't going to just *stay* like Khol had demanded. I wasn't a damn puppy.

I made my way downstairs to the kitchen, and even though I was supposed to be at school, my parents were both at work so I knew I'd be in the clear. I scooped up the keys to my father's car, knowing that it would be here because he carpooled into the office and it wasn't his turn to drive. Normally, my father wouldn't let me come anywhere near his car. I'd even learned to drive in my mother's car, but what he wouldn't know wouldn't hurt him. At least I hoped he wouldn't know when all was said and done.

I only paused for a second before starting up my father's brand new Audi something. Honestly, I don't speak car, so I had no idea what model it was, just that it was an Audi. *And new, and shiny, and very pretty*, I thought as I inhaled the fragrant aroma of new car smell. I really hoped I didn't wrap it around a telephone pole or run it into a ditch. I certainly wasn't receiving any good driver awards anytime soon. I was lucky I'd passed my driver's test at all—it only took me three tries.

I tentatively eased my way out of the garage, which I didn't hit, so that was a step in the right direction. I stopped at the end of the driveway and adjusted the mirrors one more time before peeling out onto the street. My lips turned up in an involuntarily smile as I sped off to my destination. Thirty minutes? More like fifteen at the speed I was driving.

I was about five minutes away from the school when something, or rather someone, caught my attention: Emo Boy. I stomped down on the brake, screeching to a halt, causing him to swivel around to look at me. Why hadn't Jeremy or Khol caught him? Where the hell were they? I sat frozen in the driver's seat of my father's car just staring at Emo Boy, when I saw him reach

HIDDEN GATES

back into his trench coat. I swore as I watched the shotgun emerge from hiding and point in my direction. Uncertainty sprang to life in me. I didn't know if I should simply duck and cover, or run him down. After all, he was pointing a gun at me. The alien smiling from inside Emo Boy was enough to let me know that he was about to pull the trigger, so I ducked just as the front windshield of my father's car exploded all over me. *Shit, he'd definitely notice that.*

Without looking, I hit the gas pedal and hurtled down the street for a short distance before slamming into something hard and immovable. My forehead bounced off the steering wheel—hard. More shots rang out, shattering the remaining glass in my father's car. But the fact that I didn't resemble Swiss cheese yet pointed at Emo Boy's lack of aim and hopefully my chances of survival. I scrambled to get my seatbelt off and open the door while staying slumped down in the seat. As soon as I made it out of the car, I attempted to make a mad dash to cover, but something slammed into the back of my head. Stars danced in front of my eyes as I hit the ground. I barely managed to catch myself before my face met the pavement. I tried to crawl on all fours, but I was suddenly pushed roughly over, and I stared up at a very angry looking Emo Boy.

"Guess you're out of ammo?" I quibbled, unable to keep my mouth shut apparently, even in a life and death situation.

"How did you know?" Emo Boy snarled as he reached down to grab me by my jacket. "How did you know what I had planned?"

The alien inside Emo Boy seemed to shine more brightly from inside him, and I found myself reaching up to touch his face with some kind of eerie fascination. "Can you see it when you look in the mirror?" I mumbled, now feeling pretty sure I had a concussion. "Or do you even know he's in there? Who has control? Or do you share?"

Both Emo Boy and the alien residing inside of him looked at me with shock. "You *see*? That's not possible."

I smiled, feeling more than a little woozy, blinking as something warm and sticky ran into my eye. "Obviously it's not . . . impossible." Sirens suddenly rang out in the distance, signaling that help was on the way. Emo Boy dropped me abruptly, causing me to hit my head on the concrete. "Ow. That's not very nice," I mumbled as my eyes, feeling suddenly too heavy, slid shut. "And you didn't even answer my questions."

All went dark.

"You were supposed to keep her safe," Jeremy's voice vibrated with anger, "not let her put herself in the goddamned hospital."

"I left her in her bedroom. I thought it was beyond even her to find trouble that quickly," Khol responded flatly. "And do not think for a second it doesn't cause me just as much pain to see her like this." Strong emotion flared in his voice as it went low and gruff.

"She's gonna be fine, guys. No need to fight," Jenna said, obviously trying to play the mediator.

"Yeah, but she could have died. We don't even know how close she came," Jeremy grated. "He was *shooting* at her."

"But she's not dead. She's fine. That's the important part," Jenna interjected. "And I don't want the two of you fighting and scolding her when she wakes up either." I heard a grunt from Khol and silence from Jeremy as a response.

I inwardly sighed as I worked on opening my eyes. "Does my dad know about his car yet?" I muttered. At least my mouth was working. It seemed nothing ever put it out of commission.

"Your parents are on the way," Jenna answered just as I finally managed to peel my eyelids open. She was sitting in a chair next to my hospital bed, and both Khol and Jeremy were standing towards the foot. It looked like the two of them had been pacing. Both of their faces held a mixture of worry and anger, but Khol was the first to say anything.

"I told you to stay," he growled.

I narrowed my eyes at him. "I'm not yours to order around, contrary to what you might think." I tried to cross my arms over my chest, but the IV got in the way. I turned my anger on Jeremy next. "And don't you say a word either. I do *what* I want *when* I want."

"I wasn't aware you wanted to get yourself killed," Jeremy snapped crossing his arms over his chest, his brown eyes flashing with anger.

I tried to sit up, but stars danced before my eyes, accompanied by a sudden wave of nausea. "That wasn't what I was going for," I mumbled as I slouched back down into my pillow, the nausea rolling to a stop.

Khol stalked around the side of the bed and came to stand beside me, blocking out my view of Jenna. "Let me help you."

"How?" I asked as I eyed his still angry expression warily.

"I can heal you, if you let me."

"Then why the hell haven't you healed her already?" Jeremy demanded.

Khol tensed, anger at Jeremy making his jaw tick, but he locked gazes with me. "I have to kiss you . . . touch you . . ."

Understanding dawned. "Oh," I whispered.

"Absolutely not," Jeremy said as understanding dawned on him as well. "I'm not going to stand by and watch you maul her in the name of healing. It's the most—"

"Then don't watch," Jenna snapped. "He needs to do what he needs to do to heal her, Jeremy. Would you rather she stay how she is? Would—"

"Fine," Jeremy groused. "I'll be outside waiting for her parents. Tell me when he's done *healing* her." I watched Jeremy stalk out of the room so I didn't have to meet Khol's eyes. My heart had sped up the second I realized what was needed to heal me. A part of me was looking forward to it, while the rest of me felt like a traitor to Bryn for feeling that way.

Jenna cleared her throat. "I'll be outside, too." She turned at the door and winked at me. "Try not to do anything I wouldn't do."

I stared after her, my heart quadrupling in time now that Khol and I were alone. "So . . ." I said, my face flushing as I met Khol's heated gaze. "Umm . . ."

He leaned down and kissed me, the normal shot of heat from him hitting me and then intensifying. His body felt on fire, and I arched up to meet him. His large hands cupped my face and ran through my hair, sending a tingling sensation along with heat through my system; somehow I knew it meant he was healing me, and it felt really, really good. *Better than good*, I thought. I heard a small moan escape from me as his hands slid down my torso, skimming over my hardened nipples on the way. My brain screamed for me to tell him to stop, that Bryn was the only one who had ever done anything besides kiss me, and it should stay that way, but my mouth was too busy kissing Khol to protest out loud. His healing magic wrapped around me, making me whole again, all the while his hands slowly exploring my body.

My breathing was coming in small little pants, and I gasped as Khol slipped his hand up underneath my gown to touch me between my legs. "No . . ." I moaned, the cliché of every woman everywhere who knew she shouldn't be doing what she was doing, and protested even though she didn't really mean it. Or did I? Did I really want Khol touching me the way that he was, helping me betray Bryn in the worst possible way? The answer of course was no, and yet I couldn't seem to help myself.

HIDDEN GATES

"Let me make you my Anam Cara. Let me lay claim to you," Khol rumbled his voice rough with promises of pleasure.

Alarm bells went off in my head. Like we had talked about before, he didn't just mean sex—no, he wanted to claim me for his Dragon mate—his *Anam Cara*. He would take me away from Bryn forever if he could, and I couldn't let that happen. I would surely die without Bryn. "No. Stop." I shoved at Khol's hand and scooted away from him, my face heating with sudden embarrassment. I couldn't believe I'd let him touch me that way. Bryn should be the only one. Tears began to leak out of the corners of my eyes. "That's not what I want . . ." At least not with him. *Bryn—only Bryn.*

"With me," Khol stated flatly, picking up on my emotions, "It's not what you want with me, at least not yet."

"Never," I whispered, pulling the sheet up to cover me as if it were some kind of shield.

Khol's lips turned up into a small smile, his eyes blazing brighter. "Never say never, my little Seer." And as usual, he just disappeared.

Jenna and Jeremy picked that moment to come flying back into the room. Thank God they hadn't come back a few seconds earlier, I thought, as my face heated again. I felt so ashamed for letting things go so far with Khol. Why did I have such a hard time resisting him when I didn't really want him, at least not like I did Bryn? The guilt caused my shame to creep up to new levels the more I thought about it. Khol and Jeremy kept taking me to new lows emotionally. Had it only been such a short time ago that I'd been a virgin and had barely been kissed? I'd given myself to Bryn because I loved him, not just because my body craved his. I'd always wanted any relationship I had to go beyond the physical, I'd always wanted *more*. More . . . That word mocked me now, thanks to Khol. He'd said I'd come to crave it, and now I had.

"Oh my God!" Jenna exclaimed. "We just saw the news in the waiting room and—"

"I see you're all *healed*," Jeremy said with heavy sarcasm. "That was pretty fast. And where is he? Did he leave with what he wanted?"

I met his eyes with shock. Why was he being so mean? And there it was in his face; he now thought exactly what everyone at school did—that I was a slut. Fresh tears rolled down my cheeks. "He's gone. And no, he didn't get what he wanted." My voice cracked as I tried to keep from breaking down into sobs. I liked Jeremy. And I liked that he respected me, or had respected me. I averted my eyes from his, no longer wanting to see the look of incrimination that was directed at me.

"Hey," snapped Jenna. "Don't you talk to her that way. She's been through enough today, don't you think?"

Jeremy sighed. "Yeah, I'm sorry, P.J. I didn't mean it; it's just that—I don't know—I guess I'm just jealous is all. And who the hell is Khol anyways?" His voice rose with fresh anger. "We all know he isn't human. How do we know we can trust him?"

I lifted my eyes to meet his. "We can," I said simply.

"He wants you for himself. He uses every opportunity to try and push his advantage. He—"

"You mean like you do?"

Jeremy opened and closed his mouth before he responded, bringing his hand up to push through his hair. "Okay, you might have a point." At least he had the decency to look embarrassed, something that Khol most certainly never did.

"Back to what we saw on the news," Jenna prodded impatiently.

Jeremy stood up straighter, his face going very serious. "There was a shooting at another school today. Add that in with what happened to you, which made the news, by the way, and all of a sudden Senator Bill Wexington has a lot firmer platform to lean on for gun control."

HIDDEN GATES

I thought about what Jeremy said for a second as well as what I knew so far about the aliens. They wanted control of our world, they wanted to rule us, and what better way to start than to render us powerless, defenseless. They could situate themselves in positions of power, as in Senator Bill Wexington's case, and then push for bigger government control. Once they eliminated our way to fight back, they could make us do anything they wanted. It had all the beginnings of a conspiracy theory, except for one part: it was real. "Shit," I swore as I thought about what happened today and the impact such things could have. The more things like this happen, the more people will be afraid, and what better way to scare people then to attack their kids. "Shit," I swore again. "And I'm guessing this is just the beginning."

"My thoughts exactly," Jeremy said.

"Yeah," Jenna added morosely. "I think we're in a bit over our heads."

I raised my eyebrows at her. "You think?" I almost wanted to laugh at the ridiculousness of the situation. Here we were a bunch of high school kids, and we were going to try and save our world—literally.

"We need to find a way to get them out of people's bodies. We can't exactly go around killing them. Plus, I would feel kind of guilty killing the people they were in," I mumbled, thinking out loud.

"What are they though? I mean really?" Jenna asked.

"I don't know. All I know is that they aren't from our world. Not much to go on." I frowned, thinking about how little we did know about everything, even though it was a ton more than anyone else knew.

"How are we supposed to fight them if we don't even know what they are?" Jeremy asked, looking at me. It was then I realized Jenna and Jeremy were both looking to me for answers that I didn't have. They were looking to me to tell them what to do. How had I ended up in that position? I wasn't any kind of leader. I was a chocoholic, boy crazy, high school girl who worried a little too much about how she looked.

I slumped back into the hospital bed, feeling very defeated. "I don't know."

Jeremy's face softened, something resembling pity a little too closely shining at me from his deep brown eyes. He walked over and sat on the edge of the bed, taking my hand in his. "Let me be there for you. I'll help any way I can." A jolt of energy emanating from his fingertips shot up through my arm and raced through my body. I suddenly felt very revved up, as if I'd just downed a couple Red Bulls. I met Jeremy's eyes with question. He chuckled. "Better than an energy drink, huh? I'm very good at what I do." His eyes darkened as the double entendre left his mouth.

"What are we going to tell your parents?" Jenna asked. "We need to hurry up and sync our stories before they get here."

I tugged my hand back from Jeremy, who frowned at the move. "Crap. How did I almost forget about that? How the hell am I supposed to explain any of it?"

"A vision," Jeremy stated calmly as he tried to recapture my hand in his. "Tell them you had a vision about something bad that was going to happen, but it was so jumbled you didn't know what to think, so you just headed over that way to figure it out and voila."

"Yeah, that sounds like it just might work," I said, trying to keep my hand out of Jeremy's clutches without being too obvious, although the wry look he was giving me told me he knew exactly what I was doing.

"Is that what we're going with? Because you're parents are almost here." Jenna fidgeted nervously while looking down at something she had in the palm of her hand.

"How do you know they're almost here?" I asked as I tried to see what she had in her hand.

HIDDEN GATES

She lifted her head up, and a small bug of some sort rose into the air. "I had some of the local insects keeping a lookout for me."

She smiled when I grimaced. "Fabulous. Now I have to worry about flies on the wall spying on me—literally? You Speakers are a lot more dangerous than anyone gives you credit for."

"Most people don't appreciate the advantages that having one of us on their team can bring them." Jenna smiled with pride.

Jeremy looked at her and ran his hand through his tousled hair. "Yeah, I never really thought about what it really means to be a Speaker."

"Most don't." Jenna lifted her chin and met Jeremy's gaze head on. "We're a lot more than just some weirdos that talk to animals. We're just as important as—"

"P.J.!" My mom exclaimed as she burst into the room with my dad on her heels. Jeremy backed away from the bed as my mom flew to my side. "Are you okay, peanut? They said you were shot at and—" My mom's face crumpled up as she began to cry. "I was so worried."

I sat up straighter in bed and let my mom take me into her arms. "I'm fine, Mom. I shouldn't even be here anymore." *Thanks to Khol*, I added silently. How was I going to explain my miraculous recovery to the doctors so I could go home?

She sat back and ran her eyes over every inch of me in that classic mom stare, as if she would know just by looking at me if I was okay. "How are you feeling?"

I pushed her hands away with annoyance. "Fine. Like I said. Maybe you guys can talk to the doctor so I can get out of here."

"What happened?" my dad asked sternly. I wanted to roll my eyes. What was it with men getting angry when you get injured? It was like they all get insulted that you let something happen to yourself they couldn't protect you from.

"Can't we talk about this later? I really just wanna go home." I looked at my mom and implored her with my eyes.

"Well, I guess I'm gonna get going," Jenna said. I'd almost forgotten she was still there.

Jeremy cleared his throat to remind me of his presence as well. "Yeah, me, too. Call me if you need anything, P.J." He met my eyes with meaning. "I'll get a ride home with Jenna."

"Bye." I waved my hand meekly. *Great, now I don't have the friend buffer.* "How about us going home?" I added hopefully, looking at my mom again.

"Of course, peanut, I'll just go find the doctor." My mom buzzed out of the room, already excited to get me home. She probably was more interested in what was going on between Jeremy and me, if her eyes lighting up with what he said was any indication. Luckily for me, she'd most likely gloss right over what had happened with my dad's car and Emo Boy, and grill me about Jeremy. The lesser of two evils, I supposed.

"Why weren't you in school, and who told you that you could take my car?" I didn't look up from my sheet and fidgeted nervously with it and my IV. "Answer me, young lady." The tone in my dad's voice told me the big throbbing vein in his forehead was making an appearance, and even though I hated to admit it, when that thing made an appearance, it was time to run for cover; things never went well for me.

"I had a vision," I mumbled.

"What?" he said.

"I said I had a vision," I stated a little bit louder, although not much.

A crash made me look up sharply to see that my dad had knocked over a small table that had held ice water and some cups. "You had a vision that had something to do with a kid and a shotgun, and you drove *towards* the danger?"

"It was all jumbled up—the vision," I squeaked.

"That's not an excuse. You should have told us about it before you went running off to put yourself in danger," my dad snarled vehemently.

"And then what? What would you guys have done? If you believed me at all?" Anger shot through my veins, giving me courage to face off with my dad.

"You dragged Jenna and Jeremy into this with you, didn't you? And where were they while you were getting shot at?"

"We saved innocent lives!" I yelled.

"I don't care about those lives—just yours," my dad yelled back at me.

"I'm sure their families don't feel the same way!" I gulped in air, trying to remain relatively calm, although it wasn't working. "I made a difference!"

My dad gritted his teeth and stared at me a few moments before responding. "We'll discuss your punishment when we get home. It's going to be a doozy, let me tell you. You've proven time and time again recently that we can't trust you."

I narrowed my eyes and laughed darkly at him. "Oh, really? What are you going to do, forbid me to see the love of my life? Oh wait—you already did that. You've already ruined my life. Do your worst!" I screamed the last part at him, completely losing any control I had barely managed to hold on to.

My mom chose that moment to come back into the room. "The doctor is going to be in to check you out soon, and then we'll see about getting you home." When neither my father nor I responded, she looked back and forth between the two of us. "Now what's this about?"

"I was just reminding Dad here that there wasn't any punishment that you guys could give me that would be worse than what you've already done by ripping Bryn out of my life," I growled, still glaring at my dad.

"But I thought you and Jeremy were—"

"Were what, Mom?" I snapped my head around and speared her with a look of utter disgust. "Did you really think I'd get over Bryn so fast?" I raised my hand to keep her from responding. "No, wait. Don't answer that. Of course you did. But let me just tell you this. Even if Bryn were out of the picture—which he isn't—Jeremy would be my *third* choice. Not that any of that really matters because I still want Bryn."

Shock played across my mom's face. "Third? But who?"

I was going for shock value at the moment, and I knew the perfect way to twist the knife. "One of my kind. You know what my *real* father was."

My mom staggered back as if I'd slapped her. "No—you can't."

"Why? Tell me why I can't be with someone of my kind if I want to be. None of the rules of duty apply anymore now that I know. So you see, you might as well let Bryn come back because he's the lesser of the two evils now, isn't he?"

"How did you even meet one of them?" my mom asked, her face completely stricken.

"He sought me out. My power called to him apparently, waking him up." I paused to let the news sink in fully. "You don't even know what I am."

My dad spoke up, my mom seemingly made speechless from my revelation. "You're our daughter. That's all we need to know."

"But I'm not *your daughter*, not really," I said as I met my dad's sad eyes. The look of anguish on his face almost made me crack, almost made me back down, but it didn't. I know some people would kill to have a family that accepted them unconditionally whether they be blood or not, but I didn't quite feel like that was the case. I felt like my family loved who they thought I was, or wanted me to be, not who I was in reality. They couldn't accept who I was in love with because they deemed him not good enough for me. And yet, if they really loved me unconditionally, wouldn't they just want me to be happy? Bryn made me happy. Case closed.

"I have this whole other side to me that I didn't even know existed. Why didn't you tell me? Why did you keep me in the dark?" I blinked back tears and went back to studying my hands.

"We wanted you to feel accepted and loved, not different. Not—"

"Would you have ever told me? Or was this something you guys would have taken to your graves?" I brought my head up to study first my dad's face and then my mom's. The answer was clear in both of them. "That's what I thought."

I wanted out. I *needed* out. And despite what had happened between Khol and me less than twenty minutes ago, he was the first person I thought of to turn to for help. I called out to him mentally, hoping my desperation was made crystal clear. I wasn't going to do anything stupid like run away with him, but I was planning on hitching a ride home with him so I could have some much needed space between me and my parents.

Khol appeared beside my bed in all his Dragonly beauty. Looking every bit as fierce as I knew he would. My mother gasped, and my father's eyes widened with shock. "You called, my little Seer?"

"I want to go home." Khol inclined his head in question. I knew he was wondering why I'd called him for that, and why I didn't want to go home with my parents. But he didn't question me out loud. "Please," I whispered.

Khol stepped forward to scoop me up in his arms, and my mom cried out, "No! P.J., no! You don't know what you're doing. You—"

"I'll see you at home, Mom," I said with steel in my voice.

"Paige Joplin Stone—" my father started.

"Stop. I need space from you two, and I'm going to get it. There's nothing you can do. I'll see you both at home." Khol pulled me to his chest, and I wrapped my arms around his neck, meeting his eyes to signal him it was time to leave. As we blinked out of the hospital room, I heard my mom scream out in anguish.

15

I'd wanted space from my parents, and I'd gotten it in spades. They both seemed to be avoiding me since our fallout in the hospital room, and when I did see them, my mom looked at me with tears in her eyes, and my dad simply stared at me with sadness. Maybe I'd been a little hurtful, and maybe I'd taken it a step too far by calling on Khol, but I felt like they'd backed me into a corner. They were probably afraid if they didn't let me be, I'd disappear with Khol or something. I didn't do anything to discourage them from thinking that because a small part of me was hoping maybe then they would bring Bryn back. *Bryn.* I sighed loudly as I conjured up an image of him in my mind. Of course, lately with my overcharged hormones, I always pictured him as he was when we'd been in bed together that first night—the night I'd given him my virginity.

I ran my hands through his silky, tousled hair and then down over his sweaty back. He shuddered at my touch, leaning forward to kiss me with a slow languidness that spoke of shared intimacies and unspoken promises. "I love you, Peej.

More than I can even begin to explain." His voice was so low and husky it seemed to brush things on my insides, making me shudder in turn.

That night had been perfect with him. Every little detail from being with him that first time was forever etched into my mind.

"Miss Stone, care to share with us what has stolen your attention from class?"

I blinked in surprise as I snapped back to the present—Mr. Edgington's history class. My face heated as if it were written all over me what I'd just been thinking about. "No," I mumbled, feeling everyone's eyes on me.

"Then how about you at least humor me and pretend to pay attention in my class, hmm?" Mr. Edgington raised his gray bushy eyebrows at me in question. I simply nodded in response. "Right. Now where was I? No taxation without representation—" The bell signaled the end of class, and I began hastily gathering up my things. "Remember to read the next two chapters for tomorrow," Mr. Edgington called to us, but I doubted anyone was paying attention.

One more class . . . one more class and I'm done for the weekend, I silently repeated to myself over and over like a mantra.

"Hey," Jenna said as she fell into step beside me. "Wanna stay over at my place tonight?"

"Yes," I answered emphatically without having to think about it. The tension in my house was unbearable; I would welcome the chance of being somewhere—anywhere—else.

"Your parents still acting all weird?"

"Pretty much. I think I broke something with them, but the thing is I don't know how to fix it, and I'm not sure I would if I could. They lied to me about some pretty major stuff."

Jenna sighed. "Yeah, not telling you about who your real father is—well, that's pretty major."

HIDDEN GATES

I gasped and staggered against the wall. I hadn't told Jenna any of that. I was planning to—eventually, but I hadn't gotten around to it yet. "How the hell did you find out?" I closed my eyes and shook my head. "Please *do not* tell me you had a fly on the wall or something . . . literally."

I opened my eyes to a very pleased Jenna. "You just told me."

"What?" And then I realized she'd pulled one of the oldest tricks in the book. I groaned and rubbed at my face. "But how did you even suspect?"

"Aside from the fact you don't look anything like your dad?" I scrunched my face up at her. Lots of people don't look like their dads. Besides, I looked enough like my mom that it was obvious whose side of the family I took after. "But what really gave it away was when your eyes started to glow that day in your backyard. It wasn't much, but enough to make me wonder if you weren't part whatever Khol is, and you look a ton like your mom, so I don't think they found you in a cabbage patch."

My jaw dropped open. My eyes had glowed? *Holy. Shit.* "Why didn't you say something before? Did Jeremy see too?" I gulped. What other freaky Dragon things were starting to develop in me that I had no clue about?

"There really wasn't a good time to bring it up before now. And yeah, unless Jeremy is blind, I'm pretty sure he saw, too."

I clutched my books to my chest tightly and concentrated on remaining calm. The thought of having to stay in school for one more minute suddenly seemed stifling. "I'm ditching last period. I need to get out of here." I swiveled on my heel and marched towards the front door.

Jenna scurried after me. "You just gonna walk out the front door?"

"That's the plan."

After a long pause, Jenna responded, "I'll come with you. We can go scoop up your stuff from your house, and leave your parents a note that you'll be at my place. We can start our girls' night of fun early." She smiled up at me, but I couldn't manage to reciprocate.

"Hey. Where you guys going?" Jeremy appeared out of nowhere and fell into step with us. I didn't say anything and kept focused on my main goal: to get the hell out of school.

"We're ditching last period and going over to my house. Girls' night tonight," Jenna replied helpfully.

"Girls only, huh? I don't suppose I can tag along?"

"I don't know if P.J. is feeling up to it. She's kind of on the verge of freaking out right now," Jenna stated matter of factly.

"About what?" Concern seeped into Jeremy's voice.

"The whole eyes glowing thing from the other day, you know?"

"Oh. It's not that big a deal. Nothing to freak out about; neither one of us look at you any different because of it, P.J.," Jeremy said softly.

"I'm not freaking out," I said between clenched teeth. "I'm a little bit upset is all."

"About what?" Jeremy asked.

"Seriously?" I looked at him incredulously. "Finding out that I'm not even entirely human, and that my eyes are now doing some kind of weird glowy thing like Khol's? Yep. Nothing to be upset about at all."

"Whoa, whoa, whoa," Jenna exclaimed. "What do you mean you're not entirely human?"

Really? What did she think after both meeting Khol and seeing my eyes glow? "Nothing," I muttered as I quickened my pace and practically flew down the front stairs of my school. I was almost free and clear. As soon as my feet hit the front walkway, I broke into a full out run, unable to resist any longer.

HIDDEN GATES

"Hey. P.J., wait," Jeremy called, his feet pounding on the pavement behind me.

"P.J., come on. I didn't mean anything," Jenna called from farther back. She couldn't keep up with Jeremy and me with our much longer legs.

I ignored them both and ran all the way to the front door of my house where Jeremy snagged my arm and turned me to face him. "I don't care if you're not entirely human. It doesn't change anything for me."

I met his deep brown eyes briefly before looking away. "You don't even know what I am."

"So tell me." He tipped my face up towards him with his fingertips, forcing me to meet his gaze again.

"*Rua Arach*," I muttered while trying not to count the golden flecks in Jeremy's eyes. He raised his eyebrows in question. "Red Dragon. I'm half Red Dragon."

His brows furrowed together. "So Khol is a—"

"Full-blooded Red Dragon," I finished for him. "And he wants me for his *Anam Cara*—his mate."

Jeremy's hands balled into fists, and his jaw ground together. "No," he said between clenched teeth.

"I don't know if I'll be able to stop it." I sagged with relief at finally being able to say my fears out loud. "Something about him calls to that part in me."

Jeremy studied my face and stroked my cheek with the back of his hand. "Do you want that? To be his Anam—whatever—mate?"

"No," I whispered. "At least I don't think so." He leaned forward to kiss me, and I turned to give him my cheek. "But that doesn't mean I want to be with you either. I love Bryn. I still want him and only him."

He pulled away and exhaled loudly. "I know. So you keep telling me. It's just when I'm with you I feel this, I don't know, connection. And I don't see how something so strong can be one-sided."

"I feel a connection, too. But it's to your power, and to you as a friend. I know it's not what you wanna hear, but it's the truth."

"Ahem. Why do I feel like I'm invisible lately?" Jenna grumbled from a couple feet away.

"Isn't that a good thing for spies?" I snarked.

She narrowed her eyes at me and flipped her rainbow hair. "I don't do the spying, my friends do."

"I know you feel something when I kiss you, more than a friend kind of thing," Jeremy said, as if Jenna was indeed invisible or not present at all.

I rolled my eyes at Jeremy. Guys and their egos are completely insufferable. "What do you want me to say, Jeremy? You're hot, and you're good kisser. But I'm in love with Bryn. End of story."

A smile spread across his face, the gold flecks in his eyes dancing. "So I'm still in the game."

I threw my hands up in the air in exasperation. "This isn't a game—it's my life!" With that I unlocked the door and stalked into the house with Jenna and Jeremy close on my heels. Funny, I didn't remember inviting either one of them to come in. Guess what I wanted didn't matter anymore.

I internally bitched out my friends all the way up to my room where I stopped short. Someone had been here, and I wasn't talking about my parents. It looked like everything I owned had been pulled out of place and strewn around my room. It was if someone had been searching for something and got angry when they didn't find it. As it sunk in, I gasped and slapped my hand over my mouth, stopping abruptly where I was so that Jenna slammed into my back, knocking me forward. "What's wrong?" she asked before her eyes took in what I'd already seen. "What—what happened?" she stammered.

"I don't know," I whispered.

Khol appeared suddenly in front of me, his eyes glowing intensely. "Get whatever you need together quickly. It's not safe for you here anymore."

Jeremy pushed his way in front of Jenna and me to square off with Khol. "And how do we know you're not the one who did all of this"—he motioned to the mess that used to be my room—"so you had an excuse to take her out of here?"

Khol barely spared Jeremy a glance, and instead, looked to me. "We don't have time to deal with any mistrust your friends may have for me. I need to get you out of here."

Did I trust Khol with my safety? Yes. Did I think that he'd use any excuse to get me alone so he could try to coax me into being his *Anam Cara*? Yes. So the question was which one was his motivator for the current situation? I couldn't afford to make mistakes anymore. They could cost me Bryn, or my life, or both. "What happened? Why isn't it safe here anymore?" I asked hesitantly.

"The aliens somehow know who you are. They came looking for you." He ground his teeth together as if it was taking everything in him not to just grab me and disappear.

I shifted nervously, still not quite sure what to think. "How do you even know that?"

"I saw the one that shot at you leaving your house—"

"Why didn't you stop him from doing this? Why didn't you, I don't know, *get him* or something?" I asked incredulously as I waved my hands frantically at my trashed room. "And what were you doing lurking around my house?"

"I was in the area; let's leave it at that." Khol sniffed as if indignant. "And instead of *getting him*, as you put it, I decided to follow him to see if I could find out anything."

"And did you?" Jenna piped up.

"Yes, I did," Khol said gruffly. "They somehow know who P.J. is, and they want to remove her as a threat."

"Remove me?" I staggered back into Jenna who stepped out of the way for Jeremy to steady me. "You mean—" I couldn't bring myself to say it.

"How do we know we can trust anything he's saying?" Jeremy asked while glaring at Khol.

"I trust him," I said without hesitation. Jeremy made a sound almost like a growl in the back of his throat, and his grip on my arm tightened. "So where are you going to take me?"

"To my lair," Khol said. "I wish I could keep you away, at least until—" He stopped short and shook his head as if dislodging some thought from his mind. "But your life will be protected there, even if it isn't the safest place for you right now."

"I don't understand. How isn't it safe for me there, but my life is protected?" Khol crossed his arms over his chest and made a face that somehow I understood. Dragons—other Dragons—would be at his lair, and he was afraid they'd try to lay claim to me. "How will you keep that from happening?" I croaked.

"What?" Jenna asked with her head swiveling back and forth between the two of us. "Did I miss something?"

"Nothing that you need to worry about," Khol stated with finality. Lucky for me, Jenna liked to ignore such things.

"It kind of is, since I'm going with her."

"You are?" I asked with surprise.

"Yep."

"Yeah, me, too," Jeremy practically growled. "She's obviously going to need protection from whatever danger you're dragging her into."

My face flushed from my friends' reactions. I really hadn't expected them to want to go with me, and it kind of made me feel all warm and fuzzy inside, even if I could never let them go in good conscious. "Guys, I can't let you do that."

Jenna raised her chin and met me with a steel gaze that I would have recognized if I looked in the mirror. "You're not *letting* me do anything. It's happening whether you like it or not. You're my best friend, and we have to stick together."

"No," Khol said. "I won't permit it."

Jenna narrowed her eyes and stalked towards Khol. "You're not the boss of me."

"Or me," Jeremy chimed in. "Regardless of how you feel about us, you know we'll come in handy in helping to keep her safe. And you want her safe, don't you?"

Khol ground his teeth together. "Of course." He brought his gaze back to study me for another moment before speaking again. "If I bring you with us, you must listen to what I have to say. There will be many things you won't understand, and I don't have time to stop and explain everything all the time." I saw acceptance, although reluctant, wash over his face. "Fine," he said. "I will bring all three of you to my lair."

"No!" I exclaimed. "You can't mean that."

"Jeremy's right. I must do whatever necessary, however unpleasant for me, to keep you safe."

"Who's going to tell our parents? Who's—"

Jenna cut off what was about to be a stream of reasons why they shouldn't go. None of them would have stopped me if the shoe was on the other foot, but I had to try. "I'll have one of my friends tell my parents, and in the message, I'll tell my parents that they need to fill in both of your parents."

"Well, Khol said we had to leave now. You guys won't have time to go and get your stuff," I said, grasping at straws.

"That's okay," Jenna chirped, revved up from the excitement of what she probably perceived as an adventure. "I can borrow some of your stuff."

"But we're not the same size!"

"We've made it work before, we can make it work now." Jenna beamed at me, very pleased with herself.

"And as a guy, I'm sure I can figure out something there, right?" Jeremy looked at Khol, who tightly nodded once in affirmation.

Jenna began bouncing up and down. "Yay! It's settled! Now hurry up and pack so we can get going, P.J. I'm going to find a friend to deliver the message to our parents for us."

"I just—I don't—what's happening?" I mumbled more to myself than anyone else. Just when I thought things couldn't possibly spin more out of control, they had. I rubbed at my temples, positive I was about to be hit with a massive headache. And then something occurred to me. "What happened when you followed Emo Boy? I mean, besides you getting that information?" I still couldn't quite bring myself to say the rest, that they wanted me dead. Pretty harsh, even for would-be world-stealing aliens.

"I was hoping he would lead me to others . . . like him, but I was only able to pick up the information because of a phone call he made." Khol's jaw rippled with tension before smoothing out. "He would have harmed you if he found you here."

"And?" I prodded.

"And I took care of him after he ended the call." A dark smile spread across his face that sent a chill up my spine.

"What exactly does that mean?" Although I wasn't sure I wanted the answer.

"Just gather your things and rest assured that Emo Boy, as you referred to him, will no longer be an issue for you."

Referred, past tense. Did Khol kill him? The boy that the alien had been in was just a host, wasn't he? So what happened to the parasite inside him once the host was killed? Would he die along with the host, or would he simply try to move on? Maybe once the alien climbed into a host, they were joined, becoming one. Maybe I should stop thinking of them as two separate entities and think of them as one.

"Think of them as one. The creature takes control of the body, absorbing the person inside, at least as far as I can tell, and he won't be bothering you anymore," Khol said as if he'd read my mind. And again I found myself wondering if he actually could and just wasn't telling me.

Annoyance flared within me. I didn't want Khol or anyone poking around in my brain. "Stop doing that," I snapped. He shrugged as if to say he couldn't help it, and I fought the urge to smack him before I began scanning my room for clothes and such to take with me. Because I was so annoyed with the whole situation, I just started shoving stuff into my bag with the hope that I was bringing with me what I would want later. Oh well, it wasn't as if I couldn't send Khol back to get something if I forgot it. I snickered to myself at the thought of turning him into an errand Dragon. I wondered if he would actually do it if I asked. After a second's deliberation, I decided he would, in fact, fetch things for me because he was trying to get into my pants. I felt certain that males, of any species, were the same, and predictable when it came to that issue. "Ready," I proclaimed after I swept my face wash and other necessary beauty products into my already overstuffed bag. "So how are we going to do this?"

Khol raised his eyebrows at my comment. "I'll simply shift the three of you over to my lair."

I scrunched my face up at him, again, wondering why he hadn't done that with us when we needed to hurry to save that girl I saw in my premonition. "Why didn't you just do that before when we needed to get to the school?"

"Because my powers are not back up to their full strength yet, having been in hibernation for many years. I will get very tired after I do this, and that wasn't an option before."

I guess that made sense. "Oh."

"So it'll be mostly up to me to protect her until you fully recover?" Jeremy asked. Then his tone shifted angrily. "How were you planning to do that before, when you were just going to take her to your lair?"

"I would have only been taking her, and that's not as taxing," Khol said with annoyance at Jeremy's question. "Do not doubt again that I can keep her safe."

"You didn't do a very good job before." I could practically feel the tension in the air radiating from both Khol and Jeremy.

"That was different, that was—"

"Boys, boys, boys." Jenna stepped into the space between the two of them. "There will be plenty of time to fight over P.J. after we get her somewhere safe." Neither Khol nor Jeremy said anything, but they kept glaring at each other over Jenna's head.

I sighed. "Can we just go already?" There was enough testosterone in the room to smother me, and it was nothing short of exasperating.

"You must all be touching me," Khol said without looking away from Jeremy. *For Christ's sake ... men.* I walked over to him and took his hand. Jenna did the same but slid her hands around Khol's arm, sighing with enjoyment. I had to bite my cheek to keep from telling her to get her hands off of him, and I didn't like that I felt that way, not one little bit. Khol finally looked away from Jeremy so he could smile at me, obviously enjoying my little twinge of jealousy.

Jeremy finally came over to stand by Khol, and I started to get nervous about what he would do, when he reached up and touched Khol's arm with his fingertips on the same side that Khol was holding my hand. He locked eyes with me, and then we were gone.

HIDDEN GATES

For some reason, when Khol had said *lair,* my mind conjured up thoughts of something set inside a cave, or in the side of a mountain. What I had definitely *not* expected was a friggin' ginormous house, or castle really, set on lush green lands that went on as far as the eye could see. And let me tell you, that's pretty far because I have 20/20 vision.

"Wow," I heard Jenna say under her breath.

"My sentiments exactly," I muttered.

Khol smiled at me with amusement. "What did you expect, a cave or something?"

"No," I grumbled, even though by the twinkle in his eyes, I knew he'd picked up on the fact that I had been expecting exactly that.

"My Lord." A guy about six foot tall, with flame red hair and illuminated green eyes, although not as bright as Khol's, was suddenly kneeling in front of us, or more in front of Khol, really. Even if I hadn't known to expect more Dragons, I would have immediately known this guy was one; I could feel it down to my bones. I studied him with curiosity as he rose from his crouch only to lock gazes with me. He took an awkward step towards me that caused me to clutch Khol's hand tighter, which until that instant I hadn't even realized I'd still been holding. I watched as a fine tremor rolled over the new Dragon's body and his nostrils flared. "She's—"

"Not for you to consider," Khol cut off the new Dragon's words curtly.

Still staring at me with an intensity that made me want to disappear, the other Dragon took another step towards me. "Her power—it's—it's—unique, not cold like the other female Dragons I've felt. It calls to me with a warmth I didn't think possible."

An inhuman growl erupted from Khol. "Macon, back off," he said before he calmed himself. "I know the will to resist is harder for one so young as yourself, but she's not for you."

Macon looked at Khol with what I can only describe as pain on his face. "Then why haven't you claimed her yet? She'll drive us all mad until you do."

"She's part human," Khol said, as if that explained everything.

And for Macon it seemed to. "Yes, my Lord, I understand. I will try to avoid her until she bears your *Anam Cara* mark." With that, he pulled what I now had come to think of as a Khol—a disappearing act—but apparently all Dragons liked such dramatics.

I exhaled a breath I hadn't realized I was holding. "So that's what you were talking about."

"Yes." Khol nodded as he tugged my hand and began walking towards the castle.

"Why didn't you just *pop* us into the castle instead of out here?" I asked as my head swiveled around, trying to take in all the unfamiliar sights and sounds of this new place.

"Because I wanted you to see my land." There was a note of pride in Khol's voice that I couldn't miss, and it made me wonder if the old stories of Dragons and their acquisitiveness were, in fact, based in reality.

As we made our way inside through a side door, probably what would be called a servants' door, my senses prickled, letting me know that there were more than a handful of other Dragons on the premises. My skin felt tingly, like little bits of electricity were running over the expanse of my body, and I trembled with the pleasantness of it.

"Why are we going in the side door?" Jenna asked. "I wanna tour of this place."

"P.J. needs to be isolated from the others here. You can have a tour after she's settled if you wish," Khol said with a touch of annoyance. I wanted to laugh because Jenna had that effect on everyone it seemed, but the pleasant tingling had changed, and it was if my skin were burning, and my vision danced suddenly as if I were drunk.

My focus narrowed down to only Khol, and as my breaths began to come in short little bursts, I curled myself up against the side of him as we walked. "Kiss me," I purred, not caring who saw. I craved the taste of him, and I wanted his hands on me because surely his touch was the only cure for my burning desire.

"Not now. I must get you—"

I didn't hear the rest of what he said to me. Anger at him flared inside me for denying me what I wanted. If he wouldn't give me what I needed, then surely someone else would. "Macon," I called in an almost sing song voice.

Macon immediately appeared directly in front of us, and I tugged free of Khol and stepped towards him. Khol growled, but I didn't care, he had his chance, now it was Macon's. "Macon," I purred. "You'll kiss me, won't you?" His eyes seemed to grow brighter in intensity as he came to me faster than I'd seen anyone ever move—well, except Khol maybe. His lips met mine in a searing kiss that had me wrapping myself around him as a moan escaped from me. *Yes.* I thought. *This is exactly what I need.* But before I could sink deeper into the kiss, Macon was ripped away from me and slammed into the wall. Khol scooped me up in his arms, to which I didn't protest, and suddenly we were in a different room. A room with a rather large bed, I realized with pleasure.

My head was swimming as I reached out and pulled Khol towards me, capturing his lips with mine. "You know what I want," I growled. "Give it to me." I felt possessed, like someone else had taken over my body, and I kind of liked it. I'd never felt so completely free before. *Except with Bryn,* my mind whispered. I screamed and clutched at the back of my neck, it was if someone were holding a hot iron there. "Bryn!" I cried out wishing he were here with me and not Khol. Bryn's touch was always the cooling balm that soothed my heated skin; he was who I craved.

Khol grabbed me and spun me around, prying my hand off the back of my neck to see what was causing me the pain. "No. That's not possible." His voice was filled with a mixture of shock and anger.

The pain subsided as abruptly as it had begun, and left without it, I was suddenly too weak to remain vertical. I fell over onto the bed and curled into a ball, darkness already pushing at the edge of my consciousness. "Bryn," I heard myself gasp. "Please. I need Bryn." And then I lost the battle with consciousness.

16

"My Lord, how will we track them without her aid? None of us can see them for what they really are, even you, without using her power. We can't let them get an even stronger foothold than they already have." A low male voice spoke urgently.

"I'm already aware of the problems we face, but we need to take care of her first," Khol said in response.

There was a pregnant pause during which I pondered why people were always talking around me when I lost consciousness. You would think people would want to let me rest and feel better instead of jabbering their jaws around me.

"How did you not notice until now, my Lord?"

"It must have something to do with the Black Dragon's powers. He must be young, very young. Young enough to even pass for human. He might even be partially so, like her, which could explain it. He will come for her as soon as he can. He probably already feels the pull. He will know his partial claim is in threat. It will drive him mad."

"What will you do?"

"Claim her before he fully does so. Her *Anam Cara* will not be a *Dubh Arach*. She will be mine." Khol's words came out barely sounding human, which in fact, he wasn't. *I must be dreaming.* What were they talking about? I'd never met any kind of Dragon before Khol had showed up to complicate my life, let alone one from a different clan.

"What will you do if he comes here?"

"I'll do what I need to do to ensure she fully belongs to me. I wanted to give her human half the time to get used to the idea, but I no longer have that option."

"Wha? No," I slurred, trying to wake up all the way. "I trus ou." What I was trying to tell him very unsuccessfully was that he couldn't claim me without my permission. I trusted him with that fact, and he said as long as I trusted him, he would wait. It didn't matter that I never planned on giving him permission. He believed one day I would. As for the rest, I still didn't know what he was talking about. Why did they think someone was coming for me?

"Shhh, my little Seer, you need to rest," Khol said as a large warm hand smoothed hair away from my face.

"No. I need Bryn," I somehow managed to say and actually make it sound like English.

"No." Khol's voice sounded harsh. "The only one you need is me." I squirmed to try to get away from his touch, but I didn't have the energy. I began to feel very sleepy again, my body very heavy. I tried to respond, but my mouth was too tired to move. I was holding on to awareness by a very thin thread.

"She'll sleep for awhile longer, and then I will return for her," Khol said to the other Dragon. I didn't like the sound of that. "If the Black Dragon shows up, you know what to do." I liked the sound of that even less.

"What about her companions?"

HIDDEN GATES

"Confine the boy to his room, but the girl is permitted entrance."

"Yes, my Lord."

That was the last thing I remembered until I sat up with a start, in a strange bed, in a strange room. "About damn time," Jenna's familiar voice exclaimed beside me.

I turned to see her lounging on the bed, right next to me, reading a magazine. "I've been dying to talk to you." She ceremoniously folded the magazine and met my eyes with her deep brown ones, which were currently sparkling with delight. "*Sooo* . . ." she drew out, "me and Macon—"

I raised my hand to cut her off, which caused her to frown. "Give me a second to orient myself before you hit me with what is sure to be another tale about how you got the latest notch in your belt." Jenna thrummed her fingers against the folded magazine impatiently. I inhaled deeply a couple of times while I allowed my gaze to sweep my new surroundings. *Fancy*, I thought, *if not a little gaudy*. The room looked like it had been transported right out of Marie Antoinette's time; everything was marble and encrusted with gold. "Let them eat cake," I mumbled. Yep, if the outside of the castle hadn't answered my questions about a Dragon's acquisitory nature, then this room definitely did. I wondered if there was a big pile of treasure in a vault downstairs somewhere.

"Can I please tell you what happened between me and Macon now?" Jenna's whine cut into my inner musings.

"Fine," I said, punctuating it with an eye roll. I knew she was about to tell me anyways, but I figured I might as well feign control of the situation.

"Well, you've probably already guessed that we did it." I nodded, unable to keep from doing another eye roll. "But what you can't guess, since you've only been with Bryn, is just how absolutely amazing and different it is to be with a Dragon.

They're just so . . . well, they're just so . . ." She started fanning herself as she searched for the right word. "Amazing," she finally settled on. Maybe it was time I bought the girl a thesaurus.

I couldn't keep the snide tone out of my voice, "Because you've been with so many Dragons before. How do you know Macon wasn't an anomaly?"

"Hmm." Jenna turned pensive. "You're right. I think I should conduct a study while I'm here."

"For God's sake, girl, there are more important things on our plates than your sex life." Like mine, I silently added sheepishly.

"I think you should do it with Khol."

"Jenna!" I exclaimed.

"No, I mean it. At least for comparison purposes; you've only been with Bryn, and—"

Holy crap! *Bryn.* Was it possible? Everything that Khol and the other Dragon had said while I was barely conscious came flooding back. No, it couldn't be, but then again, I was half Dragon myself after all. "I think Bryn may be part Black Dragon." The words seemed even more ludicrous when I said them aloud.

"Did you hit your head?" Jenna asked with a laugh. "You'll do anything to change the subject, won't you?"

"No, Jenna! I'm being serious. I heard Khol and some other Dragon talking, when I wasn't fully awake, about how some young Black Dragon, or at least partial Black Dragon, has the beginnings of a mate claim on me. I know from talking to Khol that the only way to claim a Dragon mate is to do it during sex." Jenna's eyes widened slightly as I continued on with my crazy theory. "Well, I've only been with Bryn, and Khol said all Red Dragons have red hair in human form, even ones like me who can't change forms, and well, wouldn't it make sense for Black Dragons to have black hair in human form? And who do we know that I've slept with that has black hair?" When I put all the clues together that way, maybe it didn't seem that implausible that Bryn was part Black Dragon. I didn't think he was full blooded because he looked too much like his dad, and he did have all the usual Guardian abilities. Which meant—"Holy crap! That means Bryn's dad had an affair with a female Dragon. That's the only way it would make sense." Was that why Bryn and I had always felt so drawn to each other starting at a very young age? Had we started some kind of bonding process between Dragon mates without even realizing it?

Jenna stared at me in what looked like complete shock. "Well, say something," I chuckled nervously. "I don't think, in all the years we've been friends, I have ever seen you go speechless."

"I—well, I—damn it, when you explain it the way you just did, it almost seems possible." She shook her head in amazement. "First you, and now maybe Bryn. Maybe it's true that Speakers can't be friends with our kind because if you're right, this means neither of you are one hundred percent Seer or Guardian."

I reached up and scratched at the back of my neck. It was beginning to burn; nothing like before, but it was definitely uncomfortable. "Hey, will you see what's going on with the back of my neck? It was burning like crazy before, and now it's more burning slash itching, but it's annoying as all hell." I lifted my hair off of my neck, and Jenna scooted behind me to take a look.

"Umm . . . when did you get a tattoo and decide not to tell me?" Jenna said with annoyance. "Didn't they tell you A & D ointment is the best thing for it while it's healing? It kind of looks raw."

"What?" I pulled away with alarm. "I didn't get a tattoo. What the hell are you talking about?" Jumping out of bed, I clamored over to a large mirror that was hanging on the wall and contorted the best that I could to try and see the back of my neck, but I couldn't see a thing.

"Hang on." Jenna reached down to the floor and into her purse to produce a small compact. She then came over to join me in front of the larger mirror while holding the compact so I could see the offending area that was hiding from me.

I gasped at the image reflected back at me in the tiny mirror. Sure enough, there was what looked like a raw and chaffing black circular tattoo right below my hair line on the back of my neck. "That's impossible," I muttered while still staring in the mirror.

"Can't be impossible since there it is." I could feel Jenna studying me. "You really didn't know? How can you not know you got a tattoo?"

"I wish I knew," I said as I headed back for the bed, my head reeling. Time and time again, I kept thinking my life couldn't get any weirder. I really had to stop jinxing myself.

A loud knock on the door preceded Khol entering the room. He gave me a tight smile as he met my eyes. "It's the Black Dragon's *Anam Cara* mark."

"Huh?" Jenna and I said in perfect unison.

Khol motioned at the back of his neck. "What you think is a tattoo is the Black Dragon's *Anam Cara* mark—mate mark, or at least the beginning of one."

"What do you mean?" Jenna asked.

Khol answered while still holding my gaze. "Because it's black, I know it was made by a Black Dragon. All *Anam Caras*—Dragon pairs—mark each other."

"So..."

He picked up on my question before I could ask it. "Yes. He will bare a red mark on the back of his neck from you." Khol paused, turmoil rolling off him in waves. "This Bryn.

Your Bryn." He practically growled the words. "I can no longer wait for you to be done with him before I claim you. This changes everything."

Fear shot up my spine and caused goose bumps to erupt on my skin. "I trust you," I whispered even though I already sensed the words were little good to me anymore.

For the first time since I'd met Khol, genuine sadness filled his eyes. "And I had hoped to keep that trust with you, but I won't lose you, especially to a *Dubh Arach*."

"Whoa, whoa, whoa. What I think you're trying to say there, bucko, is completely unacceptable. You better back off of P.J.," Jenna said angrily. "Nobody forces my best friend to do anything she doesn't wanna do."

A small part of me, the part that was slightly hysterical, wanted to laugh because Jenna had just said bucko—that was something she'd definitely picked up from her mom. A larger part of me had already taken a mental vacation. I just couldn't seem to grasp what was going on. "Khol, please," I attempted. Please, what? Please don't force yourself on me and claim me for your mate when I want someone else?

"The mark isn't complete, that's why it's irritating you. His is doing the same, I can guarantee you. But once it's complete, there will be no going back. You would be his for the rest of your lives. And that I can't allow," Khol snarled. "Especially not a damn Black Dragon." He began stalking towards me, and I shrank back until I hit the wall. I wanted away from him. I wanted to go home. I was in way over my head with him. "Drake," Khol called with menace. A moment later I saw someone male appear in my peripheral vision, but I didn't dare look away from Khol. "Take Jenna to her room and make sure she stays there."

"Yes, my Lord." The same voice I had heard when I wasn't fully conscious answered.

"No!" Jenna screamed. "You can't! She trusted you! We trusted you!" But her screams were silenced as the other Dragon disappeared with Jenna in his arms kicking and screaming, leaving me alone with Khol.

"Please," I whispered, my whole body beginning to tremble. "Don't do this to me."

"I'm sorry. I don't have a choice anymore."

"It'll be rape. Are you telling me you have no choice but to rape me? I don't believe that." My words came out shaky as I tried to withhold the onslaught of tears that were pooling in my eyes.

He came to stand mere inches away from me, his voice barely a whisper. "You'll enjoy it, I promise. I know your body craves mine. That isn't rape, coercion maybe, but not rape."

He leaned forward to kiss me, and I ducked down so he missed and got the side of my face. "But my heart and soul still crave Bryn. You'll deny me that for the rest of my life? Because once you claim me for your *Anam Cara*, I won't want him anymore, will I? At least not physically?"

"No, you won't. And it's better that way." He grabbed my wrists and pushed them up over my head, causing my heart to triple in time.

"I'll never forgive you for this," I hissed.

A sad smile turned Khol's lips up ever so slightly at the corners. "But you will because only I will be able to give you what you crave when I'm your *Anam Cara*. And Dragons are quite insatiable, especially the females; you haven't even begun to experience the full scope of your Dragon side."

Bryn's image flooded my mind, and just like that time in the woods when I was almost raped, all I wished for was for him to come to my rescue. "Bryn!" I mentally screamed. "Please, somehow don't let this happen to me—to us!" I struggled in Khol's grasp, but he was much too strong for me.

HIDDEN GATES

He managed to keep me pinned with just one hand holding both my wrists as he tore at my clothes. I screamed with fury. I couldn't—wouldn't—let him do this. When he dipped his head to kiss me, I bit his lip, causing him to growl low in his chest, his eyes glowing brighter. I tasted the tangy copper flavor of his blood as he persisted, delving into my mouth with his tongue.

"Get your hands off her. She's mine," a heartbreakingly familiar voice growled with menace from behind Khol. I had a moment of intermingled relief and joy before the smile on Khol's face set internal alarm bells going off inside of me.

And then I knew—it was a trap. "Bryn!" I screamed. "Get out of here! He wanted you to come for me!" I pulled away from Khol, whose grip had loosened, and I ducked under his arm, swiveling to his left to dash for Bryn. But before I could even get two steps, his arms snaked out and restrained me around my waist. "Bryn!" I gasped, drinking him in with my eyes. He seemed bigger—more muscular than I remembered, even though it really hadn't been that long since I'd seen him. He also seemed years older, his face set with grim determination as he looked at me. And his eyes—his eyes glowed an eerie blue that confirmed the fact that he was indeed Dragon—just like I had thought. The one thing that hadn't changed though was that he was mine. My whole body yearned to be in his arms with everything in it. It felt quite possible that I would die right there if I couldn't reach him soon. Bryn's face told me he felt the same way as he stepped towards me and reached out his arms for me. "Let me go!" I screeched, clawing at Khol's arms. "Bryn!"

"Bind him," Khol commanded, just before three Dragons appeared behind Bryn with chains. Before I knew what was happening, Bryn's arms were shackled by two of the Dragons even as the third struggled to put a neck shackle on him.

"Peej!" Bryn roared, and I renewed my fight against Khol, reaching my hand back and raking it down his cheek. His blood burned my fingertips, but I didn't care; I had to get to Bryn.

Khol slid his grip from my waist to my arms, holding them behind my back. "Stop fighting me or he dies." I instantly stilled, knowing Khol wasn't bluffing.

"Bryn," I whispered as I locked gazes with him as he was forced to his knees by the three Dragons that held his chains. Having to see him that way caused hot, angry tears to flow down my cheeks. "You never intended on raping me. You just wanted me to believe it so I'd call out to him. It was all a trap."

"Yes. I couldn't leave to chance when he would come for you . He's young, his powers are just developing, and without such a motivator, he might not have been able to do what he just did." Confusion washed over Bryn's face with Khol's words. "He shifted right to you when you called out to him. He felt your bond was in danger, and the Dragon in him knew he had to get to you."

"Dragon?" Bryn's full lips shaped the word in surprise.

"He doesn't even know what he is. He probably hasn't even had time to process what happened. He reacted instinctually, which was what I was hoping for."

"What do you want with him?" I waited for Khol's answer, and when it didn't come, I knew what he wasn't saying. I choked back a strangled cry so I could speak. "Don't hurt him. I'll do whatever you want. Just please don't hurt him," I said as I watched Bryn. He was my everything, my reason for living. He owned my heart, body, and soul. How could I either choose giving myself to Khol or letting Bryn die? Either way, I wouldn't get to be with him, and yet, at least if I gave myself to Khol, Bryn would get to live. There was some small comfort in knowing that my sacrifice would keep him alive.

Bryn must have seen something in my face because pain rolled over his. "No. Peej. Whatever it is, don't do it."

HIDDEN GATES

"I can't let you die!" I sobbed.

"It'll be like I'm dead anyways without you. Since I left, that's what it's felt like—like some part of me died because I couldn't be with you, couldn't see you. I'd rather die knowing it was for your freedom."

I looked away from him, no longer able to watch the pain on his beautiful face. "I could never let you die for me." I started to turn towards Khol, and he shifted his grip to allow me. I met his green eyes with hatred. "I said I'd do anything you want as long as you don't hurt him. But you have to give me your word that you won't harm him in any way."

Khol stared at me, blood from my scratches already dried on his face. "We will keep him prisoner until I claim you, and then he may go free. Not a minute before. It will be your choice for how long he remains here."

I raised my chin to look at him defiantly, "No. He goes free now."

"No. You agree to my deal or he dies now. There will be no other compromises. It goes against all my Dragon instincts to let him live at all." Khol ground his teeth together, and I sensed he was barely holding on to control. I knew in that moment if I wanted to keep Bryn alive, I couldn't try to push him any further.

"Okay. But not even one single strand on his head will be harmed. Your word." I held my breath, waiting to see how he'd respond.

"My word to you that I will hold him as my prisoner until you agree to let me claim you. At that time, he will be released with no permanent injuries to his body or powers." Khol continued to grind his teeth together. "That's as much as I can offer."

I nodded once tightly, knowing it was the best I was going to get for Bryn. "No, Peej. You can't. We'll find a way, I promise." I wanted to believe him, and a small part of me did, the part of me that still believed he could do anything—the part of me that still trusted him so completely that if he promised me something, that in itself would make it reality.

I didn't turn to look at Bryn for fear of my heart breaking into a million pieces. I would give myself to Khol as soon as possible, so they wouldn't have time to hurt him in any way. I hadn't missed what Khol had implied with his words: no permanent damage. That still left a lot on the table for them to torture him with. "Don't make promises you can't keep," Khol growled at Bryn. "Take him away."

Bryn howled my name as chains rattled from the strength of his fight, and still, I refused to look at him. Finally, when all was silent and I knew he was gone, I looked up at Khol and tried to put all the hatred that I now felt for him in my gaze. "I hate you," I said just as my head swam and I collapsed to the floor.

17

I awoke to Khol staring down at me. "I wish it didn't have to be this way." I sensed his words were sincere, and that made them that much worse.

"Bryn and I are meant to be together. We always have been." Raw agony ripped at my insides with the thought of really and truly losing Bryn, not just for a year but forever, and it made me begin to contemplate if it would be hard to take my own life. Maybe it was my only option for an escape. But then what would Khol do to Bryn after I was dead? I had no doubt he would kill him; therefore, I would have to gain Bryn's freedom first. And that would mean having to let Khol claim me. It was hard to believe that such a short time ago, a part of me had responded so feverishly to Khol's kisses, to his touch, when now the mere thought of his hands on me left me ice cold. Maybe it had something to do with the beginning of the *Anam Cara* mark from Bryn, or maybe the reality of possibly losing Bryn forever had finally hit home. I knew positively, without any doubts, I would never love anyone else the way that I loved him—he was my home—always had been and always would be.

"If you were meant to be with him, then you would end up with him, and I can assure you that won't be happening. You will be my *Anam Cara*, not his."

A strangled cry of frustration escaped from me. "Why?" I stared at Khol, looking for some kind of clue. "Why do you want me so desperately? It's not like you're in love with me, you can't be. Why not find some other nice lady Dragon and claim her so that I can be with Bryn?"

Khol reached his hand out to touch my face, and as I shrank back from him, a look of hurt flickered across his face before indifference settled there. "Do not pretend to know the depth of my feelings for you."

Reasoning with him obviously wasn't going to work. "I'll let you claim me, but I hope you know it'll still be rape because I'll only be doing it for Bryn, and I'll be thinking of him the whole time."

Anger sparked to life in Khol's eyes, and he roughly grabbed me by the side of my face. "Watch what you say to me, my little Seer," he snarled, pressing his lips to mine and thrusting his tongue into my mouth with force before pulling back to stare at me, his face mere inches from mine. "You do not wish for me to show you the real meaning of the word rape. You would be wise to remember that I'm not human, and I'm only trying to observe human rules for your sake."

And then I did something really stupid: I reached back and smacked him across the face with as much strength as I was capable of, which wasn't much, but enough to leave a red mark. The sound of my hand hitting his face seemed to echo inside the large room. "I'm not entirely human either," I hissed without flinching away from him. I was fully prepared for him to retaliate in some way, whether it be hitting me or forcing himself on me further, but to my surprise, he rose and stalked across the length of the room, disappearing before he reached the door.

HIDDEN GATES

I exhaled a breath I hadn't realized I was holding. I had to trust in the fact that Khol had promised not to harm Bryn, so he wouldn't suffer for what I'd just done, although I felt sure that eventually I would. Khol may not have retaliated immediately, but I knew it wasn't the smartest thing in the world to antagonize him. After all, he wasn't human, as he had just reminded me.

I paced the room, strung out from my nerves. I wanted to see Bryn, talk to him, and make sure they were treating him decently, although I didn't think I'd be able to look him in the eyes knowing what I was going to do with Khol. I knew I should be worrying more about the alien infestation problem our world was suffering from, but how could I do that when my entire future hung in the balance?

My mind kept conjuring up images from me and Bryn's shared past—all the birthdays we'd had together, all the nights we'd platonically slept in each other's arms, and of course, when we'd first crossed that line, becoming more than friends. I wished I would have known at the time that those few moments I'd spent in Bryn's arms, letting him love me, would probably be the last I would ever have. Maybe I would have been able to make them last longer, drawn them out somehow. If only I could have figured out my true feelings for him sooner, we could have had so much more time together.

"Khol!" I yelled. "Just let me see him! Please! Don't cut me off from him completely!" If he cared for me at all, maybe he'd give in. He had to be sensing the anguish his actions were causing me. "I love him!" I cried out in agony. Probably not the best thing to say, but it was the truth.

Khol appeared, his face indifferent as he looked at me with his illuminated green eyes that were filled with something I couldn't read. "You know I can't let you do that. Not until after I've claimed you."

"Why are you doing this to me?" I went to him, dropping on my knees before him, ready to beg with everything I had in me to be able to see Bryn just one more time before he was ripped away from me—again.

"You're pleading is pointless. I won't give you what you want." His voice was flat, devoid of all emotion.

"Why? Why are you doing this?" I asked again. I still couldn't understand his true motivations. Why me?

"Dragons don't fall in love like humans. It's not the same." Khol's eyes flicked away from me as he spoke. "When a male Dragon falls in love, it happens fast, and it's forever. He will do anything to be with her, even fight to the death to possess her, and for that reason it doesn't work that way for female Dragons, because some of her suitors could be killed off. Her bond doesn't become eternal until an actual *Anam Cara* mark is placed upon her."

"And what happens after the female bonds with one of her suitors? I mean, what happens to the male Dragons who live but didn't get her?" I had to know what would happen to Bryn.

"They continue to love her, but they accept that she's out of their reach. Most of the time, they enter her service in some way in order to simply remain close to her."

"So they never bond with anyone else? They never fall in love with anyone else?"

"No."

"That can't be true—I mean Macon—I mean, he was with Jenna and—" I couldn't gather my thoughts properly.

"It's true that Macon would have taken you up on your oh so kind offer." Khol's jaw ticked with tension. "And he would have welcomed the chance to claim you for his *Anam Cara* because of your power, amongst other things, but—" He dropped to his knees so he could look into my eyes from the same vantage point. "He doesn't love you. He doesn't love you like I do."

HIDDEN GATES

I stared at Khol, unable to speak. If what he had just told me was true, then I could almost understand why he was being so ruthless in order to get Bryn out of his way. Because he loved me, it was either claim me for his, or live out the rest of his days loving me from afar, never being able to have me. So instead, he was dooming Bryn to that fate. "How can you love me? You practically just met me," I finally managed to squeak out.

Khol smiled. "What's not to love? You are unlike anyone I've ever met in my very long existence. My heart had no shields strong enough to keep you out. I knew I wanted you from almost the first moment I laid eyes on you when you awakened me from my slumber." He stood and walked away, talking with his back to me. "I was willing to wait. I was willing to honor your human side, for I knew your Dragon side would come to crave more, and then I would make you mine. And it was happening; I felt your willpower to resist me weakening, despite everything else. But finding out that Bryn is part Black Dragon changed everything."

"It changed everything for you, but nothing has really changed. It's been this way from the beginning. I've belonged to Bryn since I was five years old. He's my home." I put all the pleading that I could into my voice.

"*I* will be your home. *I* will be your everything. That's what it will mean to have me as your *Anam Cara*. Don't think I haven't picked up what you're feeling for him. I know your love for him is real, not the human puppy love your family all believes it to be." The tension in Khol's body was evident in his shoulders and back as he gripped his hands together so tightly his knuckles started to turn white. "And I want that. I want you to feel that way about me." He whirled around to face me again, his expression half crazed, at least by human standards. "And you will. You will feel that way about me."

"No. It doesn't work that way. You can't make me love you."

His voice softened, and his face filled with longing as he looked at me. "You'll eventually come to love me because it's in your nature. You must be in love, you must feel that kind of passion. And it'll be easier for you to give in to those feelings once you're my *Anam Cara*." He dropped down in front of me. "I never thought it was possible for me to feel this way about anyone. I would give you the world. I would do anything for you—except for one thing."

My voice cracked. "Let me be with Bryn." Of course, that was the one thing I wanted more than anything.

"Yes. Except for that." Khol rose from his crouch and began to pace. "He isn't strong enough to protect you. He doesn't have enough resources to give you the lifestyle you deserve. He is lacking in almost every single category."

"I don't care about those things. He's who I want. He's who I've chosen. It's not fair for you to take my choice away from me." My voice began to climb octaves as it sometimes did when I was upset.

"It may not be fair, but it is the way of the Dragon, and you were both born into it."

"There's nothing I can say to change your mind then, nothing I can do?" I asked with hope in my voice, even though I knew what his answer would be.

"No. There is nothing."

"Can I see Jenna? Jeremy?"

"Not for now. I think it's best if you're left alone with your thoughts so you can figure things out for yourself without your friends' influence. After all, they will never understand—they are not Dragon." He stopped midstride in his pacing and glanced my way, not meeting my eyes. "I will not come to you again until you're ready for me to claim you. Call for Drake if you need anything. You can trust him." And with that, he vanished right before my eyes.

I was a bird in a gilded cage, or more accurately, a Dragon in a gilded cage. Drake brought me any meal I wanted to eat, any book I wanted to read, and any random object I told him I wanted. It was kind of amusing to request odd things just to see if he'd get them for me, but that also got old fast. I had my own private bathroom that had a huge claw-footed bathtub that I'd taken to luxuriating in, but even a girl like me could only take so much pampering before I thought I'd go out of my mind. I had no contact with the outside world at all, and the only person I saw was Drake. He didn't seem to like me very much though, probably because he'd figured out what I was doing with my odd request game, so he spent as little time with me as possible.

    I started to lose track of time, of how many days I'd been in my gilded prison, and it was tearing me up to know that Bryn was being held captive somewhere in the very same castle, and probably not with the same level of amenities. I knew what I needed to do to free him, but every time I thought I'd built up enough courage to call Khol to give him what he was waiting for, the words lodged themselves in my throat. The thought of being with Khol, of having sex with him, made me feel sick, especially when I'd be doing it with Bryn under the very same roof. The thought of suicide still weighed heavily on my mind, but the biggest problem with that plan was that I didn't really want to die. I was just looking for a way out. And I'd still have to let Khol claim me first to ensure that Bryn would be released. I'd gone over and over things in my mind, and I couldn't come up with any other option to save Bryn. I was going to have to give myself to Khol to free him. I just had one question first.

"Drake," I called, the massive Dragon appearing seconds after I summoned him.

"Yes." He looked at me disdainfully. "What can I do for you?"

"I just have a question for you and then you can go." He nodded once at me to let me know he was waiting for me to ask him. "Khol told me that once a male Dragon was in love, he would love her forever, even if she went on to bond with someone else. What happens if she dies?" He tilted his head inquisitively at me. "I mean, if something happened to me, would Khol continue to not desire anyone else, or would he be free to move on?" The real question was: would Bryn be free to move on?

"My Lord would be free to move on if you died, whether you were bonded to him or not, in theory. Although some *Anam Cara* pairs, if they're bonded for long enough, die of grief when one of them is killed."

"Oh, okay. Thanks. You can go now." Drake eyed me speculatively for another few moments before disappearing.

Suddenly lightheaded, I slid down to sit on the floor where I was. So Bryn would be free if I killed myself. He would be able to move on and love someone else someday, and even though the thought ripped at my chest, I knew I had to do that for him—I just had to. I wouldn't doom him to becoming some kind of servant for me. He deserved better than that. I had no other options. I would let Khol claim me so that I could guarantee Bryn's freedom, and then I would end my own life. I put my head in my hands and began to sob. I really, really didn't want to die. My life had just started. And who would help track down the aliens to stop them from taking over our world once I was gone? I stood abruptly and sniffled, wiping my tears away. None of that mattered, as long as Bryn got a chance at true happiness. Bryn would always be the most important thing in my life, and I would always do whatever necessary to protect him.

"Khol," I croaked. "Khol—I'm ready." *Am I really ready to die though? Can I really do this?*

Khol appeared in front of me only a few inches away, pushed me back onto the bed, and covered me with his body as he aggressively kissed me. He was obviously ready to get down to business, and maybe it was better that way, so I wouldn't have a chance to overthink things and lose my nerve.

My body immediately responded to his heated kisses, even as my heart froze like a block of ice inside my chest. As he tore at my clothes, I found myself arching up to meet him, wanting—at least physically—what he had to offer. Too soon, or not soon enough, we were both naked, and Khol was claiming parts of my body with his touch that I had sworn only Bryn would ever know. I clawed and bit at Khol, wanting to hurt him in some way as he rocked into me, hating and loving what he was doing to me at the same time. Things with him were different than they'd ever been with Bryn. There was no soul-deep feeling of connection. There was no feeling of being exactly where I belonged. All I felt was intense physical pleasure, which maybe would have been enough, if I didn't know what I was missing.

Intense heat seeped out of Khol and wrapped itself around me as the back of my neck started to burn. "You belong to me now," Khol growled as he looked down at me capturing my gaze. "Say it."

"Yes," I said on the tail end of a moan, wishing I could deny the words, but I felt it—I felt his magic burning me, branding me, making me his.

"And I'm yours. Say it."

"Yes. You're mine." And then I arched up one last time before I blacked out.

I let Khol claim me, I remembered as I slowly fought my way back to consciousness, and it left me empty—oh so empty. When I'd been with Bryn, I'd felt so good, so right, but being with Khol had been wrong—even if he had brought me pleasure. Maybe it wouldn't be as difficult as I thought to take my own life after letting Khol claim me. Had Bryn felt our connection breaking? Surely he had to have. What must he think of me now, knowing what I'd done to make that happen?

I blinked my eyes open to find that I was alone, no Khol to be found. Well, isn't that nice? He finally got what he wanted, and he didn't bother to stick around afterwards. I lurched from bed, stumbling towards the bathroom, not caring if I was naked or not. It didn't matter for what I was about to do. I shut and locked the door and started the water running for the bath. As the hot water filled the tub, I scanned the bathroom for options. My eyes stopped when they ran over a small hand mirror. I snatched it up and broke it on the counter, picking up the largest shard. *I have to do it—I have to do it now before I lose my courage.* I stepped into the tub, hardly noticing when the much too hot water practically scalded me, and sank down in the nearly full bath. I set the glass shard on the edge. When the water covered me up past my chest, I turned it off, picked up the shard, and leaned back in the tub.

I passed the glass shard back and forth between my hands, watching the lights glint menacingly off its surface. *I have to do it—there is no other way.* I refused to doom Bryn to a miserable life. My death would bring him happiness. Besides that, the emptiness that was eating at me already, knowing I could never have him again, was enough to make me want to end my life all in itself. But I wouldn't have done it for myself. I'd always thought suicide was the coward's way out, an easy escape from problems that would only make a person stronger if they stayed to face them. What would have happened if the hero of a story died before they had a chance to become who they were really meant to be? I never thought myself capable of doing such a thing, but then again, maybe I wasn't the hero of this story. I wanted to live—even now as I readied myself for death—I craved life. There was still so much to do, so much to experience, the good and the bad. I didn't want to die now. No—it wasn't time for selfish thoughts. This is for Bryn. *Everything is for Bryn.*

I held the glass tightly in my right hand, so tightly that I drew blood, just not from the right place . . . yet. I pressed the glass to my left wrist, making sure I cut deeply and quickly, barely able to grip it in my left hand to repeat the process on my right wrist. I just had to hope it was enough. Dropping the shard and sinking back into the tub, I closed my eyes and waited for death—my *death.*

"No!" Someone roared with outrage, but it was far away—much too far away—for me to care.

"Peej! How could you do this? How could you let this happen?" Another voice sounded from much too far away. "Save her!"

But I was just sleepy . . . too sleepy to care.

18

My eyes fluttered open to bright light shining on my face. *The sun*, it warmed and comforted me. I stretched as I yawned, sitting up in the middle of a pallet set up in the center of an immense garden. Strong, warm arms held me at my waist, and I looked down with a smile as I recognized the long masculine fingers and who they belonged to. "Bryn," I murmured, twisting around to see his sleeping face steeped in the brightness of the day. I stroked my fingers down his cheek and ran my hands through his silky mane of black hair. *I must be dead*, I mused, *for certainly waking up in Bryn's arms is heaven.*

Just then he stirred, his dark lashes cracking open to allow me to see his sea storm eyes churning with emotion. "Peej," he whispered in a rough voice as I suddenly found myself on my back with him pinning me down. His face became a mixture of anger and agony. "Don't you ever fucking do something like that again. Do you hear me?"

His fingers bit into my arms, and I wriggled against him. "I don't understand." My face furrowed with uncertainty, was

I dead or not? Because angry Bryn wasn't one I wanted in my own personal heaven. Maybe I should clarify. "I did it for you. Everything was for you."

"You tried to end your life for me? Why? Why would you think that's something I could live with?" Bryn growled.

Not dead then. I closed my eyes, not wanting to see his anger anymore. "I had to free you. I wasn't going to get you either way, so I at least wanted you to get a chance at happiness. Once I was dead, you would have been free to love someone else, bond with someone else."

Bryn shook me, causing my eyes to snap back open. "When did you get to be so stupid? Dead or alive, I'm never going to love anyone else." He continued shaking me until I felt sure my teeth were going to fall out, then he lifted me up and wrapped his arms around me. "Oh God, Peej, I'll never be able to erase that image from my mind—I thought you were dead."

"How am I not?" I whispered into his chest. "And where is Khol? Why is he letting us be together now?" My throat constricted with panic. If I wasn't dead, then that meant I was bonded with Khol. *No, no, no, no, no.*

"He healed you. He was releasing me when he felt something was wrong with you, and he brought me with him since he was touching me and he was in a panic."

I stiffened and pulled far enough back from Bryn to look up at him. "So, I'm still bonded with him?" I'd tried to kill myself all for nothing. I tore my body away from Bryn's grasp and stared down at my completely unmarred wrists. Something in me snapped, or maybe it had snapped a long time ago, and I'd never been the same. I started clawing at my wrists as I cried out in frustration. "You should have let me die!" I screeched hysterically.

"Stop," Bryn commanded as he grabbed my hands to keep me from hurting myself. "You're not bonded with him anymore. You were dead for a second, or near death—I don't really know which. But your soul left your body, breaking the *Anam Cara* magic. You're not bonded with either of us."

I met his gaze with hope. "So we can be together? Me and you, like it's supposed to be?" If he still wanted me after what I'd done—and I wasn't talking about the attempted suicide, I was talking about letting Khol claim me. I'd been with someone else besides him. Maybe he wouldn't want me anymore. "Unless . . . unless you don't want me anymore," I added with a shaky voice.

Bryn looked at me like I'd sprouted two heads. "Maybe you have lost it if you think that. Why would you think that?"

"Because I was with him—I let him—oh God—" I crumpled to the ground, unable to stop the sobs from wracking my body.

Bryn took me in his arms, enveloping me with his warmth. "That doesn't matter. I'll always love you no matter what happens. You didn't betray me on purpose. I know you never would."

"But I enjoyed it. It felt good," I croaked into his chest.

"I don't get it. Are you trying to talk me out of wanting to be with you?"

"You have the right to know. You need to know that you deserve someone better than a slut like me."

"What?" He pulled me back to look in my eyes with an incredulous expression. "You think that makes you a slut? Peej—don't you know that I could never want anyone but you? I love you unconditionally. Always."

Bryn's lips came crashing down on mine, and his tongue swept into my mouth with a mixture of his taste, and salt from my tears. My hands tangled in his hair as I struggled to get closer to him. *Home*, he was my home. His hands ran over my body as if he was checking to make sure I was real before his motions changed into something with more intent. I wrapped myself around him, needing to feel his skin under my hands, needing to absorb the taste of him on my tongue. I hadn't really thought about what I was wearing, but when the cool air touched my heated skin as Bryn parted the front of my soft and fuzzy robe, I shuddered as goose bumps erupted all over me.

"Is it too soon? Do you want this?" Bryn paused before going any farther, hesitation evident in his voice and body language.

"Yes," I rasped as I pushed my bare skin up against his hands. "I need this—with you." What I left unsaid hung in the air between us. I needed Bryn, to have his touch wipe away the shameful feelings Khol's had left behind.

My words set Bryn's lips and hands into motion again, and I moaned with satisfaction. "I'll never let anyone else touch you again, I promise. You're mine." Bryn's vow seemed to wrap around me with his power in a cool caress, claiming what rightfully belonged to him. And then he made love to me, softly and slowly at first, and then faster as we were both swept away in our passions.

I scored my nails down his back and cried out his name before a feeling of ultimate possessiveness washed over me. I looked up at him, capturing in my sights his cerulean eyes that were currently glowing an electric blue, and made my claim. "You're my *Anam Cara*. No one will ever tear me away from you again." I knew it was the Dragon part of me jockeying for control, but I didn't care because all of me wanted him, and all of me *would have* him.

"Yes," Bryn rumbled as his pupils dilated, and he bowed his head to claim my lips again. Our powers rose up and twined around each other, becoming one. *It's perfect, all so perfect*, I thought as Bryn and I cried out our releases together and collapsed into each other's arms. We were one, as we were always meant to be, and nothing short of death could change that.

Bryn cradled me to his chest as he wrapped one arm around my waist while the other smoothed my hair back from my sweaty face. I had so many questions floating around in my head now that we were done getting reacquainted. Like where was Khol now, and why had he let Bryn claim me for his *Anam Cara* after all? Where were we for that matter? "Why did he let this happen now? After he fought so hard to have me himself?" I mused out loud.

"Maybe it would be better if I answered that for myself," Khol said with a sharp edge to his voice. I would think later about the fact that he still seemed to be able to read my mind somehow.

I rose quickly, refastening my robe, and Bryn wrapped his arms around my waist so I could face Khol with him at my back. "What are you doing here?" I asked nervously.

A bitter smile turned his lips up ever so slightly. "This is my land. I am free to go wherever I wish on my property."

"Why? Tell me why you let him claim me?" I figured it was time to cut right to the chase.

"I miscalculated how human your emotions are. I never thought you'd do"—he closed his eyes for a moment before looking at me again, his eyes dropping to my wrists—"what you did. And when you did, I realized I would never be able to have you for my own." The rest passed from him to me silently. It didn't need to be said out loud. In his way, he'd done exactly what I'd done for Bryn. He'd sacrificed himself for the happiness of the one he loved—me. My heart broke just a little for him.

"Thank you," I murmured, not knowing what else to say.

"I will protect you. You will stay here as planned, out of reach of the aliens."

"And Bryn?"

"He is your *Anam Cara* now. I can't expect you to stay and for him to not. We must regroup and gather our strength so that we can make our move against those creatures soon. The time for action is nearing. We can no longer wait on the sidelines." He turned as if to go and then looked back at me with sorrow in his glowing eyes. "I never meant—I never thought—please forgive me." His voice cracked, revealing some of the pain he was feeling about what I had tried to do.

"I forgive you." And I did. I wasn't sorry that I'd done what I'd done. It had led me back to Bryn after all, but I wasn't going to hold a grudge against Khol. Maybe he was too Dragon to fully understand what he was doing before, but at least he had righted the wrong.

"Thank you," he whispered just before he disappeared.

"Well, I don't forgive him," Bryn muttered under his breath.

"Bryn," I chastised, swatting him with my hand playfully. "He's not human."

"Yeah, and neither are we apparently." Bryn's face settled into hard planes as he no doubt thought of the betrayal from his parents that represented.

"At least we have each other, for real now." I wrapped my arms around his neck and stood on my tiptoes so I could reach his lips with mine.

Bryn scooped me up and settled on the ground with me in his lap. "This is all just a little surreal. I didn't even know Dragons existed."

"Yeah, me neither," I rasped against the skin of his neck as I darted my tongue out to taste him. Would I ever get enough of him? My whole body seemed to buzz in anticipation of his touch. I nibbled on his ear next, causing Bryn to fist my hair to hold me close.

HIDDEN GATES

"Oh God, Peej. Is it just my imagination or does everything feel better than before? Because I didn't think that was possible."

I had moved so that I was now straddling him, my ankles locked behind his back. "Khol said Dragons are insatiable, especially the females. He said we haven't even begun to experience the full scope of what it means to be Dragon yet, and now we're *Anam Caras*." I slid my hands over the hard expanse of his back. "And because we're *Anam Caras*." I nipped at his bottom lip, and his large hands dropped from my hair to cradle my bottom. "You're the only one who can give me what I need."

Bryn chuckled low in his chest. "I swear I've had dreams about you that began like this."

I stopped kissing him and raised my eyebrows. "Oh yeah, and how'd those dreams end up?"

He chuckled again, tugging at my robe. "I'm a guy, how do you think they ended up?"

It was my turn to laugh. "That's what I thought." I sobered as I studied his beautiful face, a face I'd known practically all of my life, and now a face I would know intimately for the rest of it. "I love you more than I can ever explain to you." My words were similar to ones Bryn had said to me the first night we had ever been together. "I would die for you."

I felt rather than heard a low growl erupt from his chest. "You almost did." He laid me back down on the pallet, and pulled my robe wide open to expose my naked skin to the warm afternoon, and yet I still shivered under his rapt gaze. "How the hell did I get to be so lucky?"

Warm liquid heat pooled in my middle, and despite having just been with him, it felt like it'd been an eternity since I'd felt his intimate touch. I met his illuminated cerulean eyes, which were still a slight shock to see, and reached out to him. "I need you," I rasped low. And he welcomed the invitation that my arms offered, staying in my embrace for the rest of the afternoon until the sun began to dip low behind the horizon.

"P.J.!" I heard Jenna yell excitedly, setting me in frenzied motion to cover Bryn and myself up. I so didn't want her to get a look at Bryn's goodies. They were for my eyes only.

"No. Not yet. I don't wanna deal with her yet." Bryn's grip around my waist tightened as he sleepily protested Jenna's arrival. "Let's pretend she's not here, and maybe she'll just go away." I harrumphed, knowing that wasn't likely to happen.

I stood in time to see Jenna and Jeremy running towards me. Bryn remained where he was, but with his hands propped under his head. He looked so relaxed and snuggly that I pouted at him, wishing I could just ignore Jenna and remain with him just awhile longer.

Jenna jumped up and threw her arms around me in a much too tight bear hug. "Oh my God! I was so worried! Macon told us what happened!" Her eyes flicked down to Bryn, and she tackled him next. "Bryn! I missed you!" A low growl rang out around us, and Jenna paused to look at me with horror. "Was that you, P.J.?"

"Just don't touch him right now, okay?" I didn't know why I was feeling so possessive and jealous. It really wasn't like me, and I knew Jenna didn't mean anything by what she'd just done. Maybe it was the *Anam Cara* thing, or maybe it was my Dragon side, or a combination of the two; but regardless, Bryn and I were going to have to find out what else being Dragon mates was going to mean for us.

Jenna stood and raised her hands into the air in mock surrender. "Touchy, touchy."

"So you're Bryn," Jeremy said with an undercurrent of hostility that made me grimace. Bryn didn't know yet

HIDDEN GATES

that I'd been hanging out with him, or that he'd kissed me. Maybe he wouldn't care now that we were mated—*yeah, right*. He'd probably want to beat Jeremy into a bloody pulp. How could I forget how he'd reacted when Jeremy and I had our first date? He was crazy with jealousy when I'd gone to see Jeremy that night, and he had barely begun to come into his Dragon powers. Or maybe his Dragon side is what drove him to be so jealous in the first place? I hadn't thought about that before.

Bryn stood abruptly, gaze locked onto Jeremy, his nostrils flaring as his eyes lit up again. The blanket that I had thrown over his middle to cover him up fell to the ground as he pulled on his pants.

"Damn," Jenna breathed as her eyes focused on Bryn's nether region. "No wonder you're in love with him. What, Khol didn't stack up? *And* he's part Dragon? You are so lucky."

I elbowed her in the side, causing her to grunt. "Keep your eyes to yourself. He's mine," I hissed. Yeah, I really had to get my jealously under control or we'd never be able to go into public again. *And the problem with that is?* A small voice inside me whispered.

"Yeah. I *am* Bryn. Who are you?" Bryn's menacing voice brought me back to the bigger problem at hand.

"Jeremy."

Bryn's gaze snapped to meet mine. "What the hell is he doing here?"

"I came to help protect P.J. We've gotten pretty close since you've been gone. Or hasn't she told you?" Jeremy said with a smile.

"She's mine," Bryn growled, and I stepped into his side, placing my hands on him. I could sense his Dragon moving closer to the surface, and I wasn't going to let him do something he'd regret, like kill Jeremy. Although with the current look on his face, I wasn't so sure he would ever come to regret it. *Geez*—Bryn and I both had gone our entire lives without knowing Dragons existed, let alone that we were half-bloods, and now we were both acting more Dragon than human. What was going on?

"Bryn," I whispered as I grabbed him by the side of his face and tugged him down so I could capture his mouth with mine. I pushed my tongue forcefully past his full lips, and it only took him a second to respond by pulling me into his body and fisting my hair. I couldn't help the moan that escaped from me as he tugged my neck back by my hair so his mouth could latch onto my throat. He nipped lightly as if to leave his mark, then he lifted me up so I could wrap my legs around his waist. His lips reclaimed mine ferociously. I forgot where we were and who we were with as I let my fresh lust for Bryn consume me completely.

I suddenly found myself back on the pallet with Bryn's body weight pinning me down. I spread my legs for him so he could settle into the cradle of my body I offered. He ground himself against my hot core, jean against bare skin, and I moaned at the delicious friction.

"Ahem," Jenna said demonstratively. "Don't mind us or anything."

Bryn and I both froze, our heads snapping in the direction of Jenna's voice. "Shit. I forgot they were here. How could I forget they were here?" Bryn's face flushed with embarrassment as he sat up slowly, carefully making sure everything of ours that should be covered actually was.

"You guys look seriously freaky with those glowing eyes," Jenna laughed.

I just wanted the ground to open up and swallow me whole. If Jenna hadn't said something, would Bryn and I have gotten down to business right in front of them? Well,

HIDDEN GATES

not that they would have stuck around—hopefully—but if they would have, for the sake of argument, would we have? My face heated as I realized the answer. "I-I'm so s-sorry," I stammered, unable to meet Jenna or Jeremy's eyes. "I just meant to distract him, and then—well, I guess we got a little carried away."

"Well, you definitely distracted everyone," Jeremy muttered bitterly.

"No one asked you," Bryn growled.

I placed my hand on his arm and met his eyes. "Bryn. I'm yours. Stop."

He shook his head as if trying to dislodge some random thought. "Yeah, I know, it's just I feel so possessive. I don't know what's going on with me."

"You're newly bonded *Anam Caras*," Macon, who appeared from nowhere causing Jenna's face to light up, stated dryly. As if that explained everything.

I raised my eyebrows questioningly at him. "And that's supposed to mean something to us?"

Macon shrugged. "Newly bonded *Anam Caras* act as if crazed for each other. But don't worry, it doesn't last forever, just a couple of decades."

My jaw dropped. "A couple of decades?" I squeaked with alarm. "So what you're saying is we shouldn't be allowed in public for a couple of decades, and then what? Do the feelings just go away?" The feelings of jealous possession could go away yesterday as far as I was concerned, but a little pang of sadness swept through me at the thought of losing some of the intensity between Bryn and me.

"No, from what I understand, the feelings never go away. You'll just get better at controlling them," Macon said with an amused smile. Maybe he could read what I was thinking from my face.

"Oh." I slipped my hand into Bryn's large warm one. I sighed in contentment as my body hummed in pleasure at the mere touch of him. It felt like we were completing a circuit.

"Great," I heard Jeremy mutter under his breath. I glared at him, wondering if he was spoiling for a fight. If he kept up with the little jibes, there would be no doubt that a battle between him and Bryn would erupt eventually.

I directed my attention back to Macon, choosing to ignore Jeremy and his annoying comments. "Is there anything else we should know about being new Dragon mates—I mean, *Anam Caras?*"

Macon's face turned pensive. "I'll have to think about it."

"Why can't there be some kind of introductory manual or something? You know, like for expecting mothers—*So you're going to be a newly bonded Anam Cara, what to expect the first few decades.*"

"I'll see what I can find," Macon said as his attention turned to Jenna. "I was looking for you."

She reached out to touch his arm while biting her bottom lip. "*Reeeally?*" She practically purred. "And why is that?"

He drew her to him, and she molded her body to his, wrapping her arms around his waist. "I think you know," he said with a lascivious smile.

She giggled. "Oh, you Dragons are so naughty."

"You know it," he growled low in his throat as they disappeared.

"Hey, get your asses back here!" I called with annoyance. "I wanted to talk to Jenna!" But I got no response except for another snarky remark from Jeremy.

"Could have fooled me. There seemed to be only one thing on your mind that you wanted to do, and it wasn't talking, and it definitely wasn't with Jenna."

"All right. That's about enough out of you," I snapped as I dropped Bryn's hand and stalked towards Jeremy. "I told you

HIDDEN GATES

from the beginning that we were never going to be anything more than friends." I narrowed my eyes at him. "I told you I loved Bryn."

Jeremy narrowed his deep brown eyes back at me. "But the chemistry we both felt when we kissed—you can't deny that was there."

"He kissed you?" Bryn growled from behind me. Damn, I was hoping to get the chance to tell him myself before Jeremy blew me out of the water. This was exactly what I'd hoped wouldn't happen.

I gulped nervously as I turned around to meet Bryn's angry face. His eyes were lit up like two flashlights. "I wanted to tell you—I was going to tell you. I didn't want you to find out like this."

Bryn's chest heaved with barely controlled rage. "Get out of here. Now. Get out of my sight."

"Me?" I asked as my body started to tremble. I knew it: bonded or not, he was pissed.

"No. Him."

"I'm not leaving you here with him like this." Jeremy crossed his arms over his chest stubbornly.

"Now!" Bryn bellowed, causing me to grimace.

"I said I wasn't—"

"Please, Jeremy. Just leave us to sort this out ourselves. He won't hurt me if that's what you're implying. He would die before he ever hurt me." Jeremy met my eyes with uncertainty. I could see he was ready to throw down with Bryn over this, and that was the last thing I wanted. "Please," I begged.

"Yeah, okay." Jeremy stalked off with tension emanating from every muscle in his body.

Bryn watched him go, not uttering a word, not moving until he was completely out of sight, and then he grabbed me and pulled me into him. "Tell me."

"There's not much to tell. He wouldn't take no for an answer, and he kissed me. End of story." I bit my lip as I studied him, hoping he wouldn't push the issue any farther.

"And?" *Crap.* Bryn knew me too well, he knew there was more to the story.

"And what?"

"And did you like it? *And* how many times did he kiss you? *And* did you kiss anybody else while I was gone?" Bryn's voice broke an octave lower than normal.

I flicked my gaze away from him, unable to meet his angry glare anymore. How would I feel if he had kissed other girls while he was away? My gut clenched. What if he had? "I couldn't help but like it. He used his Gatekeeper power on me. He can manipulate energies . . ." I let my voice trail off, hoping I wouldn't have to say any more.

Bryn's fingers bit into my lower back and shoulder. "What does that mean exactly?"

"I . . . umm . . . you know . . . when he kissed me the first time. Okay? Is that what you wanna hear?"

I could feel Bryn's body begin to tremble, and his voice came out as a low whisper. If I hadn't been so close to him, I wasn't sure I would have heard it. "Did you do anything else with him?"

"No," I squeaked.

He tipped my chin up with his fingers so I could look him in the eyes. He did it so slowly and so carefully that a wave of fear shot up my spine. "Who else?"

My eyes widened as I stared into Bryn's face. He was so different, he had changed so much, and I could feel his Dragon side was riding him hard at the moment, pushing to have complete control. I forced myself to remember that despite all that, he was still my Bryn, still the same Bryn that I'd known practically all of my life, and now he was my

HIDDEN GATES

Anam Cara. I had no reason to actually fear him. "Khol," I finally muttered.

"That's it? Anyone else?"

I started to get angry. "No. I didn't go around kissing everybody while you were gone, Bryn. I love you. I'm bonded with you. I tried to kill myself for you." I knew the last thing was a low blow and still so fresh, but it was the truth.

He released me and backed up a few steps. "God damn it, Peej. These feelings, I know they're not right, I'm trying to fight them, but—I just wanna throw you down on the ground right here and right now, and I wanna just—just—" He looked away from me, as if ashamed of what he was about to say.

"Just what?" I asked softly.

"I wanna take you so long and hard that you won't ever remember anybody else ever touching you other than me. Because there won't be any again." He growled the last part.

A thrill ran up my spine at his words. Sick, I know. I have issues. Or maybe I should say my Dragon side has issues. "Then do it," I whispered.

Bryn met my eyes with heat. "It won't be like it's been between us before."

I swallowed in anticipation. "I know. I want you to." And I did, I wanted him to do whatever he needed to do to me to make things right between us.

"You can't mean that," Bryn said the words with an undercurrent of hope. He wanted me to mean them, but didn't quite believe that I did.

I tugged my robe from my body and let it drop to the ground to pool around my feet. "I do." I trembled slightly in the cool night air as I waited for him to react. "Take me any way you want. I'm yours."

I realized Bryn's powers had gotten a major boost because he came to me almost as fast as Khol could move. He pushed me to the ground and flipped me over so I was flat on my stomach. I lay where he had pushed me, my breathing erratic, as I listened to him pull off his pants. Then he reached down and pulled my lower half up into the air, sliding into me as he held my neck down with one hand. He took me fast and hard, setting a blistering pace, and honestly, if it had been anyone else, it might have been degrading to let someone dominate me so much, but it was Bryn—*everything with him is different.* Always had been and always would be, and maybe that was the one good thing that had come out of being with Khol; I now had a way to compare exactly how different. "Mine," Bryn grunted from behind me.

"Yes," I managed to rasp. I wanted to belong to him completely and in every single way possible. Bryn branded me brutally, and I know most sane people would never label what we were doing as making love, but somehow, to me, it still was. My heart swelled that he loved me so much, that he wanted me so much he felt the need to take me in such a manner. And maybe I wasn't a sane person at all but a sane Dragon instead.

When we were finally both spent completely and I was almost hoarse from letting him know just how much I approved of this particular manner of lovemaking—not to mention what we'd done before—Bryn pulled me onto his chest and held me there tightly. I didn't protest, and merely fell asleep, content with the knowledge that I was exactly where I was always meant to be.

19

The next morning, Bryn and I walked happily back to Khol's castle hand in hand. It seemed like he was satisfied in the solidity of our relationship after marking his claim on me again and again late into the night. I wished we could have stayed in that garden for days, if not months, just enjoying each other's company, a step removed from all the problems that existed in our real lives. But I knew that was unrealistic, plus I really needed a shower, and I told Bryn there would be no more naked time until I got one. He begrudgingly agreed, and was mollified when I invited him to join me.

I glanced over at him and felt my heart speed up at the sight. Bryn was the most beautiful guy I'd ever laid eyes on in my life. The more he touched me, the more I craved him, and not just when we were being intimate; that was still a relatively new addition to our relationship. When I really thought about it, it had always been that way between us, since we were kids. There was a comfort in feeling his skin against mine, almost like a security blanket, and until it had been ripped away for awhile, I'd never realized just how important it was to me.

I hung back a few steps while our hands remained intertwined, trying to catch a glimpse of my Anam Cara mark on the back of his neck. Every time I saw it, a thrill shot through my veins. He was mine—well and truly mine.

"Are you trying to look at it again?" Bryn studied me with amusement in his dark blue eyes.

I smiled sheepishly at him. "I can't help it. Will you let me see it again, please?" I batted my eyelashes at him and bit my lip.

He groaned. "Alright, but this is the last time." He hunched over and bent his head forward as I released his hand and came to stand behind him.

I reached my right index finger up to trace it. My *Anam Cara* mark on him appeared nothing like his on me. It was a deep crimson red, shaped like a lopsided star. "This means you're mine," I whispered in awe.

Bryn spun me up in his arms, and I laughed. "We never needed those marks to know we belong to each other."

"And to think you once tried to resist me. Remember back when I first figured out my feelings for you, and you tried to shut me down?"

Bryn chuckled. "I was young and stupid. I thought you were too good for me."

I scrunched my face up at him. "Bryn, it wasn't that long ago. And what do you think now?"

"It seems like a lifetime ago though, doesn't it?" He kissed the tip of my nose before grabbing my hand and starting to walk again. "I still think you're too good for me, but I'm smart enough now to not look a gift horse in the mouth. If you wanna be with me, I'm not going to fight you."

"Yeah, whatever." Bryn was so out of my league in so many ways it wasn't even funny. I still couldn't figure out what he saw in me.

"You just don't see yourself very clearly."

HIDDEN GATES

"I see myself fine," I muttered, not wanting to talk about it anymore.

"Come on, seriously, Peej. We were born to be together, can't you see that? What were the chances of us both being half-blooded Dragons and meeting the way we did? It was meant to be, and that's all there is to it. Plus we're bonded now; it puts a whole new meaning to the words *till death do us part*." I didn't say anything else because I couldn't disagree with him. The oddities surrounding us were too much to not believe that fate had brought us together.

I sighed, thinking about all the problems we were going to have to face in the real world—and soon. "What are we going to do about our families? School? Those alien things? Everything is such a mess, Bryn."

"It could be worse. You could be bonded to Khol, or . . ." His words trailed off and his face tensed, obviously thinking about my suicide attempt. "Have you had any more visions? About those things?"

"No. Don't you think I would've said something? That's not exactly info I would keep to myself."

"Huh," Bryn grunted.

"What? It's not like I get visions on a regular basis . . ." I trailed off as I studied Bryn's face. "Tell me what you're thinking."

"It's probably nothing, but ever since I got here, I've been feeling more . . . Dragon and less Guardian. And now you tell me you haven't had any more visions with all that's going on, factor in your much more Dragon tendencies and . . ." He looked at me as if I should know where he was going with his current train of thought; I didn't.

"And?" I prodded.

"Alright, it might sound stupid, but I feel like this place is stifling our Seer and Guardian sides for some reason."

"That just doesn't make any sense though, I mean, it's not like . . ." I got a sick feeling in the pit of my stomach "Maybe we should talk to Khol."

Bryn grunted his disapproval. "I don't trust him."

"You have no reason not to. He's never lied, and he's been totally upfront about himself and his motivations since I first met him. Besides, if he wanted to keep me from bonding with you, he could have." Bryn didn't say anything in response but instead chose to glare at me. I, in turn, chose to glare right back at him for being utterly ridiculous. "Well, I'm going to talk to him whether you like it or not."

"I'm not going to let you talk to him alone."

"Fine. Whatever." I wasn't about to have this argument with Bryn right now. He had nothing to worry about with Khol. Bryn and I were bonded, and Khol had saved my life; what was the big deal? Okay, so maybe the fact that I'd slept with Khol was kind of a big deal, especially because it sort of wasn't my choice, not rape exactly, but not one hundred percent my call either, but with everything that happened after . . . Well, I was willing to try and forget about it at least. But it wasn't like it would hurt to have Bryn present for the conversation. Besides, the thought of being separated from him for even a couple minutes at the moment seemed like torture. "Khol," I called. "Hey, Khol, we need to talk to you, please." Being polite never hurt anyone.

Instead of Khol, Drake appeared. "Yes, what can I do for you?" he asked with an undertone of sarcasm. Boy, he really didn't like me. So why hadn't Khol come?

"Where's Khol? I need to talk to him. No offense," I added, trying to be nice, not that I cared all that much. I knew there was little hope of changing Drake's opinion of me now.

"He is . . . indisposed at the moment. Unless it's an emergency—"

HIDDEN GATES

"No, no emergency. I was just hoping to talk to him about some stuff. When's he going to be un-indisposed?" I asked.

Drake smiled at me condescendingly. "It could be some time. He is currently occupied with a guest—of the female persuasion."

"Oh." My cheeks heated. "But I thought—well, I thought..." I knew our bond was broken, but I thought it might take Khol more than five minutes to get over being in love with me. *Hello... blow to the ego.*

"Oh, yes, that." Drake met my eyes knowingly. "He will love you and desire you until the end of time, but he knows you are out of his reach now. So he will try to forget you the best way he can. Pointless, really, but he has little choice."

"I don't understand." Or maybe I didn't want to.

"Oh, come on, Peej, he's trying to forget you by burying himself in some other female Dragon," Bryn said with disgust.

I shook my head in dismay. "Yeah, okay, but won't he bond with her then? And if he bonds with her—nevermind, I don't wanna know anymore." I obviously didn't understand the Dragon mating process as much as I had thought.

Drake's eyes lit up as he looked at me with unmasked hostility. "But maybe you should know. Maybe you should know what he sacrificed for your... happiness." He raked his disapproving gaze over Bryn before meeting my eyes again. "He'll never be able to bond, never be able to love another, and he'll never father a child. He'll be able to desire other women, have intimate relations with them, but it won't be the same. It'll be sex, and sex only, for the rest of his very long life. Yes, the *Anam Cara* bond is broken, but a male Dragon loves forever. If only he hadn't fallen in love with you, and merely wished to claim you for your power, then he would have lost nothing. Or if you would have stayed dead. But we all know that isn't the case." My heart clenched in my chest as I thought about what it would really mean for Khol, but what could I do? Both Khol and Bryn would have been completely free if my suicide attempt had been successful. I thought that since my attempt had broken the *Anam Cara* bond, it had broken everything else. Apparently I had been wrong.

Bryn growled beside me. "It's not her fault Khol fell in love with someone that didn't belong to him. She's been mine since way before he came into the picture."

Drake growled back, his body tensing as he stared down Bryn. "You don't deserve her. You are no match for my Lord. It shouldn't matter that she is part human. He won her fair and square by the way of the Dragon, and he should not have let you have her."

"Hey!" I said as my blood began to boil with anger. "Stop talking about me like I'm some property to be claimed or inherited and fought over. I chose Bryn. Besides, you don't even like me. I would think you'd be ecstatic that Khol didn't get stuck with me."

"It makes no difference if I care for you or not, only that my Lord does. I would have served you regardless. What you did—we would have all been better off if he hadn't saved you."

"Don't talk to her that way," Bryn said through clenched teeth.

Drake smirked at Bryn. "Or what? What are you going to do about it, little Dragon? You're too young and too weak to play this game with me."

Bryn growled low in his throat, eyes blazing bright, as he stalked towards Drake, who didn't seemed alarmed in the least. "I'll make you regret that you said that."

I clutched at Bryn, but he shirked me off as if I were nothing. "Bryn, please."

HIDDEN GATES

"You should listen to your little *Anam Cara*. Maybe she's not as stupid as she seems," Drake said scornfully while still wearing his smirk.

"Hey," I exclaimed, "I'm not stupid."

"Then you would have stayed bonded with my Lord," Drake spat, "and not have chosen this baby Dragon."

A red haze seemed to drop down over my vision, and a growl erupted from my chest. How dare he insult Bryn again and again. He had no right. I charged at Drake, my hands stretched out towards him instinctually, and then before I had a chance to really process what was going on, Drake was engulfed in flames—flames that were coming from my palms. I stopped and stared as Drake dropped to his knees screaming out in pain, and yet I had no control over what was happening with my body, the flames kept on coming.

"No," I heard Khol say as he stepped in front of the flames drawing the fire into his own palms. "Control your Anam Cara," Khol snarled at Bryn.

"I don't know what to do," Bryn snapped with alarm. "Tell me what to do."

"There's no time for that." Khol stepped forward, absorbing my flames into him as he moved closer and closer until finally he reached out and interlocked his hands with mine. It felt like he was drawing out my power, sucking it away, and I suddenly dropped to my knees, weak and dizzy. My eyes fluttered shut, and someone caught me before I hit the ground.

"What did you do to her?" I heard Bryn demand. "Give her to me."

"I did what needed to be done to save Drake. She could have killed him," Khol snarled. "Follow me inside. I'll restore what I took, but not here."

"Wait," I heard Bryn say before I sensed we were inside. Khol must have just shifted us there.

"I don't feel good," I mumbled into Khol's chest. "What did you do to me?"

"I'm sorry, my little Seer, so sorry I had to do that to you, but you'll feel better soon, I promise." Khol's voice had lost all its harshness as he whispered tenderly to me.

"That's her, isn't it? I can tell by the way you're looking at her. What is she doing here?" A female voice I didn't recognize demanded with scorn.

"Leave. I don't want you here anymore," Khol responded, cold as ice.

"But—but—I at least thought—"

"You thought what? You're Dragon, you should know better. Now leave before I throw you out."

Even though I was physically weak, my mind was still reeling. Was the woman that Khol was currently speaking to the one that he'd been *occupied* with? I was almost one hundred percent sure from how they were talking that she was, and he was just going to kick her out like that? *Wow, what an asshole.*

"I'll remember this, *my Lord*," the woman hissed.

"See that you do, so next time you'll remember your place."

"She's not even full-blooded, and she's a child. How could you want her over me? In fact, how could you want her at all?" The women's voice suddenly took on the tone of a petulant child.

"The heart wants what the heart wants," Khol muttered. "Now get out. I don't owe you any explanations, Shannon."

"You're an asshole," I managed to say in a normal tone, my eyelids still too heavy to lift. "You can't just use someone and throw them away like that." I felt outraged for Shannon. Women need to stick together instead of fighting like they usually do.

She laughed darkly. "Maybe I do like her after all, even if she is a naïve child."

HIDDEN GATES

"I'm not either of those things," I grunted with annoyance as another wave of dizziness slammed into me. "I just don't feel good."

"Well, I'm leaving," Shannon said just before the door slammed. Couldn't she shift, or was she just being dramatic? I'd probably never know.

Khol lay me down on the bed, which despite my current physical condition, got an instant reaction out of me. My eyes fluttered open even though I couldn't quite focus as I clutched at him. "Ew! No! Don't put me down on used sex sheets! Someone else's used sex sheets!" I'd have to burn my skin off. Good thing I could now probably do that.

Khol pushed me back down because I was about as strong as a newborn baby. "We didn't have sex in the bed, so don't concern yourself."

"Oh." I let myself settle back down.

"Now, let me give you back what I took before Bryn comes storming in here."

"Why didn't you just—" My words were cut off as Khol's lips pressed to mine as he exhaled into my mouth. His breath was warm and sweet with a tang of power that swam onto my tongue and down my throat, wrapping itself around my core. My eyes snapped open with the sudden energy boost, and I sat straight up in bed as Khol broke contact with me. I met his heated gaze with wonder. "Wow. What did you just do?"

"I gave you back the energy I took from you. You would have eventually regenerated it yourself, but it could have taken days." He stood and backed away from me, flicking his gaze to the side. "I'm not an asshole."

"What?" Was he going to try and defend himself now?

"Shannon is Dragon, and she knows what my situation means. She chose to be with me under no false pretenses."

"Really? That still doesn't mean you had to be so callus towards her. You were just plain mean." I grimaced as Khol slumped into himself at my words. For some reason I felt sorry for him.

The bedroom door suddenly flew open and a wild-eyed Bryn hurried through its frame. "Peej!" he exclaimed. I rose as quickly as I could and ran into his open arms. "You're fine now?" He murmured into my hair as his grip tightened around my waist.

"Yes," Khol answered for me. "I returned to her the energy I stole." He began pacing. "This is why young Dragons such as yourself don't usually find themselves with Anam Caras. It's your job to keep her under control. If I hadn't shown up when I did, Drake would be dead."

I gasped, horrified that I'd almost forgotten what I'd done to Drake. "But he's going to be okay now, right?"

"Yes. But no thanks to him," Khol spat in Bryn's direction.

"This isn't his fault," I hissed in Bryn's defense. "It's mine. I don't even know how I did that."

"You're just coming into your powers, strong emotions are normal triggers. What happened was normal, but what happened after was not." Khol continued pacing. He reminded me of a caged animal, like a tiger at a zoo.

"Tell me what I need to do, so it doesn't happen again," Bryn said softly. I looked up at him with surprise, not expecting him to accept the blame that Khol was trying to place on him.

"You'll need to train to do it and even then . . ." Khol met my eyes with some unknown emotion. "I'm not sure how long it'll take a Black Dragon to be able to do what I did."

"What do you mean?" I asked, not really sure I wanted the answer.

"You're a fire Dragon, all Red Dragons are, and it's our element to control. All Dragons have some fire, but not like us, and you're stronger than even I guessed."

HIDDEN GATES

I glanced back at Bryn before I met Khol's gaze again. "What does that mean exactly?" I swallowed to try and combat the dryness of my throat.

"It could take decades before he can do what I did today, if at all."

"But why? If all Dragons have fire?"

"Black Dragons are water Dragons, and I'm what you would call ancient. I have more power than most."

"Can't I just use water to douse her flame then?" Bryn asked with hope.

"No!" Khol exclaimed with alarm. "Promise me you'll never try. With the both of you being so new to your powers and so out of control, you could kill her."

"No. I'll never try," Bryn said as his arms slid around my waist again to pull me up against him.

"Where are all these Dragon powers coming from? I don't understand why they're just appearing all of a sudden. And I haven't had any visions since I've been here. Something's wrong; in fact, that's why I called Drake to us, because we wanted to talk to you about that."

"Yes. That is a problem," Khol said, his voice growing pensive. "I will admit, I've been a little . . . distracted. There are some things I hadn't taken into consideration when I brought you here." Bryn squeezed me once as if to say *I told you so*. I glared at him briefly before focusing back on what Khol was saying. "—the gates for your power. It would explain why your Dragon natures are emerging so fully here." I had a feeling both Bryn and I were wearing the same dumbfounded expression on our faces. Khol paused to study our reactions before continuing. "You might need to go back in order for your Seer gifts to work."

"But why would being here make that much of a difference? There are gates all over the world. I'm sure there's bound to be one close enough," I said, still a bit confused.

"We exist in your world and yet . . . not. Dragon magic helps to keep us concealed here. You simply may not be strong enough to receive visions through the barrier yet." Khol shrugged.

"So being cut off from our other sides has allowed the Dragon magic to be pushed to the forefront," Bryn stated as the pieces began to click into place.

Khol nodded. "Exactly."

"So what are we going to do?" Going back to all the problems I left behind seemed like a horrible idea, and yet I knew it was my responsibility to fight the alien creatures simply because I was the only one getting visions about them.

"We're going to have to go back, aren't we?" I asked even though I already knew the answer.

"I'm afraid so," Khol responded through gritted teeth.

Fabulous.

20

After a lot of discussion—okay, argument—it was decided that our little band of misfits; made up of myself, Bryn, Khol, Jeremy, Jenna, and Macon, who seemed unwilling to leave Jenna's side, were going to venture back to Pittsburgh. The primary goals were to see if I could get any helpful premonitions/visions and to see what had happened there since Khol had taken me on an involuntary vacation to Dragon Land. I had a sick feeling in the pit of my stomach that the fallout of my leaving was going to be more than I was going to be able to handle.

Khol and Macon shifted us into the quiet dark of my parents' backyard—funny how I had already stopped thinking of it as my own backyard. It was early evening, and yet my parents' house, along with all the neighboring houses, was silent and dark—uncharacteristically so. I swallowed the sudden rise of bile in my throat and slid my hand into Bryn's large warm one. "Something's not right," I whispered into the night.

"I don't sense anyone around," Khol muttered in response.

"I don't feel any weird energies though. That's something," Jeremy said with hope, although tension was still evident in his voice.

Dizziness swept through my head, and my vision blurred, just as pain abruptly tore through my skull, whisking me up and out of my body like every other time I'd had visions before. What I saw was like watching several different channels on T.V., but all at the same time. Most of it was too convoluted for me to make sense of except for one scene, one that threatened to rip my heart right out of my chest.

Cops wearing black S.W.A.T. gear battered in the front door of my parents' house, taking mine and Bryn's families by surprise. I was guessing they had been there discussing both of our disappearances. Bryn's father was the first to react with his superior Guardian reflexes and abilities, and then everything happened so fast, or maybe I just couldn't focus on it properly. In the end, both of our families were led out of the house in handcuffs. Bryn's father was bleeding from a bullet wound in his arm, but at least he was still alive. I then watched as every family in the neighborhood that had any Seers, Gatekeepers, Guardians, or Speakers in it, was taken away in much the same fashion. And I knew why there were targeted, why they were taken to who knows where: because of me. It was obvious the alien . . . riders felt threatened by the fact that I could see them and have visions about them, so they were trying to remove all of us. Until I had tried to interfere with the school shooting, my kind hadn't even registered on the Riders' radar, but now things had changed.

I slammed back into my body and found myself in Bryn's arms. He looked down at me, his face pinched with concern, and his eyes churned with dark emotion. "What did you see?"

HIDDEN GATES

"Nothing good," Khol answered for me. "Her visions were jumbled and more confusing than normal, but I was able to understand the gist of what she saw."

I fought the impulse to demand how Khol was still able to share my visions with me since I was bonded with Bryn, especially because a small part of me was glad for his deciphering help. I'd be damned if I had to figure it all out myself.

But Bryn wasn't above demanding answers from Khol. "How did you share her vision? If anyone should be sharing her visions, shouldn't it be her *Anam Cara*? Which is me."

Khol gave Bryn a feral smile. "Yes, well, it seems your *Anam Cara* bond doesn't translate out here where your Guardian and Seer sides take dominance."

"Hey, yeah," Jenna piped up. "Those tattoos are gone from your necks. Weird."

"What?" I exclaimed, twisting to try and see the back of Bryn's neck, which was now completely unmarked. I reached my right index finger up to trace the spot where it should have been. A sadness seeped into me despite everything else that was going on.

Bryn caught my hand and tipped my face back so he could look into my eyes. His voice went low and gruff as he spoke. "I told you before, the marks don't matter, and we don't need them to know we belong to each other." It was just with the marks, it somehow seemed to guarantee that we would be together. Without them, it felt like we were right back where we started.

I fought back tears that were welling in my eyes. Bryn was right, and besides, how shallow was I that I was worried about the lack of some stupid marks on the back of our necks when our families had essentially been kidnapped? I bit my lip and turned towards Khol. "Why were they taken? I mean, what reason was given for S.W.A.T. to take them? Obviously, it's the aliens that wanted them, but they came in using the police and government under the guise of something else—what was it?"

"Suspicion of plotting terrorist acts. They have fake intel, of course, that I'm sure also implies all the families here were part of a cult."

I felt Bryn tense, and for the second time since I'd known Jenna, she was temporarily rendered speechless. Jeremy spoke first. "Explain," he said.

"They took our families—those things, those alien riders—by using the government and law enforcement as their tools. And who would stop and question them? Once all of our kind are out of the way, there won't be anyone to stop them. They'll take over—they'll rule this world just like they did all the others before this one. Oh God—what do we do now?" I covered my face with my hands and slumped against Bryn. What could we do? Who was going to believe us? It was probably all over the news about the cult that was planning major terrorist activities. In fact, the whole situation could serve as a double whammy—they'd probably "find" all kinds of weapons that this cult had in their possession so the gun control legislation had a firmer platform to stand on. *"Oh no, you can't trust anyone, gun control is for your own safety, fellow Americans."* And then there would be nothing left to use to protect ourselves from our "protectors." "What do we do?" I mumbled into my hands.

"First things first." Khol took on an authoritative tone. "We need to get all of you out of here. Just because no one is here now, or spotted us yet, doesn't mean it's safe to be out in the open like this."

Macon strode forward, as if by silent command. "Where should we take them? P.J. needs to be able to get her visions but also be somewhere safe."

"Don't state the obvious," Khol snapped.

HIDDEN GATES

Macon bowed apologetically and averted his eyes. "I'm merely thinking out loud, my Lord."

Khol spoke as if Macon hadn't said anything. "We'll set up temporary quarters in the caves just outside the boundary line of the spells covering my land. My—" Khol stopped and eyed me warily. "P.J. will be able to get her visions, and you'll be safe there until we can figure out something better."

"We have to save them!" I exclaimed. "I'm not going back into hiding and leave them to fend for themselves. I'm the reason they were taken to begin with."

Bryn tightened his grip around me. "They're obviously being kept alive because of you—us. They'll probably offer them in some kind of exchange for you."

My eyes pricked with tears again. "Because of my visions." Yep, and to think just a short time ago, when I hadn't yet come into my Seer abilities, I had prayed and wished for visions to come to me. Now look at the trouble they had caused. "Be careful what you wish for" was really hitting home for me. "I wish I'd never started getting visions. I wish we could go back to the way it was before." I turned my head and buried my face in Bryn's chest, not wanting to deal with any of this.

"But then who would protect our world? Who would know the truth?" Bryn said gently before kissing the top of my head. "Ignorance isn't always bliss, Peej."

He was right. Of course, he was right. I knew in my heart if I actually had the chance to go back to the way things were before, I wouldn't take it. I simply wished things were actually as simple as I thought they were before, even though they never actually were anything but complicated.

"Let me just talk to some of my friends before we go," Jenna said over her shoulder before skulking off into the woods. By friends, I knew she meant of the local little furry persuasion.

"At least we have an entire team with us," Bryn muttered.

"Yeah, that's at least lucky," Jeremy agreed. "Maybe we should try contacting some of the other teams that are centered around the other gates. Surely they haven't been affected by all of this. Maybe the Riders don't even know about them yet."

"I'll send out some scouts," said Khol. "We'll know shortly who our allies really are."

Jenna came scurrying back to our little group with a grim look of determination on her face. "The good news is that my friends are able to see the Riders inside of people, too. That could come in handy in the future."

"Yes. We can use any help we can get." Khol bared his teeth in a mock smile. "Now let's get out of here before we're spotted."

"I kind of liked our other accommodations better," Jenna grumbled as she slumped down onto her makeshift bed that was nothing more than an air mattress with a bunch of blankets.

Macon smiled at her indulgently. "This is only for tonight, and then we'll figure out something better. I'll stay here with you."

"Yeah, yeah," Jenna muttered as Macon disappeared to probably get more unnecessary things for her. When he was gone, she scooted over to sit by me and rolled her eyes in exasperation. "I wish he would just give me a little space, you know?"

"You seemed really into him before. What happened?"

"He just wants sex all the time. I'll be lucky if he doesn't break me," Jenna said with a sigh.

I couldn't help but laugh. "Could it actually be true? Could you have actually met your match?" *Wow. Who would have thunk it?*

HIDDEN GATES

Jenna scrunched her face up at me with annoyance and flipped her rapidly fading rainbow hair over her shoulder. "I guess I never had a guy stay interested in me for so long." She glanced around to make sure Bryn, Jeremy, and Khol were still setting other things up around the cave and not paying attention to us, before leaning in to whisper, "What do you do with Bryn?"

"What do you mean?"

"You know—when he wants to get it on and you're not in the mood, or he wants to do something you're really not into?" She stared at me waiting for my answer.

"Well, Bryn and I haven't been having sex all that long, but—" Had I ever not been in the mood when Bryn wanted me? Had I ever not been into something he wanted to do to me? My cheeks reddened as I realized the truth. I didn't know if I could actually deny Bryn anything he wanted from me. He owned me in a way I wasn't sure I wanted to let anyone else know about. Of course, I knew in my heart that Bryn would never be able to deny me anything either—he was mine as much as I was his—but things like that are still hard to explain to an outside party. "B-but—" I stammered again. I didn't want to tell Jenna, but at the same time, with her Speaker abilities, she'd probably figure it out eventually and just be mad at me for not telling her to begin with. I really didn't need the headache. "But whenever and wherever Bryn wants it, I don't deny him. I just don't want to. I love him too much."

Shock played across her features. "So you're telling me that no matter what, you'd give him what he wanted?"

I thought about it for a second, just to make sure before answering. "Yeah, I guess that's exactly what I'm saying." When Jenna didn't say anything right away, I had the urge to explain more since it was already out there. "I love him. I mean, I love him with everything that I am. I would lay down my life for his. Hell, I almost did," I said, thinking about my botched suicide attempt.

Jenna started twirling a piece of her rainbow hair around her fingers, her eyes glazing over. "I wish I could find that."

Warmth bloomed in my chest as I thought about how lucky I was to have Bryn, and I, too, wished that someday Jenna would find with someone what I had with him. "Me, too. So Macon's not him? Even with his superior Dragon lover skills?"

Jenna flopped onto her back and exhaled loudly. "No, he's not him. Even with his superior Dragon lover skills." She sighed again, making me smile at her dramatics. "I wonder what's going on with our parents right now?"

I frowned, not wanting to think of the possibilities. In fact, I had been trying very hard not to think about that subject at all, hence why I had let her distract me with her sex talk without any of my usual complaints. "I think it's best not to contemplate the possibilities so we don't drive ourselves insane." I stood and walked over to where the boys were talking quietly to each other in harsh voices. My brows drew together as I strained to hear what they were saying, but as I got closer, they all shut up completely. "Hey," I said, knowing when people were trying to hide things from me. "What were you guys talking about?"

Secretive glances passed between the three of them before Bryn rose and gave me a tight-lipped smile. "Nothing you need to worry about." He reached out one of his large hands to snag mine, but I batted it away with annoyance.

"Don't think you can keep secrets from us and tell me it's nothing." I turned my suspicious glare on each of them in turn. "Now, who's going to tell me what you guys were whispering about just now?"

By this time Jenna had come up to stand beside me with an angry expression to match mine. "Yeah. No secrets. You guys better spill it before it gets ugly in here."

HIDDEN GATES

Khol stood, his eyes meeting my gaze. "It might be best if you didn't know for now."

"No," I said, bunching my fists into tight little balls. "No secrets."

Bryn glanced back at Khol and Jeremy, letting another guarded look pass between them before he nodded once tightly at me. "All right, it's just we didn't want to upset you any more."

"Stop stalling and tell us," Jenna exclaimed as she threw her hands in the air. I looked to Bryn, waiting for him to explain.

He cleared his throat and shifted nervously before he finally told us. "We're the last ones left," he blurted out. "The last complete team of Seer, Guardian, GateKeeper, and Speaker not in custody of some sort."

I blanched. There was no way I was hearing what I thought I was hearing—absolutely no way. "Holy shit," Jenna whispered beside me, obviously just as shocked as I was.

"It's true," Khol said. "My scouts just reported back to me. Those creatures—"

"You mean the Riders?" Jenna asked for clarification.

Khol tilted his head and looked at her. "Yes, the Riders, if that's what we're calling them now. They appear to have planted themselves in every major government in the world. They—"

"So it's all up to us?" I interrupted. My world tilted, and I clutched at Bryn for support. The full implications of what Khol was saying were finally sinking in. "We're the world's first and last hope—literally?" Bryn's warmth engulfed me as he wrapped his arms fully around me. "We haven't even graduated from high school yet, and it's up to us to save our entire world?" The cave grew silent as everyone thought about what was now fully resting on our shoulders.

How the hell were we going to pull this one off?

21

"It's just not fair," Jenna whined for the umpteenth time as she studied herself in the mirror before meeting my gaze in the reflection. Her deep brown eyes brimmed with unshed tears that she furiously batted back with her eyelashes. "I'm so plain now—just plain ugly." With that the dam broke, and wetness flowed down her face.

I struggled not to roll my eyes at her obvious pain and returned my attention to my own drastically altered image in the mirror. My long, silky, dark auburn locks had been shorn off into a short angled bob, the front longer than the back. I still had chunky pieces of auburn in my hair, but the majority of it was now a midnight black. "I'll trade you," I said with a sigh. Jenna's only response was a guttural sob.

"You look beautiful," Macon cooed to Jenna as he appeared and dropped down on his haunches in front of her. He lifted his arm to show her the offering of flowers that he had brought to cheer her up. "You'll never be plain; you just look more . . . natural now."

I grimaced at his choice of words. Clearly, just because Macon had been having sex with Jenna, didn't mean he knew her at all. "Natural?" Jenna stood and snatched the flowers from Macon's hands. "Who the hell wants to look natural?"

Unable to resist, I waved my hand in the air and scrunched up my face. "Umm. Hello? Me. I would love to have a shade of hair that looks like I could have been born with it. Not this"—I tugged at my black and red do for emphasis—"punk rock wet dream."

"My hair is brown," Jenna hissed at me. "It's the color of shit."

"You know what, Jenna? It actually is the best I've seen your hair since I've known you, but besides that—well—" I tried to clamp down on my anger the best that I could. "It's not about just us anymore. Do you think I want my hair to look like this? Do you think my self esteem is soaring when I look at myself in the mirror?" I breathed in and out a few times before continuing on. "Do you think I want to live in these caverns, even if they look like one of those home makeover shows got a hold of them? It's up to us to save our world, and if going through some unwanted makeovers—both in our appearance and living conditions—helps, then you're going to just have to suck it up."

"Easy for you to say, your hair doesn't look like shit—literally."

I threw my hands up in the air in utter exasperation. "I can't deal with you anymore right now," I said as I swiveled on my heel and stalked out of the room. Jenna was my best female friend, and there was a time when I probably would have been as distraught over my hair as she was hers, but . . . things had changed. *I had changed.*

I let my feet carry me blindly as my thoughts turned pensive. What if our efforts all turned out to be useless? What if my little band of misfits just didn't have what it took to defeat the alien riders that were trying to take over our world?

HIDDEN GATES

"I feel your worry, my little Seer." Khol's deep voice startled me from my internal list of worries—the *what ifs* of self doubt.

I looked up to see his large 6'7" frame leaning against a tree to the right of me, his dark auburn hair illuminated by the late afternoon sun making it blaze like fire. I decided to overlook his term of endearment for me because, after all, with me being bonded to Bryn, it had little meaning anymore—except to him maybe. "I really don't like that you can still feel my emotions. That shouldn't be happening with me being bonded to Bryn."

Khol pushed himself off the tree and strolled towards me, but I didn't miss the bitterness that showed from behind his glowing green eyes. "As if you have any idea what's normal or not with an *Anam Cara* Dragon pair." He let out a long deep sigh. "Besides, the two of you are hardly typical, neither of you being fully Dragon." He began to walk, and I followed behind him, a part of me wanting to comfort him. Khol was in love with me, and being fully Dragon meant he always would be—not my fault—but I wished it didn't have to be that way. I wished that he, too, could find true happiness like I had found with Bryn.

"I don't want your pity," Khol rasped harshly, turning to face me. "Never give me your pity." I stopped abruptly where I was and stared up into Khol's angry face. I knew the anger was simply covering his pain, so I wasn't frightened. I knew that he would never hurt me. He had already sacrificed his own happiness for my own when he let me take Bryn as a mate despite his prior claim. Even though it only took my attempted suicide to make him understand that I would do anything for Bryn, and that he stood no real chance.

"No pity," I said as I reached my hand up to touch his arm. "I just wish I could comfort you, make you feel better. I . . . regret the way things have turned out for you."

Khol shifted into my touch, and I felt him relax just a little. A sad smile turned up his lips slightly. "What I would need to be comforted, you would be unwilling to give."

I let my hand fall away from him. "No, you're right. I'm not willing to give you what would really make you feel better."

Khol's hand snaked out to grasp some of my hair between his fingers. "I'm glad you listened to me and left some red in your hair." He frowned as he watched my baby fine strands slip out of his grasp. "It's necessary to alter your appearance, but you still must hold on to the core of who you really are: a *Rua Arach*." I had the feeling he was talking about more than just my hair color. Had he been sensing some of the intrinsic changes that had been slowly taking place over the last couple of weeks? It was as if my hair was simply another symptom—a visible one—of my internal makeover. The old P.J. was too soft, too concerned with unimportant things. I had to become someone who could handle whatever my new life would throw my way.

It was then that Bryn appeared suddenly beside me, his dark blue eyes narrowing briefly at Khol before he swept me up in his arms with a laugh. "I think I finally got this teleporting thing down, Peej." His full, supple lips met mine, and I allowed his tongue to sweep in briefly to explore my mouth before I pulled away.

I met Khol's sad eyes, and I gave him a weak smile. "Don't worry, I wouldn't feel like me if I didn't have some red in my hair. I guess that's the Dragon side of me."

"Yes. Most likely," Khol responded flatly before popping out. I was no longer surprised when he did that, but it didn't make it any less rude. *At least say goodbye or something to let a girl know you're about to disappear. Geeze.*

"I don't like you being alone with him," Bryn grumbled.

Choosing to ignore Bryn's ever present jealously of Khol, I gave Bryn a genuine smile. "I'm so happy for you that you have the whole teleportation thing down." I stuck my lower lip out in an exaggerated pout. "But it's so not fair that I don't seem to be able to do that, not to mention your other abilities from your Guardian side."

"Nice aversion tactics, Peej. The queen of subtlety, as always."

"It's not like I care if you know what I'm doing. You're being ridiculous, and you should know it. It's just I'm not really in the mood to tell you that—again." I crossed my arms over my chest and glared at him.

He let out a loud, long, and pained sigh. "I just can't help feeling territorial around you with him. Blame it on my Dragon side. I don't know, even with knowing how things are, I still . . . Well, I still . . ." Bryn's voice trailed off as he let his eyes fill me in on what he couldn't say out loud. He still couldn't get the mental image of Khol and me in bed together out of his mind. He hadn't actually seen it with his own eyes, but we all know that sometimes what we imagine is so much worse than the truth.

"I—well, I—" What could I say that he didn't already know? I had let Khol claim me to save Bryn's life. Yes, it had brought me physical pleasure, but it had ripped my heart out in the process. Seeing the pain in my face, Bryn grimaced briefly before stepping forward to take me in his arms. "That wasn't fair. I'm sorry. I'll get over it. I love you too much not to."

I leaned back in the confines of Bryn's arms to study him. His was the face of a fallen angel, or what I imagined one might look like. Pale, flawless skin was drawn taut over high cheekbones, a perfectly sculpted straight nose hung over full supple lips, and his black hair all made him a study in contrasts. I'd known his face practically all of my life, and when I looked into it, I felt at home in every sense of the word. "I hate it, too, Bryn. I wish that I hadn't had to let him claim me to save your life—but I had no other choice. You know that." Tears that I hadn't known were forming spilled from my eyes and rolled down my cheeks. "I wish my number was still one." I choked back a sob as I thought about the fact that I could never again claim Bryn as my only lover. I wished for maybe the millionth time for that fact to be untrue, but I couldn't change the past, no matter how hard I wanted to.

Bryn buried his face in my hair and inhaled. "It doesn't matter. None of it does, not really. We're together now—*Anam Caras*—and we love each other. I hate that I let it get to me sometimes."

"No, Bryn, it's not your fault. I don't know how you do it. I would curl into a ball and die if the situation were reversed." I fisted his T-shirt in my hands and closed my eyes. "I kissed Khol and Jeremy while you were gone, I betrayed you in more ways than one . . ." Another sob stole the rest of my words. If I had found out he had done the same thing to me, I probably really would have curled into a ball and died.

Bryn squeezed me tighter to him. "Let's not think about any of that anymore. We're together now. Forget about the rest." He dipped his head to nip at my earlobe before nibbling on the side of my jaw. I exhaled all the tension I had been feeling and melted into his embrace. "I love you, Peej, more than anything."

"I love you, too," I murmured as Bryn's hands slid down my body to mold my languid form to his firm, hard one. I let myself luxuriate in the feeling of being surrounded by him for a few moments before pulling away. I met his eyes briefly before focusing over his shoulder, not wanting to get sucked in by the heat for me I saw in them. "We really don't have time for that now. We need to get back—" My words were swallowed by Bryn's fierce kiss, temporarily blanking my mind, which I'm sure was his goal. I moaned into his mouth as his large callused hands slipped under my sweater to skim my suddenly overheated skin.

HIDDEN GATES

"We have time," Bryn whispered hoarsely as he nibbled his way down my neck, causing white-hot heat to pool in my middle. Sometimes I hated how easy it was for him to manage me, even though I knew the reverse was also true.

"I'm so sick of seeing you guys groping each other everywhere I go. Can't you two be a little more considerate of the rest of us?" Jeremy's angry voice was like ice water being poured on me, and I wrenched away from Bryn's grasp. I looked up to see Jeremy's eyes glittering with dark jealousy and something else I couldn't read.

I flushed under his scrutinizing gaze. "I'm sorry," I croaked.

"Well, I'm not." Bryn pulled himself up to stand at his full height, which although wasn't as tall as Khol's, was a good deal greater than Jeremy's 6'1", not to mention Bryn's larger frame and muscles were more daunting as well. Jeremy was by no means a tiny or scrawny guy, but he certainly looked it standing near Bryn.

"Of course you're not," Jeremy said. "You're more than happy to rub it in all our faces that she's yours anytime you want."

"Hey!" I exclaimed indignantly. "That's not what this is all about."

"Like you'd be any different with her," Bryn growled as he took a step towards Jeremy who squared off with him, not intimidated at all.

"Why don't you give me a chance to be with her and we'll see."

"I don't share," Bryn's jaw turned to stone.

Did Jeremy realize how close to pummeling him Bryn really was? Did he realize how close *I* was to pummeling him for that matter? I strode forward and smacked him across the face with as much force as I could muster. His head snapped to the side before his startled brown eyes met mine. "Don't you ever talk about me like that again." I inhaled and exhaled deep shuddering breaths, trying to rein in my temper. Thank God we weren't in Khol's realm at the moment because Jeremy would have probably been toast—literally—from my Dragon fire gift. Even as it was, I felt my palms heat, ignited by my fury.

Fresh anger replaced Jeremy's surprise from me slapping him, and his lip curled up in a sneer. "If he would have stayed gone a little longer—"

"Don't say it." My voice vibrated with fury. "Don't you dare say it."

"—I would have gotten my chance to seduce you, too, and then maybe you would have made a different choice."

"It's not all about sex!" I screeched, my voice going up a few octaves. "You knew I loved Bryn from the beginning!"

"And yet you still kissed me—"

"You kissed *me*!"

"You enjoyed it. Or was your orgasm all for show? Imagine what I could have done if I actually touched you." Jeremy laughed darkly. "Khol got his shot, what about me?"

Images of Khol and I in bed together skittered across my brain, followed by what I had attempted to do right after—take my own life. The soul-deep agony that was still there but that I never let myself feel washed over me and pulled me under in one brutal wave. I dropped to my knees and screamed as flames erupted from my palms. They weren't anywhere close to the strength they had been when I had burned Drake, but I could feel the power to do more damage lurking just below the surface. And I didn't think I could control it any more than I had the first time. Bryn rushed forward, and I read the panic in his face as he reached for me. "Peej!" he exclaimed.

"No! Stop!" I croaked. "I don't wanna hurt you!" I met Bryn's eyes as he dropped his arms and let them fall helplessly at his sides. "Khol," I whispered. Before his name had completely

HIDDEN GATES

rolled off my tongue, Khol appeared in front of me and grasped my palms within his to draw away my flames. The sudden lack of heat and power caused my world to go dark around the edges, and I fell forward. Warm, strong arms caught me and scooped me up before everything went completely black.

22

"Why the hell do I have to be the one who keeps passing out?" I grumbled as my eyes fluttered open to a dimly lit room. I met Bryn's worry filled eyes and wondered why I still felt so tired. The last time Khol had siphoned off my power to control my fire, he had re-energized me shortly thereafter—*so what gives?* "Why am I still so tired?" I asked out loud.

"Khol was trying to teach me how to give you some of my power. He thought it would be a good way to learn the pull and push that I need to know to do what he does." Bryn looked away, his face falling into shadow. "But I'm not very good at it." He then stood abruptly, his back facing me. "I'm not very good at any of it."

"Hey," I said, pushing myself up onto my elbows with a grimace. Good thing Bryn was facing the other way or he would have felt worse at seeing how much I was struggling. "We're both new at this. And we wouldn't have to deal with all of this so soon if I could keep my temper under control."

"Maybe Khol was right. Maybe being with him was the best thing for you." Bryn's whispered words caused my heart to flutter.

"You don't mean that." He was just upset, I told myself. I sucked in a deep breath, trying to combat the feeling that my chest was going to cave in. "Don't ever say something like that." When he didn't move or respond, I began to shake. "Bryn?"

In a blur of motion, Bryn took me into his arms and dropped his face into my hair. His muffled voice rumbled low near my ear. "I'm sorry." He didn't say anything but continued to hold me tightly in his arms. Afraid to speak, I let him.

What was he thinking? Was he having regrets about being with me? Was I, with my newly emerging powers, too much for him to handle? "It's too late for buyer's remorse," I joked, trying to make my voice sound lighthearted. "You're kind of stuck with me because of the whole Dragon *Anam Cara* thing . . ." My voice trailed off as more self-doubts swirled around in my head. Ever since Bryn and I had left Khol's realm and our Dragon sides hadn't been dominating us, our *Anam Cara* marks had disappeared. We hadn't returned for fear of me missing out on an important vision, but the worry that out here—in the real world, so to speak—Bryn and I weren't really bonded was ever present in my mind. Maybe Bryn saw it as a way out, a loophole for him to back out of being with me. "Bryn?" His name seemed to hold all the questions I was unable to speak out loud.

"I would never let anyone else have you." Bryn's voice shook with strong emotion. "I love you. You know that. Always."

"But then—"

Bryn cut me off, obviously knowing where I was going with my line of questioning. "It just makes me sick that you have to rely on him for anything. I want to be the one who you turn to for everything. The fact that I can't take care of you kills me a little more every time something like today happens." I kneaded his shoulders where I could reach in an attempt to comfort him, but he pulled away and stood with his back to me again. "Some days I feel every bit the baby Dragon he thinks I am. And I hate it." I watched as Bryn's fists clenched and unclenched in frustration. "I need some time alone," Bryn muttered before popping out ala Khol style.

"Damn it!" I growled as I feebly punched the bed in my own frustration. "Not you, too now." It was annoying enough that Khol popped in and out all the time, but now Bryn seemed to be following suit with that unacceptable behavior. *Stupid Dragons!*

"They're killing the wolves!" Jenna exclaimed in a panic as she burst into the room brandishing her laptop. "We can't let them kill the wolves!"

"Okay, calm down. What are you talking about?"

"The government is letting people kill off the wolves in Idaho and Montana!" Jenna said in a rush. "I found info about it online!" She paused to inhale and exhale a few times, her face flushed with anxiety. "You know who it really is: the Riders! We can't let them do it! Oh my God, I can't breathe!" She gasped and clutched at her throat. "Can't breathe!" She started clawing at her throat as her breathing became short little gasps and her face flushed even more.

Holy shit! Was she having a panic attack or could she really not breathe? "Khol!" I cried out. "Khol!" Maybe with his healing abilities, he could help her. It was worth a shot anyways.

Both Khol and Macon appeared. Macon rushed to Jenna's side, worry creasing his brow. Khol turned his eyes to me. "What's the problem?" he asked calmly.

I waved my hands frantically in Jenna's general direction. "I think it's pretty self explanatory!"

"She's having a panic attack. They're not unheard of," Khol stated blandly.

I narrowed my eyes at him. "Well, can't you fix it or something, you know, with your healing powers?"

Khol frowned at me. "Since there isn't anything actually wrong with her physically, and since the panic is caused by her mind, there is nothing I can do. It will pass, and she'll be fine."

My gaze shifted to Jenna. Macon had scooped her up in his arms in an effort to comfort her. She was still gasping for air and babbling about us needing to save the wolves. "She says they're killing off the wolves—the Riders. What can we do?"

"We must pick our battles. Right now, the most pertinent problem on our hands is rescuing your families, or would you disagree?"

I swallowed at the sudden lump in my throat. As much as I wanted to help the wolves, I, of course wouldn't rate their lives above those of my family, and I didn't think Jenna would either. "No, I don't disagree," I whispered, almost ashamed to say the words out loud. Unfortunately, in a war there would always be casualties, and if I wasn't mistaken, we were technically at war with the Riders.

Khol nodded once tightly at me and then disappeared. "Yep, thanks for your help," I grumbled to myself.

"Don't worry, I'll take care of her," Macon said to me just before he disappeared with Jenna still in his arms.

I looked over to see Bryn standing perfectly still in the shadows cast by the slightly ajar door. I was beginning to wonder how long he had been standing there when he spoke. "And again you called to *him* for help," he said, his eyes dark with unfounded jealousy.

"I—well, I—" I started to stammer, emotionally steeling myself. I loved Bryn and had no reason to feel guilty for calling out to Khol for help. After all, Bryn didn't possess the healing capabilities that Khol did. "He has healing powers that you don't. I won't feel bad for asking for his help. He's a part of our team now, Bryn—get used to it."

HIDDEN GATES

Bryn ground his teeth together as he glared at me, his sea storm eyes raging with dark emotion. "Yeah, well, maybe you can ask for his help tonight to keep you warm." He swiveled on his heel and stalked away from me.

I remained paralyzed in shock for a few moments before I gave him chase. "Bryn! Wait!" I scurried to catch up to him, and when I did, I grabbed at his arm to stop him. "Bryn! What the hell is the matter with you today? Stop being so ridiculous!" I yelled at him with exasperation. "You have no reason to be jealous, so why are you?"

Bryn finally halted, exhaling loudly and slumping his shoulders. He stared at the ground in front of him for what seemed like an eternity before lifting his head to meet my eyes. "After everything . . . I still don't feel good enough to be with you sometimes."

My mouth opened and closed a few times, like a fish out of water, before I found my voice. "You can't be serious. I thought we were past that. If anything, you're too good to be with me." I still sometimes couldn't wrap my head around the fact that Bryn loved me. He was so perfect in every way, and well—I'm just me, enough said. How could we both think the other one was too good to be with us? Or was that just a part of being in love, putting the object of your affection up on a pedestal?

"Bryn," I tried again, this time reaching up to run my fingers through his shorter, spikier hair. A part of me mourned the loss of his longer locks, but just like the rest of us, I knew he had to change his appearance the best he could in case we were out in public and spotted by *Regs* on the lookout for the wanted and missing cult members' children. Thinking about how I missed his hair, I wondered if he thought I was as pretty with my new, shorter, punk rock style hair. "Do you still think I'm pretty?" I couldn't keep the words from spilling out of my mouth. Maybe I was just as bad as Jenna in my own way.

Bryn turned to regard me with a twinkle in his eyes that reminded me of the old carefree Bryn, the one from my childhood. "Just because you've gone all punk rock slash Emo on me doesn't mean I'd kick you out of my bed," he teased.

I punched him in the arm, which didn't even cause him to flinch. "Hey," I said self-consciously. "Don't be mean. It's not like I had much of a choice."

His face grew serious, and he reached up to touch my hair before cupping my face. "You'll always be beautiful to me, Peej, no matter what." I closed my eyes and sank into his hand. To have someone like Bryn love me, despite the utter mess I knew I was—how did I get to be so lucky?

"I love you," I murmured, opening my eyes to stare up into his beautiful face.

Bryn's hands moved down my back, and he pulled me closer to him. "I need you," he stated gruffly, his voice breaking an octave lower than normal. "Now."

His words ignited a wave of heat inside me that quickly spread throughout my body. I suddenly needed him now, too. But he didn't make a move. He just stood there looking down at me with enough heat in his eyes that I was almost afraid he would actually burn me. I bit my lip and pressed my body against the length of his, wrapping my arms around his neck. "So . . ." I prodded. When Bryn was in this kind of mood, I knew he liked to take charge, and I didn't mind at all, but if he didn't get a move on it soon, I was going to be the one tearing his clothes off.

"I want it—"

"Rough, I know. I've told you before, I'm yours—any way you want me." My voice came out low and sultry, which let him know exactly how okay I was with letting him take me any way he wanted.

HIDDEN GATES

Bryn's eyes glittered with pure male satisfaction, and without anymore preamble, he whirled me around and pushed me against the wall face first. I braced myself with my hands as he pulled down my pants and underwear all in one motion. A shiver ran down my spine as I stood there waiting, fully exposed to him. And then when he slid into me I called out his name and rocked back into him. The things he made me feel—not just physical pleasure, but emotional intimacy—I knew only he could give me. I'd only fully come to understand that after I'd been with Khol, and I wished I could make Bryn fully understand that as well, because if he did, he would never be jealous. It always felt like Bryn was making love to me even when he was being his most brutal.

"You're mine," he growled. "Never forget that."

"Never," I gasped out as my whole body shook with ecstasy. It was then that he leaned over and bit my neck in the general area of where neck meets shoulder. And I'm not talking about a love bite. I'm saying that he Bit. My. Neck. His teeth sunk in as he snarled his possession of me again upon my skin, and then I felt him find his own release.

When he finally pulled away from me and released my neck, I whirled around and glared at him. "That. Hurt," I said with annoyance as I brought my hand up to the tender spot on my neck and pulled it back again. It was covered in blood. I stared wide-eyed at the red liquid and then brought my gaze up to Bryn who looked almost . . . surprised. "You drew blood. What the hell, Bryn?"

"Yeah, I don't know what happened." He looked away sheepishly. "I'm sorry, Peej."

I pulled up my pants and stalked over to the small mirror that was hanging on the wall. I ground my teeth together when I saw the damage he had done. He'd bitten me so hard that I could clearly see where all his teeth had been, marked by bright red oozing out of the little indentations. "This better not scar," I said as I met his eyes in the reflection of the mirror. He had come to stand behind me, and his gaze then dropped down to his handiwork, a small smile tugging at his full lips. "Hey. That better not be a smile on your face, Mr. O'Bannon."

It was then he looked back up at me, and a full, patented smile, complete with dimples, spread across his face. "I don't know why, but"—he reached his forefinger down and lightly touched my wound—"this makes me happy."

"You can't be serious," I ground out, trying to keep my temper under control. Luckily for Bryn, my energy was so low I wouldn't accidently set him on fire, because I was that pissed at him in that moment.

He bit his lip in a vain attempt at containing his smile, but it only seemed that much brighter when it slipped his grip. "I can't help it. Something inside of me feels . . . happy that I bit you, and the thought of you scarring, well"—he looked away from me—"that makes me almost ecstatic."

I gaped at him. "You're kidding, right?"

"I wish I was," he muttered, running his hand through his hair.

"Yeah. I'm gonna go check on Jenna," I said as I stalked past Bryn towards the door. He didn't make any move to stop me and didn't say anything else. *Smart man.*

I swung out of our room and stomped down the hall towards Jenna and Macon's room. At least I hoped I was, I hadn't exactly memorized the lay of the land yet. *I'm probably going the wrong way.* I was so caught up in thoughts about why the hell Bryn had bitten me, that I almost ran face first into Khol's chest. "Oh," I muttered. "Didn't see you there." Why the hell was he standing smack dab in the middle of the hallway anyways? *Stupid Dragon.*

HIDDEN GATES

"His behavior is beginning to concern me," Khol said softly, worry etching his sculpted face.

"What are you talking about?" I asked, even though I had a feeling I knew exactly what he was talking about. I absentmindedly brought my hand up to touch the wound on my neck from Bryn's bite.

"I think you know what I'm referring to," Khol murmured as he brought his hand up to move mine off of my wound. "You should let me disinfect and bandage that. It could scar."

I frowned. "I think that's what he wants—for it to scar." I looked up to study Khol's face as his eyebrows arched up to practically skim his hairline.

"Did he say that? That he wants it to scar?"

"Yeah, actually he did. He said something inside of him felt *happy* that he had marked me, and that the thought of me scarring from it made him feel almost *ecstatic*."

Understanding passed over Khol's face before he schooled his features to appear neutral. "Mmm-hmm," was all he responded with.

"Oh, don't give me that. I know that you know what's going on now. I saw it in your face. You're not the only one good at reading people, Khol." I crossed my arms over my chest and glared up at him as his lips quirked up slightly at the corners.

"Very well. It seems that his Dragon side is struggling with the disappearance of your *Anam Cara* mark. He feels the need to mark you in some way—any way—to satisfy his Dragon half. We need to figure out a solution before his Dragon side loses control and he does something reckless."

A knot of worry twisted in my stomach. "Like what? What could he do?"

"Come." Khol motioned for me to follow him. "We will talk more as I dress your wound."

I brought my hand up instinctually to cover Bryn's mark on me. "No!" I exclaimed. "Just leave it alone." I couldn't fight back the unexplained panic that rose up in me at the thought of losing Bryn's mark.

Khol stopped short to study me, and I backed up a few steps while trying to get my breathing under control. "It appears your Dragon side is having some issues as well."

"No, it's not," I snapped. I was angry that Bryn had bitten and marked me, wasn't I? I mean, wasn't that why I had stormed out of our room to go check on Jenna to begin with?

Khol quirked one auburn eyebrow at me. "You could have fooled me."

I exhaled loudly and slumped in on myself. I supposed there was no point in trying to deny it. "Fine. Bryn and I are both having some . . . issues. So what do we do about it?"

"I don't know," Khol stated flatly.

"What do you mean you don't know?" My voice began to climb octaves. "You're like this ancient Dragon, so you have to have run across something like this before, right?"

"In actuality, I have never, in fact, run across a situation even remotely resembling your and Bryn's."

"What?" I asked incredulously. "How is that even possible?"

"Most half-blooded Dragons end up with full-blooded Dragons, and that pretty much solves the problem. With the two of you, only time will reveal the solution—if there is one." Khol turned his face away from me when he said the last part, causing my pulse to speed up.

"Explain," I squeaked.

"If you had remained bonded with . . . me for instance . . ." Khol paused long enough so I didn't miss the longing in his eyes. "Then my magic would have been strong enough to sustain the *Anam Cara* marks for the both of us, until and if yours matured enough to be up for the task. As it is now with the two of you, neither one of you has fully matured into your powers, and it appears that outside of my realm, your human magic is more dominant than your Dragon. It could take some time for them to balance out. In the meantime, the Dragons inside of you are struggling to clarify the *Anam Cara* bond. Out here, it's as if you haven't been fully bonded yet. It's why the marks didn't appear the first time you were together sexually, but only appeared when in my realm."

My heart was pounding in my head. "So theoretically, out here, our *Anam Cara* bond is still in danger."

"Yes."

"Oh." I gulped. "That means that some other Dragon could still force me to be his Dragon mate."

"I won't let that happen," Khol stated firmly as he stepped forward and tipped my chin back so he could look me full in the eyes. "You have chosen, and I won't let someone take that away from you."

"Take your hands off of her," Bryn growled from behind me. "I've heard about enough. I know what you're trying to do, and it won't work. She has chosen—and she belongs to me." Bryn seemed to take up more space than he normally did, and as I turned to face him, I swore that his eyes flashed a bright Dragon blue. It happened so quickly, I wasn't sure if I had imagined it.

"Bryn—Khol was just trying to help. He was—"

Bryn bore down on me, and when he was close enough, he swept me up in his arms. "He was trying to help himself to you is what he was trying to do," he snarled. "He was trying to take away my mark."

I looked up pleadingly into Bryn's face as he moved swiftly back towards our room with me in his arms. "Bryn, please." And that time when his eyes flashed bright Dragon blue, I was sure I wasn't imagining things. I swiveled my head around to peer at Khol over Bryn's shoulder, and when I turned my pleading eyes towards him, he took a step back and raised his hands as if to say he wasn't getting involved. I scowled at him, letting him know it was a little too late for that, but he simply shrugged and disappeared. *Typical.* "Bryn, you acting like this is completely unacceptable. I feel like you're dragging me back to your cave by my hair." I ground my teeth in anger when he didn't even dignify me with a response. I smacked at his chest. "Put me down. Now."

When we made it back to our room, Bryn deposited me gently on our bed and backed away from me slowly. His face was a mixture of anger and torment, making him appear much older than his eighteen years. "I'm sorry. Again." He spun around and punched the wall with all his might, causing bits of rock to rain down on him. "You just have to stay away from him—at least for now—until we get this figured out." His shoulders rose and fell as he tried to get his breathing under control. "It's just everytime I see you with him, I can't stop myself from losing it, Peej. I want to kill him. No joke—actually rip him limb from limb."

Much to my shame, I started to cry. Huge racking sobs tore at my body, and I curled into a ball and hugged myself in the middle of the bed. I was trying to be strong—really, I was—but everything was such a mess. Our families had been kidnapped by crazy aliens hellbent on taking over our world, we'd been forced to go into hiding and drop out of school, Bryn was acting like some sort of overly possessive caveman—I didn't know who I was any more. I was not currently acting like the new tough me that I so desperately wanted to be—and, and I hated my new hair! Things couldn't get much worse.

Bryn came and scooped up the little ball that was me and held me in his arms as he stroked my hair. "Things will get

HIDDEN GATES

better, I promise, Peej." He chuckled dryly. "Because they can't really get all that much worse."

"Bryn, we just don't have time to figure out all of our Dragon bullshit right now, not with everything else that's going on." I sobbed into his shirt.

"Yeah, I know," Bryn said reassuringly. "It'll work out. I swear it will." And yet the old feeling that I used to get that just because Bryn promised me something, it would come true wasn't there anymore. I knew he would do everything in his power to keep his promise to me, just like he always had, but somewhere along the line I had begun to doubt him. None of it was his fault—after all, he was human . . . mostly—I just wished I still believed anything was possible just because he said it was. I guess that meant I was growing up. *Growing up sucks.*

"Please do not tell me this weak sniveling *child* is the P.J. you chose over me." A girl's voice I didn't recognize asked sharply from the open door of our room.

"Nala?" Bryn said with surprise. "What the hell are you doing here?"

Why the hell do females keep referring to me as a child? I lifted my tearstained face from Bryn's shoulder and blinked away the blur from my eyes. I inhaled sharply and wiped at my face self-consciously because in our doorway stood a friggin' supermodel, or at least someone who looked like one. She was at least my height, if not taller, with the long, lean muscles of an athlete. She wore black leather pants that were molded to her body, and a matching black leather bustier. Her hair hung long, black, and silky halfway down her back, and her eyes were almost the same bright blue as Bryn's—except they glowed. *Dragon,* I realized belatedly. She was absolutely gorgeous, and if I wasn't mistaken, Bryn knew her. I turned my face questioningly towards his and saw that surprise was still the dominant emotion displayed on his, so I decided to take the lead, despite my current emotional breakdown.

"And you are?" I sat up and arched my brows at the girl.

She crossed her arms over her—yes, of course—more ample than my own bosom, and gave me a haughty sneer. "I don't have to answer to you. Bryn knows me."

I fought back the urge to say something snarky, and I turned back to Bryn instead. "Well?" I said with annoyance. "Care to fill me in on the random Dragon girl who seems to know *you* and that *I* don't know." He had to have met her when he was away. There was no other explanation. My stomach knotted at the thought. And then her words from when she first appeared came back to me ... "Bryn?" His name held all of my unspoken questions, and when I saw the look on his face I knew. *I just knew.* "Oh my God." I stood, and my hand fluttered to my mouth. "I told you—but you didn't tell me. *How could you not tell me?*"

"Peej." Bryn reached for me, anguish in his eyes—and guilt. There was definitely guilt there, too.

"You let me babble on and on about how awful I felt about what happened with Khol and Jeremy while you were away and—" That's when it fully dawned on me. With everything that had been going on, I had absolutely no idea what Bryn had been up to when he was away—hell, I didn't even know *where* he'd been. "And you just kept saying not to worry about it, that none of it mattered because we're together now." Anger began to course through my system. "Oh God—how could I be so stupid. You just didn't want to tell me what happened—or *who* happened while you were gone."

"Her hair isn't even really black, is it? She's not even a Black Dragon. What is she, Bryn?" The bitch Dragon's scornful voice sliced into my head like a red-hot poker. I whirled around and faced down the bitch who thought she was going to steal

HIDDEN GATES

Bryn from me. Sure, I was currently angrier than I ever had been with him, but who was I to call the kettle black? In the end, I didn't want anyone but him, and no stupid bimbo Black Dragon was going to lay one finger on him.

"I didn't even know what I was before—or her, or you. I just—"

"Shut up, Bryn," I hissed. I was, for the first time, mentally reaching for my fire, and even though I was still weak, I could feel it bubbling up inside of me. I was going to fry this bitch until there was nothing left of her. I was going to make her pay with her life for what she tried to do.

"Oh shit!" I heard the bitch exclaim just as I felt the flames burst to life in my palms.

"Peej, no!" Bryn exclaimed as he rushed towards me.

But before I could do any real damage, Khol appeared in front of me with a strange look on his face, and he grabbed my palms, essentially dousing all hopes of me killing the bitch Dragon. "What's going on?" he asked, much too calmly for my taste.

"Did you sleep with her?" I demanded of Bryn with a white-hot fury I'd never felt before. "*Did* you?" I belatedly realized I hadn't passed out after Khol had taken my flames. *Go me.* But I had little time for patting myself on the back. I needed answers from Bryn, and I needed them *now*.

"I would never—" Bryn started but was cut off by bitch Dragon's high-pitched voice.

"She's *red?!* She's a fucking *crazy* Red Dragon?"

"Are you actually standing there openly insulting me and my faction, when we both could strike you down with barely any effort at all?" Khol's voice was calm, but I could feel the anger rolling off of him in waves. "What are you even doing here? I don't recall issuing an invitation to any *Dubh Arachs*."

"I came for Bryn," bitch Dragon said, with false bravado because I could see the fear in her eyes.

"I don't want you here, Nala," Bryn said. "What happened between us didn't mean anything to me. I love P.J., and I always will."

"You don't love her. She's a Red Dragon—you're black." She tapped her leather-clad leg impatiently as if it explained everything.

"He's mine!" I screeched as I struggled to get to her, but Khol was a lot stronger than I ever hoped to be.

"Give her to me," Bryn growled at Khol as he stepped in to take me from him. His eyes flashed Dragon blue again, belying his true feelings.

"Don't touch me!" I hissed at Bryn, and even though I was still within the confines of Khol's arms, my flames were pushing to erupt from me again. I was that angry.

"It would be best if you left her to me for the time being," Khol informed Bryn.

But he wasn't having any of it. "I said to take your hands off of *my Anam Cara* and give her to *me*."

"*Anam Cara?*" Bitch Dragon said with shock. "I don't see any marks."

"It's complicated," Khol stated dryly.

"Maybe I should go—for now." Bitch Dragon eyed Bryn with a longing that set my blood on fire, which caused actual flames to burst up from my palms again.

"If you come anywhere near him, I'll burn you alive," I seethed. And in that moment, I absolutely meant it. I had attempted to take my own life for Bryn—I wouldn't hesitate to take another's if they stood in our way.

Bryn didn't seem to care about any of that anymore though. His only goal was to get me away from Khol. He crowded closer to me as Khol desperately attempted to get me under control.

HIDDEN GATES

"Give her to me," Bryn repeated, this time with utter coldness. I could sense he was on the verge of snapping. *Fabulous.* That would make two of us.

I threw my head back and screamed in frustration and fury. Raw power like I'd never experienced before rushed through me, but only for a second, one painful second, before everything went completely black.

23

A familiar song being hummed by a familiar voice lilted into my ears as I struggled to wake up. "Mom?" I murmured as my eyes finally fluttered open.

"Hi, peanut," my mom said, smiling as she leaned over to touch my face while I lay in bed—my bed, or rather, my old bed in my old room that I grew up in.

"I'm not really here, am I? This is a dream, isn't it?" I asked my mom as I let the sadness that she wasn't really here wash over me.

"No, I'm not really here, and neither are you. But I am communicating with you through your dreams. I'm asleep where I am now as well."

I sat up and eyed my mom keenly. "Yeah, so we are kind of really here then." I smiled at her before tears began to slide down my face, and she took me in her arms. "I'm so sorry. All of this is my fault. Are you okay? Is Daddy? You guys know I didn't really mean all that stuff I said, right? I love you both so much."

"Honey, we know, and we both love you very much, too. I hope you'll always know that."

There was a note of sadness in my mom's voice that caught my attention. "Mom?" I sat back and looked into her face, which had suddenly grown very serious.

"You need to listen to me, peanut. I don't know how much time I have here."

"Okay," I said with unease.

"They're going to kill us. Exterminate all of us."

"No!" I gasped. "We're going to save you! We're coming for you! We just need a plan!"

Defeat was etched into every plain on my mom's face. "You mustn't try. The only reason I'm able to come to you now is because I think they're letting me. They expect you to come for us—it's all a trap—and that's why you can't."

"No," I said with determination. "We're going to save you. None of the rest matters."

"Our world matters and protecting it still does. You and your friends will be the last hope this dimension has. If they kill you, then this world will die, too. You can't let that happen. This is what we're here for—this is what we've all trained for all these years—even though no one ever thought it'd really happen. I'm so sorry we've failed you, so sorry all of this falls on you." My mom's face crumpled as she fought to stave off tears of her own.

"Mom, no—"

She brought her index finger up to silence me. "Peanut, please, you need to let me finish. I need to say these things to you." She was saying goodbye to me, I realized. My mom was saying goodbye to me before she would be taken away from me and murdered by the alien riders. Tears flowed more freely down my face, but I nodded so she could continue. "I'm proud of you, honey, so proud. And I know things aren't turning out for you the way you had hoped. But you have good people surrounding you—people who love you—don't forget that. And Bryn—I'm so sorry for everything your father and I did—you're going to need him now more than ever. Do you love him? Truly love him?"

"Yes. More than anything, Mom," I sobbed.

She smiled at me through her tears. "Then don't let anything stand in your way. Our people have forgotten many things, forgotten that love is more important than anything sometimes, because life is short—too short." She wrapped her arms around me again. "We'll always be with you, peanut. We both love you more than I can say." She sat up and looked off into space as if she were seeing something somewhere else, and who knows, maybe she was. "I have to go now. I love you."

"Mom, no!" I reached for her, but she was fading away right before my eyes. "I need more time!" And then she was gone. "No!" I screamed. "No!"

I sat straight up in bed and blinked my eyes open to the dim light inside of my and Bryn's room. Bryn opened his sleep-encrusted eyes and reached for me. "Peej," he whispered, "What's wrong? She's gone. Don't worry."

"We have to save them now! Before it's too late!" I stumbled out of bed in a panic.

Bryn slid out of bed and caught me by the elbow before I could do a face-plant. "Who? What are you talking about?"

"Our families of course! Who the hell else?"

"Did you have a vision? Tell me what happened."

I stopped and turned to look into Bryn's worried face and let everything that my mom had just told me fully wash over me. My lower lip trembled as I talked. "We're not going to be able to save them, Bryn. It's going to be too late. My mom—" I stammered. "My mom said they're going to exterminate all of them—soon. It could be happening now."

Bryn's whole body went rigid, and then he slumped back onto the bed with a vacant gaze. "I just thought—maybe hoped—that they would try to ransom them or something, give us some time. Oh God—*all* of them?"

I nodded numbly.

Bryn abruptly stood, determination replacing the empty look of sorrow that had been in his eyes just moments ago. "I'm going to go gather everyone together for a meeting. Get dressed and I'll see you in the common room in ten," he said as he pulled on sweatpants and a T-shirt and stalked from our room without another word.

I didn't know what he hoped to accomplish with the meeting, but at least we'd have everyone in one place so I could tell them the horrific news I'd just received.

Everyone was already assembled in the common area by the time I got there about ten minutes later. Judging from the tension in the room, Bryn had already filled them in on what I had told him.

"What are we going to do?" Jenna blurted out before I could even settle down beside Bryn.

I bit my lip and tried not to let her expectant face tear my heart out. She really thought that I had a plan or an answer of some sort. "There's nothing we can do." I cringed at my own words.

"What? You're just going to let them die? You can't mean that!" Jenna stared at me in shock.

"This is about more than just us, Jenna. I wanna save them just as much as you do—God damn it!" I swore, letting my anguish and frustration take control of me for a moment before I calmed down. "My mom came to me in my dream. Told me what they were planning. I got the feeling"—I swallowed at the lump that had formed in my throat—"she was saying goodbye. They're probably already dead." The truth of it washed over me, and I started to shake. "They let my mom reach out to me when they haven't before so we'd be in a hurry to get to them. But we won't find them alive if we go."

"We have to try!" Jenna cried out in anguish as she collapsed against Macon, who wrapped his arms around her.

"We have to save this world—our world—from the Riders. We really are this dimension's first and last hope. Before, when we found out everyone but us had been captured, we knew everything fell on our shoulders, but there was still a chance for reinforcements—still a chance that we might get help."

"Now we really are alone," Bryn chimed in, his voice flat.

"You're not alone. You have the support of the Red Dragons." Khol's voice echoed through the room loud and clear and plucked a note of hope deep inside of me. "We can't let their deaths be in vain. We can beat the Riders. I know we can." Khol placed his hand on my shoulder, and I looked up into his eyes. "We will succeed."

I nodded once tightly in affirmation of his promise. "What about the other Dragon factions? Do you think they'd be willing to help?"

"I can guarantee you the Black will," Bitch Dragon said as she strolled into the room as though we'd been expecting her.

I must have noticeably tensed, because Bryn slid his large warm hand over to cover mine, and I moved closer to him and out from under Khol's touch. This was war, and sometimes you had to work with allies that in normal times—well, I don't know—let's say who you might want to burn to a crisp. I loved Bryn and I knew he loved me, and that's what really mattered. We'd have our little talk about what happened while he was away later—and in private.

"I'll send a messenger out to the Gold and Silver factions immediately," Khol informed us before he disappeared.

I stood and walked over to where Macon was still holding a sobbing Jenna. I reached my hand out tentatively to touch her but let it fall without contact. "Jenna," I whispered. "We'll make them pay. I know it won't bring them back, but we'll make them pay."

She hiccupped once and then abruptly stopped crying. Her head lifted up just enough from Macon's chest so she could meet my eyes. "Good," she croaked.

We stared at each other for a few moments, neither one of us saying anything aloud, but we reached a silent understanding. We were on the same page with this. The Riders would pay for what they did, and we would be the ones to deal them their hand of justice.

I turned to look at Jeremy next, who also met my gaze with the same grim determination as Jenna just had. It was good to know that despite his feelings of bitterness towards Bryn and me, Jeremy would have our backs where it counted.

"Tomorrow, after we've all had a chance to rest as much as we can, and after Khol has hopefully heard back from the other Dragon factions, we're going to come up with a concrete plan of action. No more waiting around. We can't afford to for one second longer." With that, I strode back over to Bryn, took him by the hand, and headed towards the door. When I got close to bitch Dragon, I flipped my new shorter hair and turned my nose up at her. She could covet *my* Bryn all she wanted, but he always had, and always would, belong to me.

As I lay in bed sprawled across Bryn's bare chest, I let my thoughts wander. I knew there was little hope for any real sleep for me, and I could tell Bryn wasn't really sleeping either, but I was too tired to talk, and I knew he was, too.

HIDDEN GATES

There would be a time for me to question him about bitch Dragon, but it wasn't now. And maybe it wouldn't be for a long time. We were at war, and who knew how long we'd get to be together before something happened to one or both of us. Everything was unstable and uncertain about our future, all of our futures actually, so we had to take refuge in all the small comforts as they came our way.

I tried not to think about the fact that our families were dead. I just tried to think of them as being somewhere far away from us, somewhere that didn't get U.S. postal service or long distance phone coverage. I knew I wasn't coping and was in some sort of denial—or maybe that was my way of coping. I knew our cause couldn't afford for me to have any more emotional breakdowns. Somehow I had taken on somewhat of a leader position in our little group, and with that came greater responsibility. So instead of shattering into a million pieces like I really wanted to, I thought of my mom, and took inspiration from one of her favorite movies.

"After all, tomorrow is another day," I said into the dark with a small smile on my lips.

Oh yes—the Riders would rue the day they messed with me.

ACKNOWLEDGEMENTS

Well this is the part where I get to thank all the people who made this book possible. I really hope I don't leave out someone important. *internally cringes*

First I'd like to thank my amazing Hubby, who is supportive and patient beyond the realm of what I imagine any normal man is . . . dah dah da duuuh . . . Super Hubby!

Next I would like to thank my parents for encouraging my love of reading and crazy imagination during my most impressionable years. Carnegie Library rocks!

Then of course there's my lovely squad of beta readers for this book: Joy A. Ball, Kristin Bingham, Kellee Fabre, Tiffany Mahaffy, Laura McGee, Jillian Omerine, Erin Rathbun, and Lauren Reidy. Thank you so much for all your feedback and support! You ladies rocked it . . . beta style!

Of course I need to thank Lindsay Tiry for her amazing cover design, and Jordan P. Fremgen for his amazing logo designs for The P.J. Stone Gates Trilogy. Both artists extraordinaire!

Lets not forget Monique Larroux, who took my awesome author photo. She clearly is very talented, as evidenced by her getting a quality photo out of me without a beer in my hand or my making a funny face.

I also need to thank my editors Kenya Wright, Kelly Hawkins, and Greta Maloney. You ladies rocked it as well!

Of course I'd like to thank Dragonfairy Press, Kenya Wright and Alicia Wright Brewster to be specific, for believing in me and my book, and for putting up with me during this whole process. I love you guys!

And last but certainly not least: thank you to all the Book Bloggers and fans who keep me going! I wouldn't be anywhere if not for you guys! I love each and every one of you!